Leave Tomorrow Behind

Books by Judy Clemens

The Stella Crown Series
Till the Cows Come Home
Three Can Keep a Secret
To Thine Own Self Be True
The Day Will Come
Different Paths
Leave Tomorrow Behind

The Grim Reaper Series
Embrace the Grim Reaper
The Grim Reaper's Dance
Flowers for her Grave
Dying Echo

Leave Tomorrow Behind

A Stella Crown Mystery

Judy Clemens

Poisoned Pen Press

First Edition 2014
Large Print Edition

10 9 8 7 6 5 4 3 2 1

Library of Congress Catalog Card Number: 2013933213

ISBN: 9781464202063   Large Print

Poisoned Pen Press
6962 E. First Ave., Ste. 103
Scottsdale, AZ 85251
www.poisonedpenpress.com
info@poisonedpenpress.com

Printed in the United States of America

For all of my readers who asked when they would get to spend time with Stella again. I hope you enjoy her new adventure. I sure did.

Acknowledgments

Much thanks goes to:

Lydia and Sharon Hartzler for sharing their knowledge about cows and 4-H, answering my questions practically before I asked them, and giving me great ideas. I'm glad my questions about manure could offer family suppertime conversation.

KB Inglee and Elizabeth "Bodge" Inglee-Richards, and Ron Baldridge, DVM, for their veterinary expertise and willingness to answer strange questions about medicines and animal health.

Cindy Luginbill, for answering questions about salons and day spas.

Lee Diller, for being a great boss at my "other" job.

Nancy Clemens for being an awesome and speedy first reader, and always encouraging my dream.

Steve, Tristan, and Sophia Smucker for being wholly supportive and enthusiastic about my writing life, and for being the best family I could ask for.

My wonderful, wonderful readers, who asked many times when Stella would be coming back to visit. I'm so glad you insisted.

The team at Poisoned Pen Press for their camaraderie, flexibility, and way of making this job so fun.

If I changed information about 4-H, or veterinary meds, or beauty salons, or the recording industry, it was purely because of literary license. The people I named all know their stuff.

Dance, dance, dance little lady
So obsessed with second best
No rest you'll ever find
Time and tide and trouble
Never, never wait
Let the cauldron bubble
Justify your fate
Dance, dance, dance little lady
Dance, dance, dance little lady
Leave tomorrow behind.

—Noel Coward

Chapter One

The conversation was simple. Miranda, my future sister-in-law, would make a suggestion, and I would say no. Like this:

"Off-the-shoulder?"

"No."

"Three-quarter-length sleeves?"

"No."

"Puffy ones, then."

"No."

It was early. Well, early for some people. I'd been up since five-thirty, when I'd milked the cows, and now I was supposed to be eating breakfast and watching the morning news. But sometimes plans fall through, and we have to soldier on. That's what I was doing. Except I'd be hard-pressed to find an actual soldier who would want to face the grilling I was getting.

Miranda had, in a moment of what she called "insanity," kept me from being impaled by a pitchfork earlier in the summer, but that hadn't made us instant bosom-buddies. In fact, sometimes it seemed she regretted her whole impulse to save my life. I can't imagine why.

Back in the whole annoying conversation, she sighed. Heavily. "Fine. We don't have to talk about the sleeves right now. How about the skirt? Full? Floor-length? Flared?"

"No."

"You have something else in mind?"

"No. I mean…no, there's not going to be a skirt."

She blinked, then gave a little clap. "You mean you're going to wear slacks? Oh! Silk pants! That could be nice."

"I am not wearing silk pants."

"So, what, then? I suppose you're just going to be naked?"

"I'm not going to be naked, Miranda. I'm going to be wearing jeans."

"Jeans? You can't wear jeans!"

"Can so."

She took a deep breath and closed her eyes. And then she was suddenly smiling, like one of those manic televangelist ladies with all the makeup and the big hair. "Okay, Stella. I get it. If you don't want to talk about your dress right now, we can talk about something else."

"I am not. Wearing. A wedding dress."

She waved a colorful brochure in the air. "Cake. Let's talk about cake. Now, I was thinking, maybe, one of those multi-tiered cakes, with the flowers, and the little figurines on top, you know, made to look like you and Nick. Or, we could get the guy on that TV show, the Cake Boss guy, he could make a themed cake, like with—" she swallowed "—cows, or motorcycles, or houses, like our family's development company builds—"

"Ma's making the cake."

She laughed and flicked her hand at me, like I was the silliest thing she'd ever seen. "My mother couldn't make a cake to save her life."

"Not your mother. Ma Granger. She's making the dessert."

"Ma Granger? I don't know, Stella. Do you really think she's equipped to make that much?"

"She raised eight boys. I think she can make enough dessert for fifty people."

She blinked, a whole lot, like she had dust in her eyes. Which wouldn't have surprised me, actually, since we were in my old farmhouse, and it was a dry summer, and I wasn't exactly on top of the dusting.

"Um," she said, "I believe I just heard you say fifty people?"

"Yeah, around that. Could be sixty, maybe, with all the Granger kids."

"Kids? But wait, there are almost three hundred guests on the invitation list. And none of them are children."

"What invitation list?"

She poked around on her iPad, then swiveled it toward me. "This one."

I scanned the names. I didn't recognize any of them. "Who are these people?"

"Folks from Virginia, mostly, although your friends are on it, too, of course, somewhere. You know, it's mostly our family's friends, church members, employees, neighbors—"

I shoved the tablet back to her. "You can pick twenty-five."

She choked. "But…but the venue. It's huge. We'll be swallowed up."

"What venue? I think the yard here will hold seventy-five people just fine."

"Yard? Here? I don't think…"

"Hey, there." My fiancé, Nick, entered the kitchen, his hair messed up from sleep, but otherwise looking mighty fine. He walked over and planted a kiss on my mouth. "How're you this morning? Cows all good? Queenie?"

"Nick." Miranda's chin stuck out toward New Jersey. "You have got to talk to her."

"I am talking to her. I asked about the dog, and work, and how she's feeling."

"I mean you have to talk to her about the wedding."

"What about it?"

"She won't agree to anything!"

"She agreed to marry me. That's the most important part." He went to the counter and poured a cup of coffee. "Nice to have you here, Sis. Otherwise, I have to make my own brew." He took a sip and sighed contentedly.

Miranda shook the iPad at him. "Twenty-five people, Nick. That's what she said I could have."

"For what?"

"The invitation list!"

Nick slid out a chair and sat next to me. "Twenty-five sounds fine." He frowned and put his arm on the back of my chair. "But the Grangers will be more than that. We're not limiting them, are we?"

"No," I said. "They're on my part of the list."

"And she said she gets sixty!" Miranda pointed at me, just in case Nick wasn't sure who she was talking about.

"It is her wedding." Nick took another sip.

"It's yours, too."

He smiled. "Exactly."

Her mouth opened. Then it shut. "Oh, for

heaven's sake. I don't know why I'm helping you two, anyway. It's not like any of it is appreciated." She whisked all of her lists and brochures and magazines and samples together, whacked them on the table to even them out, then stacked them on her iPad. She stood up, knocking her chair against the wall, and stalked out of the room, leaving some flowery scent in her wake.

Nick took another sip of coffee.

"The cows are good," I said. "Want some breakfast?"

Chapter Two

"You sure you got this?" I watched Lucy, my farm-hand, who was supervising her daughter Tess, now nine years old, as she bottle-fed the newest calf.

"I said I got it. Go. Take Zach to the fair. We'll come later and see him, when he's settled."

It was too hot to do much, anyway. Even Queenie, my collie, had decided to take the day off. The last I'd seen her, she was lying on the plain cement of the barn floor, well out of the sun. If I stayed home I'd end up doing something like mowing the lawn, or fixing some rotted boards on the far side of my garage, and I really didn't feel like doing either. Besides, I'd promised Zach, and he'd be showing up any minute, ready to transport his calf to the barn at the county fair.

"Mom!" Tess squealed. The nipple on the huge bottle had collapsed.

Lucy took the bottle, pinched the nipple until it popped back into form, and returned it to her daughter. "Nick going with you?"

"Don't know. He seems to be feeling pretty good today, so maybe."

"He seems to be feeling pretty good all the time now."

Nick had been diagnosed with MS, multiple sclerosis, during the last year, which of course had taken its toll on the two of us and his family. But lately, with a new diet and medication regimen, along with exercise and Nick's generally positive way of looking at life, things hadn't seemed so bad. In fact, some days I almost forgot he wasn't the same guy I'd fallen for a year before. No, that's not right. He was the same guy. Just…different.

"He'll probably come along," I said. "To get away from the wedding planner, if nothing else."

Lucy grinned. "You never know. Miranda might have a good idea tucked away in there, somewhere."

"If you're someone else, maybe."

The calf hiccuped, and the bottle popped out of her mouth, sending a stream of colostrum, the mother's first milk we couldn't use in our regular tanks, shooting all over her face. She backed up on knobby legs, shaking her head and spraying droplets all around. Tess, giggling, used the towel Lucy handed her to wipe the calf's face, then got the nipple back in its mouth. The calf sucked so hard she almost pulled Tess over, but somehow the girl remained standing.

I congratulated Tess on her success with the calves, and went to find Nick. He sat on the sofa in the living room, laptop open, hands on the keys.

"You have to talk to her," Miranda was saying. She perched beside him on the sofa. Both of them had their backs to me. "This wedding is not going to happen if she doesn't let me…if she doesn't make any plans."

"How do you know she hasn't?"

"Fine. Show me a plan. Anything. Building rental. Flowers. Invitations. A date."

"We told you a date."

"You said, 'We're thinking of maybe July 27.'"

"That's a date."

"But nothing concrete. 'Thinking of maybe?' What kind of commitment is that? And it's next month."

"Miranda." Nick paused, then shut his laptop and set it on the coffee table. "Look, Sister. I appreciate what you're trying to do. No, really, I do. But you've got to understand, Stella is…she's a lot different from you. In a lot of ways."

Miranda snorted. "I do realize that. I'm not an idiot."

"Didn't say you were. But listen. You want to make a nice wedding—"

"The best wedding."

"But are you wanting the wedding you would want? Or the wedding Stella would want?"

"I'm planning—or trying to plan—the wedding any woman would want. Any normal one, anyway."

"Well," Nick laughed, "maybe Stella's not normal."

"Who's not normal?" I stepped into the room, and Miranda jumped up so fast I thought her ass was on fire. Nick merely turned and smiled at me. "You, of course."

"Never claimed to be. So, hey, you want to go to the fair with me and Zach?"

"But…" Miranda fluttered her hands.

"You're welcome to come, too, although you'll have to drive separately. We can only fit three adults in my truck, and if we go by foot size, Zach is now officially a grown-up."

Miranda's jaw worked, and then she smiled, although it was a little like the smile adults give children when they really can't stand being around them.

A car pulled into the drive and I peeked out the window. "He's here. You ready?"

Nick got up and held his arms out to the side. "As long as I'm dressed okay."

"For the fair? Before it's even open?" I surveyed his jeans and Phillies T-shirt. "You look perfect."

"Not as perfect as you."

Miranda made a gagging sound and stalked to the stairwell, where she slammed the door behind her.

"Shall we?" Nick said, and we went outside.

Mallory, Zach's older sister, climbed out of the driver's seat of the old sedan to pet Queenie, who trotted out from the barn to see who had arrived. Mallory's boyfriend, Brady Willard, unfolded from the car, too. All six feet of him.

"Where did that come from?" I asked.

"What?"

"You're taller than me now."

"Dad's tall." Brady's father was the town's one and only detective, and he'd helped me out when my farm had been threatened. And when my life had been threatened. And...well, we were friends.

"Yeah, he's a big guy, but when did you get so huge?"

He shrugged.

Zach rolled out of the back seat. "So, where's Barnabas?"

"Where you left him, lazy butt. It's not my job to get him ready."

He dropped his bag in the grass and loped off toward the barn. Queenie followed, tail wagging.

"So," Mallory said, "Mom and Dad will probably call you, like, ten times to make sure he gets settled okay." She rolled her eyes. "Like the fair is such a dangerous place."

"It is," Brady said. "Dad says cops will be all over because of everything that goes on there."

"Like people dying from eating deep-fried Snickers?"

"No, like drug dealing, fighting, prostitution, gambling, drunk guys peeing in the fairway. Or puking."

Mallory put her hand over his mouth. "Stop! Gosh! I'm sorry I asked."

I glanced at my feet. "Glad I'm wearing boots."

"You should be," Brady said, in all seriousness.

"So are you guys going, too?" I asked.

Mallory made a face. "Not after that."

Brady shrugged again. "Later this week. For the derby or whatever."

Demolition derby, he meant.

"Which one?"

"Combine, of course. I got a friend in it. His ride's called Smashmaster."

A combine demolition derby. Yes, you heard right. It's huge in Ohio, apparently, and now Pennsylvania had decided to get in on the fun. Farm kids use rusted, outdated combines, paint them all up, and bash them into each other in the hopes of a prize. It's loud and muddy and fairly safe. Pretty entertaining, actually, if you like that sort of thing.

Mallory tugged on Brady's arm. "Come on. I told Grandma we'd help with corn today, and we're already late."

"Right. Yippee." He swung his arm in an "all right" gesture.

Mallory swatted him. "You know you love it." She looked at me. "Grandma makes all these awesome desserts, and the only way you get any is to help with the corn."

I nodded. I'd attended more than one corn-freezing day at Ma's house. And I had eaten more than my share of chocolate cake. "Better get going then, before your dad inhales it all."

Brady's eyes widened, and he practically dove into the car. Because Mallory's father, Jethro, can really pack it away.

Once they were gone, I headed into the barn.

"He look okay to you?" Zach stood in the stall beside Barnabas, the beautiful Holstein calf he would be showing. The yearling waited, chewing his cud and looking about as bored as a calf can look. He'd been born the summer before, raised right there on the farm. I'd given him to Zach as a baby, just after Zach had lost another calf, and he'd been Zach's ever since. Zach had bottle fed him, brushed him, and named him. I hadn't done anything except supply the barn and the feed. And the occasional taking care of when Zach was gone.

Zach had been a good worker for me for years, so I was happy to offer what I could to pay him back. Beyond the cash I'd already given him.

"He looks perfect. But he'll look even better once we get him to the fair and you wash him up."

"I guess."

We led Barnabas out to the trailer, which I'd already hooked up to my truck, and he waltzed right in without a fuss.

"He'll be okay in there?" Zach peered into the back. "He won't be scared?"

"Zach, you're acting like an amateur. How many times have you helped transport cows?"

"I know. Sorry. It's just, he's so small compared to the milkers." He trotted over to grab the bag he'd left in the grass, and met Nick and me back at the truck, where I was explaining to Queenie that she would be staying at the farm.

Zach hesitated, shifting from foot to foot.

"No," I said before he could ask. "You are not riding in the trailer with Barnabas. Get in the cab."

After a little who's-going-to-sit-in-the-middle dance, Zach slid onto the bench, and Nick took the seat by the window. We waved at Queenie and headed off to start Zach's adventures at the fair.

I really wish we hadn't.

Chapter Three

"There's a place! No, there's a place!"

"Zach, will you shut up? I have eyes." I drove slowly, making my way through the grass field toward the dairy barn. Kids and cows and trailers were everywhere, and I really didn't want to run over any of them.

Zach hugged his bag and leaned forward. "There's Bobby and Claire! Stop! Stop, Stella!"

Bobby and Claire Kaufmann. Twins, Zach's age. Zach knew them from school and 4-H, and I knew their folks, good dairy people from the other side of the county.

"Stella!"

"I'm stopping, I'm stopping. Give me a second."

I eased the truck to a halt in the middle of the lane, and a horn blew behind me. I waved out the window for the driver to hold his horses. Or cows.

Nick slid out, and Zach vaulted to the ground to attack Bobby. Bobby jumped about a foot, but once he realized it was Zach, he relaxed and punched Zach's arm. Claire's face turned pink, and she stepped back, crossing her arms.

"Uh-oh," I said.

Nick hopped back in the truck. "What?"

"Claire's got it bad for Zach. Look at her."

"She looks mad."

"No, she's uncomfortable. Watch her eyes." Her eyes were flicking to Zach's face, then away, then back again. "And her shoulders." Up and tight, her arms hugging her stomach. "Classic signs of a shy girl who thinks a guy is cute."

"I don't know. She sort of looks like she's going to be sick."

"As I was saying."

"Zach!" A new guy sauntered up—Randy, Zach's buddy who would be showing a calf I'd sold him. His black eye from getting punched by his ex-girlfriend's new squeeze had finally faded, and he looked more like himself again. I hoped he felt more like himself. I was recovering from an injury, too, but it was a bit more complicated than Randy's eye, since it included a broken bone in my foot. But I was off the crutches and out of the boot, and healing up just fine, thank you very much. It was only at the end of a long day, or if I stepped wrong, that I had a twinge of a reminder.

I held out a fist as Randy walked past my door, and he bumped it. He was a nice kid when he wasn't getting into stupid fights about stupid girls. Really. The girl was stupid. As was the fight. But saying "I told you so" is never helpful, especially when speaking to a teenager, so I'd let it go. Randy seemed to have learned his lesson. I certainly hoped so, anyway. Zach was going to be staying with him in his camper for the week, since Jethro and Belle were busy working and doing other stuff, like freezing corn, and wouldn't be able to run him back and forth as often as he wanted. Plus, it would be fun for him to hang out with all the other kids. You'd think the Grangers could hold off on corn for a week and do the whole fair thing, but the corn was ready, and the freezing process was like a religion in their family. I was sort of surprised they were letting Zach off the hook at all, even for something as important as the fair.

A spot opened up in the "cow dispensing" area, so I pulled in, assuming Zach would find us. When he didn't, I went looking. I found him in Randy's trailer, pulling stuff out of his bag.

"Zach." I had my head in the doorway. "Barnabas, remember? The reason we're here? The calf you were so worried about twenty minutes ago?"

"Oh, right. Sorry. I'll be back!" This he said to Randy and the twins, of course. Bobby was eating a Pop-Tart, and didn't even notice Zach was leaving. Randy grunted. Claire was the only one who seemed to care. She glanced up at me, then looked away, her ears turning red this time. Zach bounded down the stairs, not giving the poor girl a second glance.

Claire wasn't bad to look at. Pretty nice, actually, but maybe that was through my "farming genes are good genes" glasses. She was as tall as Zach, maybe a little taller, with broad shoulders and a wide, friendly face. Her coloring was all brown—her hair and eyes, I mean—and her skin had that ruddy, fresh, pink look you get when you work outside. She wore the same sort of stuff I had on—jeans, boots, a Got Milk T-shirt. I liked her, and I wished Zach would at least notice she was there.

"Find a place to park?" Zach asked.

"Right next to the barn."

"Awesome."

Zach checked in and received his stall assignment, in a nice spot toward the front of the barn, where he and Barnabas would get at least a little breeze. The stall on the right was still empty, and the one on the other side had a fresh layer of wood chips on the floor, awaiting its occupant. We took a few minutes to gather up some of the free chips the fair offered, and spread them in Zach's little space. When that was done, we led Barnabas down the trailer ramp and into the barn. He trotted along behind us, like he did it every day, like he was just

happy to be there. I was thankful for his easygo-
ing personality—but then, when your whole life
consists of a teenage boy who dotes on you, what
would you have to be uptight about?

"Hey, Austin," Zach said to the guy who had
moved into the next stall, where we'd seen the wood
chips. He was a couple of years older than Zach, and
a member of Zach's 4-H club. Being a senior, this
would be his last opportunity to show at the fair.

Austin smiled and paused in brushing his calf,
holding out his fist. The same teenage-guy hello
ritual I had just performed with Randy. It felt nice
to be accepted as one of their pack.

"How you doing, man?" Austin said. "Awesome that we're next to each other. You let me know
if you ever need anything."

Zach bumped his fist. "Same here."

Austin nodded at me and Nick, and went
back to brushing. His pretty Holstein calf—named
Halladay's Dream, according to the sign on the
board—stared into space, chewing his cud like
Barnabas had been doing that morning. The two
bovine boys should get along just fine.

Nick attached Zach's official certificate to the
board above the stall, using the zip-ties Zach had
packed in his bag, then hung up another one, which
Zach had made, using some old wood siding from
my farm. It showcased photos of Barnabas from

when he'd been born, right up to the present, as well as the logo for Royalcrest Farm. My home.

"Hey, thanks, Zach. I appreciate the acknowledgement."

He smiled, and gave a little shrug. "Here, Nick, can you put this up, too?" Zach handed Nick another homemade sign with Barnabas' name in rainbow bubble letters.

Nick raised his eyebrows.

Zach's face told it all, and I laughed.

"Yeah," he grumbled. "Mallory made it. I decided I'd better stay on her good side and use it."

"You're a wise man," Nick said. "Keeping your sister happy makes life better all around." Nick tied it up next to the other one, and stepped back, eyeing his work. "Very…"

"Nice," I said. "It's very nice."

Nick cleared his throat. "Just what I was going to say."

"Now, Zach," Austin said, pausing in his brushing, "that is truly you."

Zach threw some wood chips at him, and Austin ducked, laughing. When he stood back up, his laughter stopped, and he scowled. "There they are." He stared at something across the room. "I'd hoped they would sit this year out. Give the rest of us a real chance."

I followed his gaze to a girl bringing in her

calf. Her parents were with her, one in front, one behind, their eyes darting around the room, taking in everything and everybody. My nose wrinkled.

"What's wrong?" Nick said. "Who is it?"

"The Greggs," Austin spat.

Zach snorted. "Also known as The Cheaters."

"Cheaters? How do you cheat at the fair? Steroids? Don't they check for that sort of thing?"

"Nothing that complicated," I said.

"Then what?"

I kept my voice low. "Okay, so our fair is now, a few weeks into June, right? Not that long, really, since the State Fair last September. The Greggs—" it was hard to say their name without spitting, like Austin had "—attend the State Fair, watch the judging, and buy the winner. If the Grand Champion isn't for sale, they go for whatever's closest. Problem is, they end up with the winners so many times they're running out of cows to buy."

"That's not illegal?"

"Nope, not in our county. Should be. The whole idea of the fair, and of 4-H itself, is for kids to learn how to take care of animals. Look at that girl. You think she has any idea what she's doing in a barn?"

The Gregg girl in question—there were several of them in the family, so I wasn't sure of names— looked like she weighed about eighty pounds, and was terrified of the calf. But then, one false step and the calf, not even full-grown, would crush her. She and her parents wore all the right kinds of clothes, and drove the right farm-type vehicles, but the problem was they were too clean. I don't mean them as people. We farmers can clean up just fine. But the clothes hadn't been worn. Not how you need to wear them to actually be a farmer. And the truck and trailer? They hadn't been used for anything except hauling champion cattle from fair to fair. No "memories," as Jethro liked to say, meaning scratches and dents and scuff marks.

"But don't they have to know what they're doing at least a little bit, to keep the animals through the winter?"

"Don't know what they do about that, but I could guess."

"I don't have to guess." Austin tossed his brush into his bucket. "They have one little pole barn, more suited to purebred horses than cows. They keep their precious prize animals in there, and hire a guy who takes care of them all winter, milks the dairy cows, brushes the calves, everything. The only time any of the Greggs actually touch the animals is here, where people see them."

"And you know this how?" I asked.

"Guy at my church. They asked him to do the work a couple years ago. He turned them down."

"But what's the point?" Nick asked. "If they don't want to spend time with animals, why do the fair thing at all?"

"I do know the answer to that," I said. "Rumor is the oldest daughter thought it would be fun to have a 'pet' cow. The other girls decided they wanted pets, too, and the parents don't mind the limelight, from what I can tell. The dad uses it to promote his business. He's the CEO of some recording label in Philly, so the cash isn't a problem. Not like it is for those of us who do this for a living, who are hands-on with the herd every day. They built some mansion worth a bazillion dollars, but try to suck up to the country music fans by doing some 'farming.' "

Nick took my hand and squeezed. "The way they farm they miss out on all the best parts, don't they?"

I watched the wide-eyed little Gregg girl dance away from the calf's hooves as it entered the stall. The mother slammed the gate shut as soon as the cow's hind end cleared, and the three of them stood back in the aisle, brushing off their pants, obviously glad to be done with the messy work of touching a living creature.

"Yes," I said. "They absolutely do."

Chapter Four

"Hey, you." Carla Beaumont slapped her tray down next to mine in the school boosters' food tent, and plopped into a chair. "Got Zach's little boy all settled?"

I set down my hot dog and focused on my friend, and favorite veterinarian. "He's happy."

Carla winked at Nick. "Hi, gorgeous. How ya'll doin'?" Nick smiled, and Carla faked a swoon.

I shook my head. "Crazy woman. What are you doing here already?"

Carla had been chosen as the official fair veterinarian. It was quite an honor, and for her it was the first time. Most of the other local docs were happy for her—they'd had their turns—but of course there were a few being snotty kids about it. Just because she wasn't a fifty-five-year-old white guy didn't mean she couldn't handle the job. In fact, a lot of her clients specifically asked for her when they called her multi-vet practice. They liked that she was younger, and that she was a woman. Of course there were those who preferred the old guard, but that's to be expected. The vets she worked with were all supportive and competent, and if it hadn't been that Carla was my best friend, I would have been happy for any of them to take care of my animals. But sometimes personal lives do make a difference.

She was smiling now. "My official duties started as soon as the kids got checked in, and you won't believe how many people think their precious animals are already on the brink of death. Or are at risk of contracting something from the animal next door." She took a bite of her double cheeseburger. She would somehow get through the sandwich, fries, milkshake, and piece of pie, and still be ready for a funnel cake. The woman could really pack it away, sort of like Jethro, Zach's dad. Sometimes I thought Carla was actually a teenage boy disguised as a nicely-rounded thirty-something veterinarian.

"Bryan with you?" Carla's boyfriend.

"Nope, has to work today. Sorry to disappoint you. I know how you love him."

"Hey, it's been better, hasn't it?"

She grinned. "Sure. You've been very gentle with him. But you do realize he's still afraid of you."

Bryan and I had gotten off to a rough start. I hadn't known about him at all until Carla was in an accident and he and I met up at the hospital.

He was a complete stranger to me, and I'd made the mistake of accusing him of murdering several women earlier that summer. Not my proudest moment, but I loved Carla, and I didn't want her hurt. So sue me.

"That's okay," Nick said. "I'm scared of her, too."

I kicked him under the table, reminding myself of my still tender foot.

He grabbed his leg, making an exaggerated face of pain. "See what I have to put up with?"

Carla laughed. "Oh, you two, you are just so—" Her phone rang, and she sighed, putting it up to her ear. "Dr. Beaumont. Yes. Oh, is that so? I'm sorry to hear that. I'll be over to check just as soon as…" She glanced at her hamburger. "As soon as I'm finished with this cow. All right?" She hung up.

"Really?" I said. "You still consider that burger a cow?"

"I didn't say the cow I was with was still living." She took her time eating it, and the three of us chatted, talking about the fair food and events we were looking forward to.

"There's the man of the hour," Carla said.

Zach had entered the food tent with Randy, Bobby, and Claire. The three boys sauntered up front, laughing at something. Claire followed quietly, her eyes scanning the menu posted above the counter.

"Quite the crowd," Carla said, shaking her head. "Hate to see what all they'll get up to this week."

I took a sip of Pepsi. "They're all right. Besides, if Zach does something stupid, I'll kill him."

"Good to know. In case he shows up dead."

She crumpled her napkin and tossed it onto her tray. "Guess I'd better go soothe the crazed parents before they contact the fair board. Because you know the one time I dismiss a complaint will be the exact moment a cow dies of a highly communicable disease, and I'll be drummed out of Pennsylvania to become a lowly milkmaid." She brightened. "But then, I love milk. And ice cream. And cheese. Maybe that would turn out just fine." She winked at Nick, and left, going by way of Zach and his buddies, who took a moment off from laughing to say hello. She bumped Zach with her ample hip, and was gone.

"What are you grinning about?" I said to Nick.

"Her. She's something."

No argument from me.

"These seats saved?" Zach plopped down beside me and took a huge bite of a donut.

"Nice lunch for a growing boy."

"Tastes good. Besides, I have these." Cheese fries. Much better.

The rest of the kids filled out the table, Claire ending up on the far corner, catty-cornered from Zach. She kept her eyes on her plate.

"How's Barnabas?" I asked.

"Perfect." He spoke around the pastry. "He made friends with Austin's calf by peeing so close to the side of the stall it splashed into his."

Randy and Bobby laughed. Claire didn't. I was fairly certain Austin hadn't, either, but then, excrement was one of the by-products of having 4-H animals, so to speak.

"Hello, everybody."

The laughter stopped, but the boys' mouths stayed open. I think my jaw dropped, too. Nick was the only one who didn't respond, because she was standing directly behind him. "She" being a teenage girl who, well, wasn't exactly what our teenage boys were used to seeing. Her bleached blonde hair was piled on top of her head in a messy knot, her teeth were whiter than a snowstorm, and her boobs were so large they were almost knocking into Nick's head—or maybe they were, from the look he was giving me. If he so much as turned an inch she'd poke his eye out. Across that ample—or should I say outrageously ginormous—chest was a banner proclaiming her to be a contestant in the Lovely Miss Pageant.

"My name's Summer," she said, batting eyelashes as big as garden spiders. Along with the batting came the pout of the puffy lips. They couldn't possibly be natural. "I'm going to be competing in the Lovely Miss Pennsylvania pageant Wednesday afternoon. I hope you'll come."

Claire, the only one apparently not frozen in shock—or horror—gave a tight smile. "Sorry, we'll be too busy."

"Aaaaah, I don't know," Randy said. "I might be able to find the time."

Bobby nodded, smiling like an idiot.

"And how about you?" The teenage Botox factory turned those way-too-baby blues on Zach, and I felt him flinch.

"Uh…maybe."

Claire's eyes narrowed, and she looked back down at the table.

Summer gave me a passing glance, then fixed her gaze on the back of Nick's head. She moved to the side, managing to avoid a boob collision with Nick or anything else, and swiveled to look at him. Her eyes widened, and her smile grew. Not an unusual reaction for any female confronted with Nick's gorgeousness, but something about this particular girl made my stomach turn.

"How about you?" she purred.

If she so much as reached toward him I would break her arm.

Nick held very still, then leaned Randy's way as he looked up at the girl, toward her face, although I'm not sure he could actually see past the mountains blocking the way. "Sorry. Beauty pageants aren't really my thing."

"Oh, it's so much more than that. It's about talent, and commitment to the world, and the environment…and also beauty." There went those hideous eyelashes, fluttering away, like aliens flying back to the home world. I considered asking if she had something in her eye, but decided I'd rather not speak directly to her.

"Still," Nick smiled casually, "I have other things on my schedule."

"Are you sure?" She leaned in a little closer. I recalled the CPR class I'd had ages ago, hoping I still had the skills, in case she suffocated him with her chest.

"Yes, I'm very sure. My fiancée and I—" he gestured toward me "—will be busy."

She wrenched her eyes from his godlike face and gaped at me. "Your fiancée?"

By some miracle I didn't lunge across the table and strangle her. But then, I probably would have bounced off that silicone armor.

"Summer? There you are." A woman, plucked and dyed and pressed and just as real as Summer scurried up, checking her watch. "We have a schedule, you know."

Summer pouted, her lips protruding grotesquely, like she'd been hit in the mouth one too many times. "Mooom, I'm making new friends. Inviting them to the pageant."

"You need to let me know where you are—"

"I invited him." She pointed at Nick, and her mother's face went slack. Well, it sort of did. It would have been more impressive, I was sure, if her face-lift hadn't stretched her skin so tightly she would crack if the wind hit her wrong.

"Oh, my yes," she oozed. "You certainly are very welcome to attend the event."

"As I told your daughter," Nick said, somehow keeping his composure, "I'm afraid that won't be possible."

"But you must come! What could keep you away from such a delightful display of young women?"

Nick's eyes flashed. Not with anger, or even disgust, I didn't think, but with humor. If he hadn't been such a kind, generous person, he would have laughed in her face.

I had no such issues. I sounded like a donkey choking on a bone. Except donkeys don't eat bones.

"Mom," Summer whined. "She's his fiancée."

The woman stared at me. If she would have been capable, I'm sure she would have shown horror. Or at least distaste. But seeing how her face was basically molded plastic, all she presented was blandness.

Nick kept his own face pleasant. Summer's expression went through several changes before stopping on her own variation of pleasantness, which was actually quite frightening. After a year, she twitched her shoulders, which about brought down the tent from the vibrations. "Well…five o'clock Wednesday. I hope to see you all there. Come on, Mom." She gave Nick a finger waggle, and rolled away.

Her mother blinked several times, then hurried after her daughter.

The silence they left in their wake was deafening. Until Nick snorted. And then I snorted. And then the guys' jaws snapped shut.

Claire was the only quiet one, since rolling her eyes didn't make any noise.

Chapter Five

"So what was that all about?" Nick took my hand as we walked back toward the calf barn.

"I think you know."

"Yeah. Teenage hormones."

"I think it was your hormones she was after." I bumped him sideways. "Not that I was worried."

"I should hope not. I like my women—emphasis on women, as in, not girls—one hundred percent real." He held up my hand and rubbed his finger on the tattooed engagement ring my buddy Rusty Oldham had inked there a month before. "And I haven't ever seen one thing about you that wasn't." He kissed the back of my hand.

I pulled him toward the dairy barn, separate from where Zach had Barnabas, to see if any of our friends were there. Bobby and Claire had brought animals from their parents' herd, so we could at least check them out.

We walked into the barn, and were greeted

by the warm, musky scent of cows and everything that goes with them. I breathed in deeply. "Home, sweet home."

We wandered down the aisles, stepping out of the way of arriving kids and their cows, admiring the different breeds and the high quality of the livestock. Lots of lovely ladies with long, straight bones, wide, feminine faces, and bright eyes. They weren't yet as cleaned and trimmed as they would be, since they were just moving in, but it was easy to see at a glance that I wasn't, actually, at home. I had nice cows, but finding a herd where every single one was in this kind of shape would be impossible. Or really, really expensive.

"Hey, here's Claire's." We stopped at the corner stall to admire the young Guernsey. She was gorgeous. A lovely fawn color, with clearly defined white markings. Long, curled eyelashes. Deep brown eyes. I read Claire's signs. "Her name's September Breeze."

"It would be easy to fall in love with her," Nick said. "You think I could I pet her?"

"Sure." Claire had come up beside us so quietly I hadn't heard her. She leaned on the stall. "Breezy loves attention. And people love to give it to her."

I don't think I was imagining the irony in her words. Poor Claire. Nice and sturdy, like her cow. But not stunning. Or even shocking, like the showstopper we'd just seen in the food tent.

Nick ran his hand down the cow's broad face, and leaned in to murmur sweet nothings I thought I should be the only one to receive. But then, I figured I could share with a four-legged female.

"You done eating already?" I asked Claire.

"Wasn't really hungry."

Yeah, I wasn't either after that hideous display.

"She's beautiful," I said, meaning Claire's cow.

"Thanks. Bobby's is nice, too, but she can't compete with Breezy."

Bobby's Guernsey hung out in the next stall, looking about as excited as a half-asleep cow can. She was nice, for sure. But she really couldn't hold a candle to the cow right in front of me. I wondered how it was that Claire ended up with the prettier of the pair.

"Check this out, Stella." Claire pointed toward the animal's rear, and I stepped to the side so I could see.

September Breeze had lovely long bones, straight legs, a strong back…and an udder she wielded like a trophy.

"Wow." I went around the corner and squatted to peer through the slats of the stall. The udder was just how you'd want it. Smooth, evenly rounded teats, the udder nice and high—above her hocks, or where the legs bend—a deep udder cleft, which means a nice separation between the two sides. Couldn't get much more ideal than what she'd been born with. "And just think," I said as I stood up, knees cracking. "She's one hundred percent real."

Claire's scowl held for a few moments longer, until a grin finally broke through. "And she won't try to stick them in anyone's face."

"Boob faker," I said.

Nick glanced up from his love fest with the cow. "Hey, now."

"Hey, now, what? If that girl's going to go around threatening people with her Double Es, she's going to have to be prepared for a little ribbing. Not that she could find her ribs under all that."

Claire burst out laughing. Nick shook his head, apparently not appreciating the "annoyed female" humor.

"Wait." Nick focused across the room. "Isn't that those people again?"

Claire and I followed his gaze. "The Greggs," she muttered.

I squinted, like that could help me see better all the way to the other side of the barn. "Can't imagine anything they bought—I mean *brought*— is as gorgeous as September Breeze."

Claire's nose wrinkled. "I hope you're right."

"At least you raised yours on your own. That's got to count for something."

"I don't know if that's enough."

I slapped Nick's rear. "Come on. If you can tear yourself away from your new girlfriend there, I'd like to check out the Greggs and their cows up close."

He gave Breezy one last ear rub and promised to return. Claire and I exchanged an amused glance. "See you later," I said. "Good luck."

Nick and I made our way toward the Greggs' stalls, pausing now and then to admire the bone structure or coloring or "sweet, honey eyes"— Nick's words—of the beauties lined up along the row. Kids of various ages mucked out the stalls or applied maintenance to their fences or animals, and I greeted several I knew by name. The older girls, whether we greeted them or not, took a break to watch Nick walk by. Even steadfast devotion to their animals couldn't keep them from admiring the prime exhibit parading past their stalls. Since they were teenagers, and no threat to me, I let them enjoy the view without contemplating the chances of their survival.

"Stella?"

I turned away from a grand specimen of an Ayrshire cow to see a woman I knew from dairy circles, but hadn't seen in a while. Claire and

Bobby's mother, Amy Kaufmann. She had the same looks as Claire—Pleasant. Brown. Sturdy. "Amy. How ya doin'?"

"Doing great. You?"

"The same. This is Nick. My fiancé."

Amy shook his hand. I was impressed that her pupils didn't dilate. "I heard someone finally snagged Stella here. Good luck to you."

I frowned. "Hey."

Nick put his arm around my shoulders. "She'll need as much luck as I will. Believe me." I could hear the seriousness underneath his banter. His illness. It never quite left his mind, even if he seemed as healthy as ever. I nudged him, letting him know I was on his side.

Amy looked over my shoulder at the Ayrshire. "Nice girl, there."

"Yeah." I lowered my voice. "Not as nice as Claire's, though."

She took my elbow and led me down the row in the direction we'd been headed. "I know, right? I'm not sure how we lucked out with Breezy. She is a beauty, isn't she? Poor Bobby's cow is nice, but she really can't compare to Claire's."

"Claire deserves it."

"Yeah." Her expression went wrong, like she'd just tasted sour milk. "Unlike those two."

The Greggs, of course. We'd neared their

area, and were in good view of them and their animals. The two middle girls—the original, older two had graduated and moved on to other things—had side-by-side stalls, and their Guernseys could have been twins. A little larger than Breezy, they stood tall and strong, with clear-cut markings and pretty, trimmed forelocks. Not exactly what you would see if you came to my place. But then, I have Holsteins, which have a different look altogether.

"I need to go," Amy said. "See you later?"

"We'll be around."

She left, offering one more glare toward the offending exhibitors, and we turned our attention to the family we'd come to check out.

The Gregg girls were in full-out decoration mode, hanging posters and ribbons and glitter. It was like a Hobby Lobby had exploded. The girls, apparently not content with buying a champion, had decided they needed to win the stall decoration contest, as well. Maybe that was the only way they would feel like they had actually done something to deserve winning a prize. But then, if their parents thought what they were doing cow-wise was legit, their daughters probably thought so, too.

The cows in question were pretty nice. And by pretty nice, I mean perfect. Great build, great coloring, great udders. It was no wonder they'd won at the State Fair the year before.

"Pretty, aren't they?" The Gregg mom was talking to me. She'd obviously just had her hair done, and her lipstick was on in nice, clean lines. I stifled a desire to kick wood chips on her clean pants and un-scuffed boots. Very grown up of me.

After a slight pause, during which I was biting my tongue, Nick said, "Yes, they're very nice."

We watched the girls climbing all over the stall, covering every available surface with sparkle. It was amazing how unlike a cow stall a square box made of wood could actually become.

"They have such nice personalities, too," the Gregg mom said. "We're very fortunate."

And then I couldn't help it. "They are nice cows. Practically perfect in every way. Too bad I can't congratulate the people who actually raised them."

The smile froze on Mrs. Gregg's face, and her voice rose. "What do you mean by that?"

"Mary, what's wrong?" Now the Gregg dad was getting in on it.

She took a little hiccup breath. "She was saying that—"

"Nothing," I said. "I was saying nothing."

Mrs. Gregg's chin quivered, but I didn't feel sorry for her. That's what she got for being a cheater, and teaching her kids to be cheaters, too.

"Well, you were obviously saying something, because my wife is upset." He wasn't going to let it go.

Fine. "We were just having a conversation about who should actually get the credit for your cows. Your family, or the people who actually turned them into champions."

Nick grabbed my hand and pulled. I dug in.

Mr. Gregg, all fake farmer in his pressed denim pants and plaid shirt, looked me up and down, his eyes hesitating at the steer head tattoo peeking around from the back of my neck. His chest puffed out, and he made his hands into fists, pushing against the tops of his legs. "And who would you be?"

"Nobody," Nick said. "She's nobody. Come on." That was to me, of course.

I let him drag me away this time, aware I wasn't helping matters for anybody by pointing out the Greggs' bad decisions. Except my own sense of justice.

"Hey—" the Gregg dad called after us, but Nick hustled me out of the barn and into the crowd of incoming kids and animals.

"Nobody?" I said, yanking him to a stop. "I'm nobody?"

"As far as he's concerned, yes. Do you really want to start a fight in the dairy barn? In front of all those kids?"

I turned away, glaring across the sea of people. Dammit, Nick was right. But it was just so wrong.

"Geez, what's with you?" Zach and Randy were coming back from the food tent.

"Nothing," I said.

The boys gave Nick some kind of look, and slowly walked away.

"Dude," Randy said over his shoulder to Nick. "I am so glad I'm not you right now."

"You won't be soon," I said.

Randy's head jerked around, and he walked a little faster.

Nick smiled.

"What?" I snapped.

He smiled some more. "You have such a way with people. It's no wonder you have so many friends." He slid his arms around my waist and kissed me, right there on the fairway. "So, my sweet girl. Ready to go home now?"

He was lucky I didn't slug him.

Chapter Six

Zach held his hands up as we approached his stall to say goodbye. "I didn't do anything, I swear. Please don't kill me."

"Nah," I said. "I'll just kill Randy."

Randy stepped behind Zach, as if he were really afraid.

Austin sauntered over from his stall, wiping his hands on a rag. "Can I watch?"

I made a gun with my fingers. "I'll let you know time and place."

"You mean it's not right now?"

"I enjoy the anticipation."

He gave me a thumbs-up.

Randy didn't.

"Barnabas doing good?" I reached into the stall to rub the calf's head. He butted up against my hand, and I kneaded harder as he pushed forward. I almost expected him to start purring, or to flop on the ground so I could rub his belly.

Zach laughed and patted Barnabas' back. "He's great. Seems pretty happy."

"He's always pretty happy. Aren't you, sweetie?" Barnabas looked up at me with bright, liquid eyes, and I rubbed his ears.

"We're heading out," I said to Zach. "You need anything else?"

"I'm good. Thanks for bringing me and Barnabas over."

"You got it."

"You coming to the concert tonight?" Opening night of the fair always featured a local country artist, this time Rikki Raines, a girl who'd grown up in the county and had started to make a name for herself in the surrounding areas. The teens seemed to be fans, from the different T-shirts I'd glimpsed throughout the day, proclaiming the wearers to be "Rikki's Rowdies." I'd even seen several bright white wigs, which emulated the long, bleached locks of the singer.

I glanced at Nick, and he shrugged. Country wasn't exactly his glass of milk, but it was always a good time to see people. I'm not always a people-person, but when it came to the fair, I was "fairly" assured of seeing people I liked. At least, some of them. "We'll see what we feel like by that time. If not, we'll be by tomorrow."

His eyes shifted sideways, and I turned. Bobby

had come up, accompanied by a girl. This girl was completely different from anything we'd seen so far. Not a farmer, like Claire, but also not the obscene mannequin we'd experienced at lunch. This girl was cute. Bouncy, but in a good way. And a real way, from what I could tell. She looked like an actual teenager, tallish, with good bone structure. Her long, shiny hair was sort of an auburn color, and a smattering of freckles dusted her nose. She wore sparkly flip-flops, bright pink shorts, and a white blouse, tied at her waist. If she wore makeup, it was expertly applied, so all I noticed were healthy skin and bright green eyes. She was the real deal.

"Hey," Bobby said into our silence.

Zach nodded, his eyes still on the girl.

Uh-oh.

"This is my cousin, Taylor," Bobby said. "She's from Doylestown, and, um, she's doing that pageant thing this week. Taylor, this is Zach. He's the one staying with us this week."

Nick made a noise, and I elbowed him, but I looked at the girl. "You're bunking with Bobby and Claire, too?" Because that could be trouble.

"No," she said, exhibiting perfect teeth. "I won't be staying overnight here at the fair. I don't have an animal to take care of, so…" She shrugged prettily. If shrugging can be described as pretty. "I'll leave the hard work up to these guys."

Oh, she knew how to work it.

"That's Austin," Bobby said. Austin had—geez, what a coincidence—come back over to rejoin the conversation.

Austin smiled. "Hey, Taylor, nice to meet you."

She returned his smile, then moved toward Barnabas. "Is this your calf, Zach? Ooo, he's so cute!"

Yup, definitely working it.

I glanced at Nick, and he winked. "You ready now?"

I turned to say goodbye to Zach and give him a "have fun and be careful" speech, but—what a surprise—he wouldn't have noticed if I'd suddenly grown a second head, seeing how he was introducing Miss Cutie to his calf. Nick and I started toward the back of the barn, and met Claire coming in. I saw the moment she noticed what was going on behind us. Her face went from shy eagerness to surprise, then anger, and finally to acceptance.

"Hi, Claire," I said.

But she didn't hear me. She hesitated, then turned around and walked back out of the barn, her shoulders tight.

"Poor girl," Nick said.

"Yeah."

She was already out of sight by the time we got outside. But someone else was waiting, just around the other side of the trailer where kids would be emptying their wheelbarrows of manure each day.

"You!" Mr. Gregg stomped up and leaned toward my face, way breaking that whole personal space thing. He lowered his voice, and hissed, "You stay away, you hear me? Don't you come near my family, or my cows."

"Hey," Nick said, but I held him off.

Gregg leaned in even closer, so I could feel his breath. He was only a few inches taller than me, and a little bit rounder, so I wasn't too worried about my safety. My boots could do some damage if they needed to. When he didn't move, I put my hand on his chest and pushed him back.

He slapped my hand away. "Don't you touch me."

"Then I would suggest you back up. Now. Or you're going to feel my foot somewhere you wouldn't want it."

His mouth worked, but he took the step I'd suggested. "I'm serious," he said. "You stay away, or…or you'll be sorry."

"It will be my pleasure." I smiled.

His eyes flicked from me to Nick. "You, too."

Nick blinked. "What did I do?"

Gregg didn't answer him. Instead, he twitched his nose, and stomped away. Nobody approached him, or even looked at him with interest.

Nick shook his head. "Like I said. You're always making new friends."

"Who would want to be friends with him?"

"Apparently not you."

"Or anybody else at this fair."

He watched until Gregg was gone. "I just don't want him coming after you."

"Let him."

"Stella—"

"I'm kidding. *Kidding.*"

"No," he said. "I don't think you are."

He knew me so well. How sweet was that?

"Come on," I said, putting my arm around his waist. "Stop worrying about Mr. I Buy My Kids Their Lives. Let's go home."

"Do you have friends there?"

"You know I do. Queenie loves me. And Lucy tolerates me." I rested my chin on his shoulder. "And maybe I'll show you just how good a friend of yours I am."

He looked down at me, and at my lips. "Really?"

I smiled, and raised my eyebrows, just a fraction.

He swallowed. "Just how fast can we get there?"

Chapter Seven

Later that afternoon I was headed out to the barn when my phone rang. This was not the phone in the house. It was not the phone in the barn. It was the new cell phone—with the pink, sparkly cover—Miranda had bought for me and insisted I carry at all times "in case something happens to Nick." Now, I really didn't want to start carrying a phone, and there were lots of times I didn't, like when I was milking, or scraping the barnyard, or when I was actually with Nick, because if the whole point was to take care of him, I would do better being with him in person than counting on technology. If we were gone somewhere and Lucy needed me, she could always call him—he'd had a phone ever since I'd met him. I loved him anyway.

But just at that moment, I happened to have my unwanted accessory on me. "You want to answer it, Queenie?" I held it out to her.

She sneezed.

"Fine. I'll get it. This time. Royalcrest Farms."

"Stella Crown?"

"Yeah."

"This is Becky from up at the bank."

"How did you get this number?"

"It's on your answering machine. It said if you didn't answer at that number and it was an emergency to call this one."

Miranda. I was going to strangle her. "So what's the emergency?" Although I knew it couldn't be good. The words "bank" and "emergency" should never be in the same conversation.

"You had a big bill come through today, and, well, you don't have enough funds in your account to cover it. I need to know what you want to do."

"What was the bill?"

I heard papers shuffling. "Insurance. Bi-annual premium."

"Shit." I rubbed my forehead in case it helped. It didn't. "Can't you just use some money from my savings, like you always do when I overdraw?"

"See, that's why I'm calling. There's not enough in your savings, either, so the only other possibility would be to take it out of your line of credit, but that would push you right up to the limit of that, also. It would be the last time you could use your LOC until you paid some off."

I stood in the middle of my driveway, staring

at my barn, but not really seeing it. Red was the only color I could identify, because that was the color of every bank account I'd ever had. Also because I was plenty pissed off. At Becky, the bank girl. At the economy. At Miranda, for changing my answering machine. At Nick, for having money I didn't want to ask him for.

"Ms. Crown?"

I sighed. "Use the line of credit. I'll figure something out for the next big bill."

She cleared her throat. "You'll have to figure out something for the little ones, too, I'm afraid."

I hung up on her.

"Stella?" Lucy was standing in the doorway of the barn. "Everything okay?"

"Sure. Everything's just dandy."

She frowned, swiveling sideways to let Queenie and me through. "That didn't sound very convincing."

"No? That's probably because I was lying." I kept walking straight through to the office, Queenie on my heels. I slammed the door behind us and dropped into my desk chair, my head in my hands. Queenie lay on the floor beside me, her nose on her outstretched paws. Her eyebrows shifted as she watched my half-hidden face, and I reached a hand down to rest it on her head. The door opened. I didn't look up. "Did my slamming the door not give you a hint that I wanted to be left alone?" When Lucy didn't respond, I looked up. Miranda. Even better. "What?"

"Geez, don't bite my head off. I only came to get you to think about something, okay? Just let me finish before saying anything."

"Miran—"

"Uh-uh. No talking." She waggled a finger in my face. I wanted to break it. Or bite it.

She kept on going, like I'd given her the go-ahead. "I know you think this wedding should be how you want it, and of course it is your wedding. But think about Nick. It's his wedding, too. Don't you want it to be nice? Here. I have it all budgeted out, because I know you're concerned about the money." She pulled a paper out of a pristine manila folder and slid it across the desk. "Everything, down to the penny. I've been calling in favors. We do have a lot of friends in Virginia, you know. But look, see? The caterer, flowers, musicians, photographer, videographer, dresses—including your dress, tuxedos, honeymoon, going-away clothes, transportation…it's all there. Take a look and let me know what you think."

Something very cold and very ugly was creeping up my throat, and I knew there was no way Miranda or our relationship would survive it. It didn't matter what she'd written on the paper. No matter how many favors she'd called in, no matter how many "friends" she had, there was no way I could afford whatever wedding she thought we should have. More than that, there was no way I wanted to afford it.

"Miranda," I said.

"Yes?"

"Get out."

"Excuse me?"

"Get out. Please."

"Stella—"

"Out!" I banged my fists on the desk and stood up, leaning toward her. She slipped out of the chair, grabbing the arms, then scuttled to the door. She looked back at the piece of paper on my desk, but decided not to come after it. Wise choice.

When she was gone—leaving the door open, of course—I sank back into my chair. Queenie had stood up when I'd yelled, and now she did a little back and forth dance, eyeing me suspiciously. "Oh, come on," I said. "You've never seen me lose my temper before?"

She harumphed, and lay back down.

I slouched at my desk, staring at the family pictures that Zach's Uncle Abe—one of my best friends—had hung on the wall. My folks and me, when I was a little tyke. Me with my mom, when I was a teen. And then me with Howie, my longtime farmhand-slash-father figure I'd lost a year earlier when a crazy person had gunned him down in my milk parlor. What would I tell all of them if I lost the farm? Could I ever look at the pictures again?

Nick had money. More money than I could imagine. He and his family owned a housing business in Virginia and, even with the current economic situation, they weren't lacking for work. Miranda had once accused me of only wanting Nick for his money, but of course that wasn't true. It had started out that I'd wanted him in spite of his money, but now it was just…part of him. He'd offered to help out in the past, and I'd always turned him down, because I could always squeak by, but now…

Family farms were becoming a thing of the past. A cute, almost quaint kind of symbol with vegetable stands and specific customers. Tourists looked them up, hoping to get a glimpse of "the old days," and people from the city visited to quench their two-hour longing for "the country." But I didn't want to be a blurb in a "Discover Pennsylvania" book. I wanted to do what I'd always done—to make my living by milking my cows and running my farm. Nick had moved up to Pennsylvania to be with me. He'd left his family and business in Virginia—with the help of the Internet—and seemed as happy as…well, as Barnabas was in his new stall.

"Hey." Lucy leaned up against the doorjamb. "You okay?"

I looked at her for several seconds, then gestured to the chair. "I've got problems."

Her mouth twitched.

"Yeah," I said. "Funny."

"You said it, not me."

"Sit. Please."

She came in, her brow furrowing. "You're serious. What's wrong?"

I leaned forward, rubbing my face. "You know how I've been asking you for the past few months about your job here—"

"Are you firing me?" The color drained from her face.

"No! No. Just listen." I took a deep breath. "You love it here—"

She nodded.

"—and I love having you here. In fact, I couldn't do it without you." Nick couldn't physically hold up any of the hard work. Well, he could once in a while, but with his MS he had to be careful. Besides, running a dairy farm wasn't his thing. It was mine. I couldn't expect him to change his life that much. He'd already made the move to PA. He didn't need to do an entire career switch, too. And run a dairy farm on my own? After having a partner my entire life? Not going to happen. Not if

I wanted to live past my present thirty years, which had clocked me over the head earlier that summer.

"You're prepared for the fall?" Lucy had made money for the farm the year before by offering autumn activities—hay rides and a pumpkin patch and one of those vegetable stands I had really wanted to avoid.

"Sure. Everything will be ready, you know that. Stella, what's going on?"

I pushed myself out of my chair and strode to the window, where I stared out at the quiet, empty driveway. "I'm running out of money. I can't make enough to keep things going how they should be. Not anymore. The bank can't do anything else, and the cows certainly can't, either, not unless we go to three milkings a day, and I don't think I could do that."

Lucy was quiet.

I looked over my shoulder. "You don't want to do that, do you?"

She shook her head. "So what are you saying, if you're not firing me?"

"I have to...ask Nick."

"Sure. It's always good to talk things over with your husband. Or your fiancé." She smiled.

"No, I mean I have to ask him for money."

"Oh." She studied my face. "Are you okay with that?"

I looked out the window again, letting my eyes run over the heifer barn, the yard, the house. The house itself wasn't anything special, no architectural masterpiece. It was just an old farmhouse with all those farmhouse problems. Drafty in the winter. Insulation that had sunk to the bottom of the walls. Damp basement. Creaky stairs. But it was my house. And it had been my parents'. And now Nick was here. It was his home, too.

I turned back to Lucy. "You know, I think I am." I surprised myself—and Lucy, I could see—by smiling. "He made his choice to come up here and be with us. I guess that means he's a part of it now, too. It would be wrong *not* to ask him."

Lucy sat there for a few moments before getting up and wrapping her arms around me. Not something she did on a daily basis. I stiffened, but after a few moments allowed myself to relax into it.

Lucy sighed. "Oh, Stella."

"What?"

She leaned back and looked into my eyes. "I do believe you're growing up."

Chapter Eight

I found Nick in the kitchen, his laptop open, papers all over the table. He was staring at something on the screen so intently I figured it must be something really important. I wasn't sure if I should interrupt, or not.

"Nick?"

He glanced up, then gestured me over. "I'm glad you're here. I need your help understanding this."

"Nick, you know numbers aren't my strong suit." Little did he know just how weak I was feeling at the moment when it came to those pesky digits, especially the ones with dollar signs—or negatives—in front of them. But I went to stand behind him, anyway, and set my hands on his shoulders, expecting to get an instant headache from the spreadsheet. But instead of columns and numbers I saw a picture of a cat. Or, sort of a cat. It was a weird black one, standing in an awkward position, but it was definitely a cat.

"What is that?" he said.

I leaned closer. "I was going to say a cat, but—"

"You see a cat?"

"Of course. It's right there. Can't you see it?" I felt his forehead. "Are you having an episode?"

He pulled my hand away, keeping hold of it. "I'm fine. But I can't see the cat. All I can see is the silhouette of a dancer."

"A woman or man?"

"Woman. Standing with her back to us, her toes pointed, her face tipped our way."

I squinted, and tilted my head. "Nope. Can't see it. Just the cat."

He sighed. "Oh, well. I guess between the two of us we see them both. That's good enough for me."

I laughed. "Me, too."

He turned toward me. "Were you looking for me?"

"Yeah. You have a minute?"

"For you? Always." He scooted his chair away from the table and held out his arms.

I sat on his lap and looked down at his face. "You know how I've wanted to run the farm on my own? How I haven't wanted to take anything from you?"

"Sure."

"And you believe me? That I've never been after your money?"

He laughed. "Of course."

"Good. Because it's true. It's always been true." I hesitated.

He wasn't running away screaming yet, and he had to know what was coming. My stomach churned. I'd always forced away any thoughts of accepting his money, and now I expected myself to just ask? Like it was nothing? I scooted off his lap and leaned against the counter, gripping it so hard my fingers hurt.

"Stella." His voice was kind. "If you need money, you know you only have to ask."

I took a shaky breath. "Nick, I…I was wondering how you would feel about maybe contributing something to the running of the place. Since… since it is your home now, too."

He blinked. And he stared. And then a smile broke out on his face, like the sun coming up after the Apocalypse. He came over, resting his hands on the counter on either side of me. So close I could hardly breathe.

He brushed a finger over my eyebrow. "You just said this was my home."

"Well, it is, isn't it?"

"Any place with you is my home. But, yes. This lovely, drafty old place, and the barns, and the cows, and the yard that needs mowing every other day. They're all my home now. And I can't believe you're going to let me help take care of it. How much money do we need?"

Happiness radiated off of him. Out of him. And I could feel myself smiling right back. He leaned in to kiss me.

"I knew it!"

Nick's nose crashed into my forehead. He spun around to stare at Miranda, his hand over his face. I wondered just how much blood was spurting out of his nostrils.

"I knew she was after your money!" Miranda screeched. "I told you! I said it at the very beginning!"

"Miranda." Nick used his free hand to pat the air, like it would calm her, even though she was in her raging crazed woman mode. "You're eavesdropping."

"Am not."

"And you didn't hear the whole conversation." He took his hand off his nose and looked at it. There wasn't any red.

"I heard enough." She glared at me. "I heard you ask her how much money she needs. Like you're going to say no to anything when she's got her hands all over you."

I took a breath to say some not very nice things, but Nick glanced back at me, his eyes pleading. I looked at the floor, clamping my lips together.

"Miranda." He was using his calm-but-mad-big-brother voice. He'd had lots of practice with that. "You were listening to a private conversation."

"About our family's money!"

"No. This conversation was about my family's money."

"But I am your—" She choked off her sentence, then pointed a shaking finger my way. "She is not your family until you sign on the dotted line. And if she has her way, that's never going to happen!"

I jerked my head up. "What?"

"She won't even talk about the wedding." Still not addressing me. "I gave her a way toned-down budget today, and she wouldn't even look at it! I don't think she wants this wedding to happen at all! She just wants…" She shot daggers at me with her eyes—or maybe the pitchfork she'd saved me from a month before. "She just wants you to save her precious cows."

I pushed myself off the counter. "Now look here, Miranda—"

"Stella." Nick swiveled, putting himself between me and his sister. He laid his hands on my shoulders, and looked down into my eyes. "Do you trust me?" he whispered.

I couldn't speak.

"Do you trust me?"

"Of course I do."

"Then, please. Let me handle this. Okay? Why don't you go back outside? Go hammer something. Or break something. Or kick something—but not with your sore foot." He smiled, but it wasn't his usual carefree one. Nothing like the one he'd had just moments before when I'd asked him for money. Go figure.

"Okay."

He kissed me lightly and let me go. I slipped out of the kitchen, not looking back at Miranda. I wondered just how long she was going to be staying in our house.

Chapter Nine

Miranda screamed out of the drive, slinging gravel as far as the next county. She'd only been in there with Nick for maybe ten minutes, but apparently that was enough.

"She going home?" I tried not to sound too eager.

Nick rested on the gate, next to where I was taking his advice and hammering a new fence post into the ground.

"She said she was."

My breath caught.

"But she didn't take any of her stuff."

Crap.

"So I expect she'll be back sometime after supper, when she's had her fill of Doylestown, or wherever she's going to go to shop and eat."

"We'll just plan on being gone by then."

"Where are we going?"

"To that Rikki Raines concert, remember? If you want."

"Sure. But speaking of food, I'm hungry. Want me to make something?"

"Unless you want to eat at the fair again."

He made a face. "I think I'd rather have something not deep fried this time."

"I'll be in soon."

Lucy pulled in the drive, back from picking up her daughter, as Nick walked toward the house. Tess bounded out of the car, yelling hi to Nick and doing a cartwheel. She was nine, and every bit as energetic as you'd think.

"No Lenny?" I asked Lucy when she came over. Lenny was Lucy's husband, also my friend and biker buddy.

"Working late. People want their bikes all fixed before the fair's poker run later this week." She looked after Tess, who was running around the house, Queenie on her heels. "Plus, Tess went over to work with him today, after lunch, so he wasn't as productive as he would've liked."

"You know she's always welcome here."

"Of course, but when she gets it in her head to be with her new daddy, I don't want to get in the way. And he won't say no." Her voice caught, and I looked away to give her some privacy. She loved Lenny, and he was a great dad type, but he would never replace the dad Tess had had before. Or the husband Lucy had lost. But then, Lenny wasn't trying to replace him. He was just trying to pick up where the other guy had left off. A long road for all of them.

"Talked with Nick," I said. "He's game."

Lucy smiled. "I'm not surprised. Are you? But something's wrong."

I recounted the whole Miranda experience.

"I wondered why she was driving like a teenager. She almost blew us off the road on our way in." She shrugged. "She'll get over it, and come back."

"I don't know, she was pretty pissed off. She's probably off telling her mom and sister all about how I'm going to drain the gold from the kingdom, and next thing you know the entire clan will be here trying to drag Nick away."

"You said his mom and older sister are different from Miranda."

"I guess. But who knows what Miranda will tell them, and what they'll believe?"

"Nick is levelheaded. Someone had to teach him that. Maybe his mother."

"I hope so. With my luck the only sane one was his dad, since he's the only one not around anymore." Nick's father had died a year and a half earlier, prompting Nick's travels to Pennsylvania, when he'd shown up at the farm disguised as a barn painter.

"Hang in there. Unfortunately, when you marry someone, you get the whole family in the bargain, whether you want it or not." She should know. Her late husband's family had tried to get her arrested for killing him, even though it had been an accident. They'd finally relented, and while their relationship with Lucy wasn't exactly friendly, at least they weren't siccing the cops on her anymore.

"Well," she said. "I'm headed in to milk. You guys taking off again soon?"

"That was the plan. Unless you want me to stay and help. I'm not dead set on getting back to the fair. Rikki Raines is okay, but not on my top-ten list, or anything." That would be hard, since most of my top-ten list were either dead or not performing anymore. Stevie Ray Vaughan, Lynard Skynard, the Eagles.

"No, go ahead. Milking is my Zen time, and Tess is fine with Queenie, or catching up on her TV watching."

She left, and I packed up my tools. Nick had some spaghetti and salad ready by the time I got in, and before long we were cleaned up and on the road, this time in Nick's Ford Ranger. The fair was busier this time around, since the public was now allowed in, just for the concert. The exhibition buildings wouldn't be open to them until the next day. Nick drove around to the 4-H entrance, since my being Zach's sponsor got us in for free. We found a parking spot and walked into the family area, where all the 4-Her families had set up their campers. A path through the middle would take us to the main fairgrounds.

"Hey," Nick said, "isn't that your buddy Gregg, who threatened you this afternoon?"

My "buddy," the ever-charming Mr. You're-Going-To-Be-Sorry, hovered under one of the trailer awnings. Hardly anyone else was around in the makeshift campground, so he was easy to spot. And he wasn't alone. Someone else stood just out of sight, hidden behind a light post, and Gregg was not happy with whoever it was. He was throwing his arms around, and pointing, and doing the whole hunched over thing he'd done when he'd threatened me that afternoon.

I stepped into the shadow of another trailer, and pulled Nick into hiding, too, up against a camper. I peered around the corner. "Who is that with him? That's not his wife. At least, I don't think it is. It's hard to tell with that pole in the way."

"Not really any of our business, is it?"

"That's got to be the Greggs' trailer. If you want to call it that." It was more like a full-fledged RV, you know, the kind for old folks who travel to Florida every winter.

"Not really any of our—"

"—business. I know. You said that before."

"But sneaking around behind trailers does

have its advantages." He pressed closer to my back, and ran his hands up my sides.

"Nick…"

"What? You weren't complaining earlier." He kissed my neck.

I laughed. "Yeah, when we weren't surrounded by trailers that might or might not contain teenagers. And their parents."

"Oh. Right." He gave me one more kiss, then leaned over my shoulder to look toward Mr. Gregg. "Hey, it's a woman. She moved, so I can see her."

"And it's our business now?"

"If I can't make out with you, I might as well do something interesting."

Nick was right. About the person, I mean. The woman was standing directly in our sight lines now, and she definitely wasn't Mrs. Gregg. This woman was taller, curvier, and just a little…classier. Now, Mrs. Gregg, as you remember, was clean as a dairy cow on show day. Neat and tidy and all done up to appear like a gentlewoman farmer. But this lady, I don't know, she was simply gorgeous.

"Wow," Nick said.

"Yeah, I know. What is it about her?"

"She's perfect."

"Excuse me?"

"I don't mean for me. You know you're the only one who's perfect for me."

"Not according to Miranda."

"Were we talking about Miranda? I don't think so. Anyway, this woman's just…look at her. Everything's how it should be, and it doesn't seem fake."

Yeah. Made me want to go over and kick some dirt on her. Or mess up her hair. Just like I'd felt earlier that day about Mrs. Gregg. Except if I did that, I'd have to talk with Mr. Gregg, and we all know he would have a cow about that.

"Who do you think she is?" For not wanting to poke his nose in other people's business, Nick was sounding awfully…nosy.

"Have no idea. I've never seen her before." But something about her looked familiar. I couldn't tell what it was. Her hair was reddish, but I couldn't tell if that was from the light, or because of its actual color. Her skin was ivory, and that *smile*. It was a surprise when it came out, since its brightness was almost blinding, but also because it was aimed at Mr. Gregg. Not somebody I would imagine received a lot of those smiles.

Nick cleared his throat. "Um, what they're doing right now reminds me of us about a minute ago."

Yeah. Not exactly how a married man and another woman should be standing. Except it wasn't really her. It was him. She was backing up, her hands out. Pushing him away. She wasn't smiling anymore. I could see even from this distance that she was pissed off now, backing away. But he wasn't giving up. He grabbed her upper arms and pulled her closer, bending his face toward hers.

Nick moved, like he was going to run around me and go after Gregg, but I held him back. "Wait. She's going to—"

She kneed Gregg in the crotch, and he bent over double, letting out a grunt we heard all the way at our spot. The woman said something else I was sure he deserved, then spun around and marched off.

Awesome.

Nick looked down at me. "You knew she was going to do that?"

"I could see it in her face. And the way she was preparing her knee." I took his arm, loving that he had been ready to go defend her. I would have done the same if she'd needed it, of course, but I could tell she was up for the task.

Gregg stood up gingerly, his fists on his hips.

"Let's get out of here," I said.

"Agreed. Seeing that made me feel…"

"Like you were going to heave?"

"I was going to put it a bit more delicately, but yes."

I was not a delicate lass.

Just as we were pulling back, Gregg looked our direction. I stumbled, stepping on Nick's foot. He gasped and hopped backward, crashing into a trash can and knocking it over. He leaned down to pick it up.

"Hey!" It was Gregg. He'd seen us. Or heard us, more like.

I grabbed Nick's hand, and we ran. We ducked around the last row of trailers and sprinted to the far side of the concrete bathrooms, dodging wayward parents and jumping over a cooler and several teens who sat on the ground playing a card game. I pressed my back against the building and peeked around the corner, but I couldn't see Gregg anywhere. It seemed we were safe.

I let out my breath, giving a little laugh. "Well. That was interesting."

Nick took several deep breaths. "Why do I feel like an idiot?"

"Don't worry. You're still cute."

He made a face, then grabbed my hand, and we headed toward the calf barn, which is where we'd been going in the first place, before that little excursion into the dark side. "So." Nick sounded a bit awkward, because coming across a scene like that was weird, and if he was feeling anything like I was, he was just a little creeped out. He looked up at the cloudless sky. "Nice evening."

"Too hot."

"Whiner."

"Am not."

"Are too."

I turned to argue just as we went through the calf barn entrance, and ran right into Mrs. Gregg. She bounced off of me into a burly teenager, who barely stopped on his rush past, screaming, "Don't let her go there! Don't let her—oh, shit." His shoulders slumped, and he stopped running to plod forward toward the mess his cow had just made.

"Hey!" Mrs. Gregg said, just as her husband had a couple minutes earlier, only her version sounded afraid, rather than angry.

I held up my hands. "Didn't see you. Sorry."

Her lips trembled, and she glanced around, as if she was worried someone was watching. "Have you seen…my husband?"

Oh, boy. I glanced at Nick, but he was no help, avoiding my eyes. "You lose him?"

"He's somewhere around here."

"Maybe the dairy barn?"

"I was just there. I didn't see him."

Of course she hadn't, because he hadn't been there. He was busy assaulting some unknown woman.

From Mrs. Gregg's appearance, it seemed she'd been searching for him everywhere, including the manure pile. Her clothes, which had been pristine earlier that day, bore signs of actual work, which, if it were true, made me feel a little bit better about her. Not great, mind you, but it was something. And it made me feel even more dirty about what I'd just witnessed her husband doing. Her knees were smudged, she had a small rip in her shirt sleeve, and there was a piece of something—a wood chip?—lodged in her hair. If I didn't know better, I would say Mrs. Gregg had been for a roll in the hay. Without her husband. What was going on with them?

"Mom?" The two older Gregg girls, the ones with the dairy cows, wrinkled their noses in unison. From their French braided, light brown hair, to their clean pastel shorts and skin-tight, lacy tank tops, they were practically twins.

"Where have you been?" the older one said. "Where's Dad?"

"I'm sure he's close by, Madison. Did you try calling him?"

The girl rolled her eyes. "I texted him. He didn't answer. But then, does he ever?"

From the sarcasm, I would guess the answer to that would be "no."

"He's very busy," Mrs. Gregg said. "He's probably helping your sister."

"Of course he is. Because Melody is so way more important than we are."

"Like, right," the other one said.

"Now girls." Mrs. Gregg glanced at Nick and me, obviously embarrassed. "Let's go see where he is."

"You go look," the older one said. "I'm going to the concert. Come on, Annie."

The two girls spun like countrified synchronized swimmers, and stalked away.

Mrs. Gregg looked like she was going to say something, like maybe, "I'm sorry you had to witness that, and that I have two spoiled brat kids," but instead, she pulled her head in like a startled turtle and scuttled away.

"Any guesses?" I said. "Has he been after that other woman for a while, or did he just want to take this moment to screw another 4-H mom in his trailer?"

"Stella!"

"What? You think he wouldn't do it?"

"I don't know anything about him!"

"Except he's a cheater in one way, with the cows. So why not another? You saw him over there, practically smothering the woman."

Nick frowned. "Sometimes you disturb me."

"And why did she look like that?"

"Who? Like what?"

"Mrs. Gregg. Dirty."

"Maybe she was cleaning out the girls' stalls. Seems like something those parents would do instead of making their kids do it."

"True." I hesitated. "Should I have told her where he was?"

He shrugged. "No-win situation right there."

"Absolutely. So let's forget them, okay?" I pulled him toward Zach's stall, but our boy wasn't there. "Where's Zach?" I asked Barnabas.

He didn't answer.

Austin, Zach's next-door neighbor, was cleaning out his stall, putting the dirty wood chips into a large wheelbarrow. He leaned on his pitchfork. "I think he already left for the concert."

"Aren't you going?"

"Yeah, soon. I wanted to make sure Halladay here had a clean place for the night."

"Good man." I looked around, wondering where Zach had gone. Barnabas looked just fine, so I assumed Zach had done what was needed, and then headed out.

"I'm sure he's okay," Nick said. "Let's go get seats for the concert."

"You sure you want to?"

"I thought that was the whole point of coming again."

"Well, it really was just to be social."

He shook his head.

"What?"

"Who are you?"

I punched his shoulder, and he grinned. "That's more like it. So, what do you say?"

I said goodbye to Austin, took Nick's hand, and started toward the grandstand. "We can always leave if you can't stand it anymore."

"Or if you decide you've had too much socializing."

I kissed the smirk right off his face.

Chapter Ten

Zach was standing toward the front of the crowd with his friends, but Nick and I wanted a seat in the stands, not having any desire to be on our feet for an hour and a half. Besides, I also didn't feel like dealing with the unavoidable drama—I could see that cute girl Taylor standing right next to Zach, and him looking like a lovesick calf. Claire was close by, too, doing her own looking at Zach and the other girl. Nope. Didn't want to be anywhere near that.

I heard someone calling my name, and I searched the faces in the stands until I saw Jethro, Zach's dad, standing up and waving. We were fortunate the stands didn't collapse with his bulk swaying around like that.

Nick and I clambered up toward the Grangers, offering a lot of "Excuse me's" and "Sorry, I didn't see your lemon-shake-up there's," and squeezed in between Belle and Vernice, whose husbands made us feel like a particularly smooshed up sandwich. Jermaine was as large as Jethro, but had landed solidly at the other end of the color spectrum, his skin resembling eighty-percent dark chocolate. Yum. He'd come to the Granger family as a Fresh Air kid from Philly way back when, and had been adopted into the white-faced Granger clan for good. He was a great addition to the group, and everyone in the area just thought of him as "one of Ma's boys."

"Country music?" I asked Vernice, whose gorgeous skin was more of a gentler sixty-percent cocoa.

She smiled. "I think Jermaine's a bigger fan than his brothers. I never could quite understand his fascination with it, but then, there are worse vices. It's especially funny, since the girl is as white as they come, including that bleached hair of hers, but he assures me it's the music he loves."

I thought back to a few months earlier, when Jermaine had been working security at a different concert, one that had all gone to hell. Jordan, yet another Granger brother, had lost his girlfriend in the aftermath, and he hadn't been quite himself since. Not that I could blame him.

"No Jordan tonight?" I asked Belle.

"Nope. Just couldn't bring himself to come. I don't know that he'll ever enjoy concerts again, poor guy. We left him at home with Ma, cleaning up from today."

"Lots of corn?"

She flexed her fingers. "Thought I was never going to be able to move again, my hands were so stiff. And even after a shower I still feel sticky."

I searched through the teens down at the lower level, but couldn't find any I knew, other than Zach and his crew. "Where's Mallory?"

Belle pointed. "She and Brady are down there."

"With Zach?"

"Are you kidding? She'll stay as far away from those boys as she can. One of the reasons she likes Brady so much is he doesn't think burping and farting are funny anymore."

"Zach still does?"

Nick laughed. "It never ends. Believe me."

The lights on the stage brightened, and background music started. The kids—and Jermaine—whooped and hollered, and before long the whole place was rocking. I had to give it to the girl, Rikki Raines—she had quite a set of pipes. It was a wonder we hadn't seen her on "American Idol," or one of those shows. But then, maybe she didn't need that. She danced around the stage in her white cowboy boots, denim skirt, and fringed vest, like she'd been doing it for years. The lights reflected off of her trademark bright blond hair, making me squint.

"Local girl, right?" Nick said.

"From our county. Got noticed somehow, and has been making the rounds in the area."

"She's amazing."

He was right. Even I—die-hard classic rock fan—enjoyed the show. Jermaine hooted and screamed while Vernice clapped politely, and the kids down front went nuts.

"How old is she?" Nick asked in-between songs. "Can't quite tell from here."

"Almost twenty, I believe," Belle answered.

"Ask Jermaine," Vernice said. "He probably knows her exact birthdate."

"First CD came out last year." Belle frowned. "What was it called?"

"*Rainestorm*," Vernice said. She looked at me. "Not 'rain storm,' like you'd think, but her last name and 'storm' combined. A play on words. The song she's singing right now."

"Yeah, I got it." I wasn't that dumb. Did I look that dumb?

"Haven't I seen her somewhere?" Nick said.

Vernice laughed. "Only if you've gone to the grocery store and scanned the gossip magazines in the checkout line. Or watched the news. Or listened to the news. Or the radio. She's everywhere these days. What's the latest thing? It's not about her music…"

"Valerie," Jermaine said, proving that he really could hear a conversation while dancing in his seat to a country song.

"Right, Valerie."

I sighed. "All right. I give. Who's Valerie?"

"Poser," Jermaine said.

Vernice patted his leg. "Valerie Springfield, another up-and-comer, a little more mainstream than Rikki, from the Lancaster area, and fresh on the scene. Supposedly Valerie and Rikki are having a fight over some new young star from that zombie TV show. Can't remember his name. Jermaine?"

"Don't care! Listening to music!"

Which I guess was more than a little hint.

Almost two hours later the girl wound it down, said her first goodnight, sang two encores, and finally finished with "Forever Your Country Girl." The audience eventually settled down and began to file out.

Nick had turned pale, and I didn't like that. "Hey. You okay?"

"I'm fine. Just tired."

"Come on. Let's get home." I pulled him up from his seat, and we said goodbye to the Grangers, who invited us to come freeze corn the next day. I begged off, and we picked our way down the bleachers.

Halfway down we had to wait for parents with toddlers to clean up the disaster that had been their seats, and I let my gaze wander over the stage, on the other side of the fence, separate from the crowd. Black-clothed stagehands efficiently dissembled and packed microphones, signs, speakers, everything necessary for the concert. Several security guards remained, backs to the stage, watching the crowd, eyes constantly on the move. County fairs weren't notorious for riots or crazed fans, but as Brady had mentioned earlier, there were plenty of hometown folks who hit the beer stands a little too hard. I didn't blame Rikki, or her manager, or the fair board, or whoever, for having pros keeping an eye on things.

A flash of white behind the stage caught my eye, and suddenly there was Rikki Raines, with her cowboy boots. She was talking to someone I couldn't see, arms flinging animatedly. She paused, hands on hips, then turned to go, shaking her head. A hand shot out and grabbed her elbow, and she yanked away, pulling the person into the light.

It was Gregg. Manhandling a second woman for the day. Who knew how many more there had been? The man was a menace. He'd changed out of his fake farmer clothes into a suit and a bright red tie. His recording studio executive costume, apparently. He obviously wasn't happy, but then, was he ever? I hadn't seen the man smile once that day. Not even when he was with his daughters, getting their should-be-illegal cows settled.

Rikki wasn't happy, either. She poked Gregg in the chest, and he grabbed her wrist, pulling her close, although this time it didn't look like he was thinking about sex. He wrenched her arm, and she writhed, her back twisting.

Why were the security guards not seeing this? Because their backs were to her, dammit. To protect her from outside people. They had no idea what was going on right there, on the "safe" side of the fence.

"Nick, we have to get over there."

"Where?"

I pointed, but before he saw them, Rikki stamped on Gregg's foot, and he jerked back. She yanked her arm away, and took several quick steps back, holding her wrist. She said something else, then spun around and marched off. Gregg made a move like he was going to follow, but a woman came up to him, holding an electronic tablet. He shoved it away, and she leaned back, holding the tablet to her chest. Gregg followed Rikki with his eyes, but she was too far away now, and more people had come between them. He waited a few more seconds, then walked stiffly away, the woman with the tablet trotting along behind.

"What's happening?" Nick said.

"Nothing, anymore." I explained what I'd seen.

Nick's face darkened. "What is wrong with that man?"

"A lot."

"He obviously doesn't like women. Another reason for you to steer clear of him."

"Not a problem. Too bad everybody can't."

The toddler family had finally made way for us, and we continued down the grandstands, meeting Zach and his bunch at the bottom. Taylor was standing right next to him, with Randy and Bobby hanging around behind them. Claire hovered off to the side, arms crossed, looking anywhere but at the other kids.

"Hey," I said. "Like the concert?"

Zach shrugged.

"It was great!" Taylor said. "She's so talented. It's so wonderful how she's growing her name on her own, and all the work she does with charity, and now the fair! And she's so nice, too!"

I glanced at Zach to see how he was taking the girl's little speech, and it seemed he was taking it just fine. In fact, he looked like Taylor had just spoken the most profound words ever. In a fantastic, gorgeous way.

"Yeah," I said. "She's quite the performer." On and off the stage.

"Oh, Taylor! There you are." A woman sauntered over and gave Taylor a one-armed hug. And not just any woman. It was the woman we'd seen with Mr. Gregg a few hours earlier in the trailer area.

Taylor smiled. "Hi, Mom! When did you get back?"

And it hit me. No wonder I had thought the woman with Mr. Gregg had looked familiar. She was an older, slightly taller version of Taylor the Bouncy Teen. I swiveled my eyes to meet Nick's, and he nodded. He'd recognized her, too.

"Hi, Aunt Daniella," Bobby said, and she gave him a little hug.

Claire didn't look as eager to jump on the whole reuniting with family thing, but she said hi and let her aunt put her arms around her. Claire didn't exactly hug her back.

"So, who have we here?" Taylor's Mom said, eyeing Randy and Zach.

Taylor pointed them both out and introduced them, her hand staying on Zach's arm as she gave me a blank look. "I'm sorry. I don't remember your names."

Nick nudged me.

"Huh?"

He held out his hand. "Nick Hathaway. This is Stella. She's Zach's sponsor for the fair."

"Daniella Troth," Taylor's mom said. "Very nice to meet you both." Daniella had a very firm grip, I'll give her that. Like she needed any more glorious attributes to go along with her perfect—according to Nick—appearance.

"Taylor," she said, "are you ready to go?"

Taylor deflated. "We were just going to go ride the double Ferris wheel."

"No problem. I can find something to do for a few minutes yet. Just text me when you're ready."

"Bye, Mom. Thanks!" Taylor grabbed Zach's arm and pulled him toward the fairway. He didn't say goodbye to us. Randy and Bobby followed like they were attached with a tow rope. Claire trudged along behind. I wasn't sure why I was feeling so sorry for the kid, except that I knew Zach was a great guy, and I could feel her pain. It's hard to compete when a girl like Taylor is in the picture. Especially if the guy you liked had never really seen you in the first place. And the girl is your cousin.

"So I take it the fair is an annual event for you folks?" Daniella smiled at us, and I hoped Nick was still feeling my perfectness for him, rather than the golden aura that seemed to reflect off of this woman.

"It is for Stella," Nick said. "My first time, actually, except for when I went to the fair as a kid."

She focused her smile on me, and rather than sensing the whole pushy mom thing I would expect with someone whose daughter is in a beauty pageant, she seemed to really be interested in what she was asking. Imagine that.

"I live with cows," I said.

Nick snorted.

"I mean, I'm a dairy farmer. Zach gets his animals from me. I grew up bringing my own."

The three of us walked away from the crowd, toward the fairway. "I always wanted to raise an animal for the fair, but it wasn't what my family did." She sounded regretful. "So when Taylor got old enough, I thought maybe she'd want to be in 4-H with her cousins. Their mother, my sister, married into a farming family, so it comes naturally for them, and they've offered a second home to Taylor since her father died. She spends more time with them than at our place, some weeks."

"Amy Kaufmann is your sister? Claire and Bobby's mom."

"That's right. She's been such a blessing during this time."

I wasn't sure if she was giving an opening to ask about her husband's death, but I didn't really want to take it, if she was. Nick, apparently, did.

"How long has your husband been gone?"

"Several years now. Cancer. Taylor was young, but she remembers him."

Nick's expression had gone all thoughtful, and I knew he was thinking about how he could die young, too. Not that I would let him.

"So Taylor and 4-H?" I said, wanting to change the subject.

"My brother-in-law offered to let Taylor take care of one of their cows, or even raise a calf. But she didn't have the interest. She was more into... girl stuff."

"Like the pageant." I tried not to let my irritation with the whole judging-by-looks thing come through in my voice.

She glanced at me, a grin teasing her mouth. "Right. I guess I don't really have anything against it. I own a salon in Philadelphia, so I deal with a lot of girls—and their mothers—who are involved. But it was never really my thing. I don't really socialize or anything with the moms. I guess we don't have much in common."

Hard to believe, looking like she did.

"But Taylor thought it would be fun, and she has met a few nice girls through it. It's not the same as me with the moms. Taylor and those girls are all connected on Facebook, and Twitter, and Face Time...I don't even know all the right names. They share their contact lists, their photos, everything. You'd think they were all sisters, or at least cousins. And as far as the pageant itself, at least it offers something other than just the beauty portion. It's taken cues from some of the larger organizations, and the contestants have to do community service, make good grades, and display a good deal of talent."

"What's Taylor's talent?" Nick asked.

I expected something like baton twirling, or doing a cheer. Yay.

"She's fluent in American Sign Language. She'll do a song translated into that, kind of like a dance."

"I've seen that sort of thing," Nick said. "It's beautiful."

"I agree. Plus, she can use it as part of her service portion. She's already translated at many events, and in schools." A doorbell sounded in her purse, and she pulled out her phone. She frowned at the screen.

I didn't like her new expression. "Are the kids okay? Daniella?"

Her head jerked up. "No, I mean, yes, the kids are fine. It's…someone else." She gave a brief smile, but it lacked the warmth of the earlier one. "It was so nice meeting you both. I hope to see you around some more this week." She tucked her phone into her purse and strode away.

We watched her go. "Gregg, do you think?" Nick asked.

"If it was, I hope she's got her knee ready."

She disappeared into the crowd.

"So," Nick said, "she's nice *and* pretty."

"I believe your earlier description of her was 'perfect.'"

"Which I meant in a completely non-competitive way, compared to you."

"Uh-huh." I stared at him, but his pleasant, honest expression didn't waver. "Whatever."

"So," he said, "maybe some funnel cake?"

I laughed at the change of subject. "I thought you were done with fried things."

"Well, I was earlier, but that smell…"

"Then let's go. I don't want to deprive you of the best the fair has to offer."

He grinned like a little boy.

Chapter Eleven

We bought a fresh pastry and ate it at a table in the school food tent, where we saw lots of familiar faces and had more than one conversation about the crappy economy and whether or not there would be any farm kids left for next year's fair. Gloom and doom. That's us. Welcome to the world of livestock and agriculture.

After a while Nick and I brushed the powdered sugar off our shirts—and he brushed some off my face—and we wandered back toward the parking lot.

"Leaving so soon?" Carla was just exiting the calf barn as we walked past. Only this time she wasn't alone. Lugging her veterinarian tool kit was "the love of my so far disappointing life as far as guys go."

"Hey, Bryan," Nick said.

Bryan shifted the toolbox to his left hand and shook Nick's, like the proper "aw shucks" guy that he was. "Nick. Good to see you."

He glanced at me, and I bared my teeth in what I hoped was a convincing smile. He tipped his cowboy hat. Carla rolled her eyes.

"So are you?" she said.

"Are we what?"

"Leaving?"

"Yeah, we're all tuckered out."

She gave me a look, like what the heck was I saying, but seeing Bryan and his NASCAR accessories always made me feel like I needed to talk hillbilly, or we'd leave him out of our conversations. I know. I'm an ass. But, come on. Does he really have to wear the ginormous Jeff Gordon belt buckle and T-shirt and the watch with all the fancy timers? Was he afraid that without those identifying markers he would disappear?

"Sorry," I said, "we're just tired. This is our second time here today, and Nick's doing his ghost impression."

"I'm better now," he said. "That funnel cake helped. We can stay longer."

"Nick—"

"Ooh, funnel cake?" Carla grabbed my elbow and turned me around, walking me back toward the fairway. I glared at Nick, and he grinned. I'd make him pay later. In a good way.

"So," I said. "You get things worked out from earlier today?"

Carla blinked, like she was having to reroute her thought processor from focusing on fatty foods. "What things?"

"You know. The parents who thought their animal was going to get sick from the neighboring stall."

"Oh, them. Talk about drama. You'd think these people had never seen a cow before. But then, maybe these people haven't."

"Who?"

"That family. The ones who always buy their animals from the State Fair."

"You know about them, too?"

"You kidding me? All us vets know about them. It's not as if the champions don't get listed everywhere, with their photos all over the place."

"So the Greggs were the ones complaining?"

"Them and about a dozen others. It's like people get off their own farms and forget to bring their brains along. Ooh, look! Elephant ears!"

"I thought you wanted a funnel cake."

"Doesn't matter. As long as it has fat and sugar, I'm happy. Right, honey?" This last was to Bryan. "That's why you and I get along so well. I've got all the fat, and you've got all the sugar!"

He smiled at her, his eyes glowing, and she let go of my arm to go snuggle under his.

I, on the other hand, had neither fat nor sugar.

I suppose I was the gristle. And Nick was the icing. Good enough to lick.

"What are you grinning about?" He walked up beside me.

"I'll show you later." I put my arm around his waist and hooked my thumb through his belt loop.

His eyebrows rose. "I like this. The fair makes you frisky."

"And hungry."

"Stop!" Carla shrieked.

I spun around, ready to defend her. But she was pulling Bryan along to the homemade ice cream stand. Nick and I watched as she ordered a large waffle cone.

"That woman," Nick said.

"Yeah. Isn't she great?"

"Want to get a table?" Bryan asked Carla, when she'd returned with a cone as big as her head.

"No. I want you to win me something."

He winced. "I'm never any good at those carnival games."

"Oh, come on. It'll be fun."

So the four of us wandered around the games, losing quarters—and dollars, which made me cringe—and marveling at how the international carnies lacked so many teeth. And hygiene skills. And names we could pronounce.

"Hey," Nick said while we waited for Bryan

to shoot ducks with a water pistol. "Isn't that the Gregg guy again?"

Gregg was still in his suit, walking quickly down the fairway, head swiveling side to side, like he was looking for somebody. I hoped it wasn't me. I really wasn't in the mood for a fight.

Nick's eyes narrowed. "At least he's not threatening anyone at the moment."

"Until he finds who he's looking for."

Two more men in suits followed Gregg, also searching the lines and stalls. These guys didn't look like executives. They looked like bodyguards. Or thugs. Not from the same security company who had worked the concert. Their suit coats fit snugly around bulky arms and chests, and what promised to be a gun holster, and the men stood at least a head taller than the regular fair crowd. One of them caught my eye and held my gaze just long enough for a chill to sneak up my spine. But then he was gone. I shuddered.

"Stella!"

I searched for the source of the voice, and Nick pointed up. Zach was on the double Ferris wheel, peering over the edge, tipping the car forward. Taylor peeked over the front, too, and the car tipped even further, swaying as she waved.

"Whoa." I held my hands up, like I could keep them from falling, should they tumble out.

The wheel kept turning, and the next car in line held Randy and Bobby, with Claire squished between them. She wasn't having as much fun as Taylor, that was easy to see. And then they were gone, spun up toward the sky, and I was left feeling a little dizzy and carsick.

"Guess Taylor's not ready to go yet, huh?" Nick said. "Her mom's going to be wondering."

"I'm ready, though," I said. "I've got to be up in six hours."

"Is it really that late?"

"So who's that little vixen up there with Zach?" Carla's eyes sparkled, maybe because she was interested in Zach's love life, maybe because Bryan had just won her a gigantic purple puppy. Or something that sort of looked like a puppy. With horns.

"She's a competitor in the Lovely Miss Pennsylvania pageant," I said.

Carla blanched. "Not that horrible girl I saw hanging around the food tent earlier."

Nick barked a laugh. "No way."

"This girl is actually nice," I said. "She's Bobby and Claire's cousin from Doylestown. She seems genuine."

"In every way?"

"From what I could tell, although I wasn't really looking."

She angled her eyes toward Nick, and he held his hands up. "Not even going there."

"But her mother," I said, "is perfect, according to Nick."

"Stella…"

"Just kidding. She seems pretty perfect to me, too."

Carla wrinkled her nose. "She's not one of those crazy moms who puts her three-year-old in beauty pageants, dresses her up in skanky clothes, and makes her dance to 'Maneater'?"

"No." I laughed. "Taylor, the daughter, doesn't look like that. And her mom seemed like a normal person. She said the whole pageant idea was Taylor's, and the only reason she let her do it was because of the community service element, and the pageant's focus on talent."

Carla harumpfed. "Twirling a baton in a skimpy outfit?"

"I didn't know batons wore outfits," Nick said.

I elbowed him. "Actually, Taylor's talent is sign language."

Carla nodded. "Okay. I can deal with that."

Zach yelled again, coming around on another spin, and we waved up at him.

"Remember?" Nick said in my ear. "We were going home?"

Right.

"Carla—" I turned to tell her we were leaving, but she was busy being kissed by Bryan. Or by the gigantic horned puppy he'd won for her. It was hard to tell. I cleared my throat, and Carla pushed the stuffed animal to the side to see me. "We're going."

"Okay, see you tomorrow!" She grinned and hid behind the puppy again.

Nick laughed. "Guess the fair makes her frisky, too." He swung my hand as we walked away. "See, Bryan's not so bad, right? You just spent over an hour in his presence, and no one died."

"Whatever." Actually it really hadn't been that bad. He didn't talk to me much, and he made Carla as giddy as…well, as Taylor was around Zach. Interesting.

We made our way down the fairway and had just passed the calf barn when screaming split the air. We stopped like dogs on point, and listened. More screaming. Close by. We ran toward the sound, and found a teenage girl up on the manure trailer, shrieking, her hands on her face. An overturned wheelbarrow lay on the ground, obviously tipped off the trailer, its contents spilled into the path. I leapt over the dropped manure and ran up the ramp. The girl grabbed me, crying and saying things I didn't understand, her face pushed into my shoulder.

Nick ran up the trailer behind me. "There."

I followed his finger toward the pile of manure. I didn't understand why the girl was so freaked out, because cow crap was a matter of daily business. Maybe there was a rat, which would be gross, but not unheard of. Or maybe she slipped and thought she was going to fall off. But she kept screaming, and blurting out unrecognizable words, and I took a closer look where Nick was pointing. He'd gone even paler than he'd been before the funnel cake, and I realized something was out of place. A person was lying on the pile—but no, not on it. In it. All I could see were jeans and farm boots. The entire upper half was covered.

Other people had arrived, and I wrenched the girl off and shoved her onto someone else. Together, Nick and I grabbed the legs of the person and pulled, but whoever it was was really stuck. A few more people joined us, and with a few hard tugs and some careful use of shovels, we were able to slide the person onto the bare floor of the trailer. Impossible to see who it was, with all that crap everywhere. Nick peeled off his shirt and I used it to wipe the person's face, doing my best to clear the nose and mouth. It soon became obvious that it was a woman, and also that my actions wouldn't do any good. She wasn't going to be breathing again no matter how clean her airways became. Not with the way her eyes were staring, and the way her chest wasn't rising up and down.

And then I sucked in my own breath. Because I saw something else mixed in with the muck surrounding the woman's head. It wasn't straw, because I would recognize that right off. But it was bright white, where it hadn't been ground into the manure. Stunned, I rubbed Nick's shirt over the woman's head, clearing enough of the dirt that I could see that the white strands were attached to her scalp.

I had just seen that hair earlier in the evening, when it had been flowing beautifully, a part of the woman's easily recognizable persona. I took another look at the victim's face, realizing with horror who I was seeing.

It was Rikki Raines.

Chapter Twelve

"No, I didn't know her. I never talked to her." I'd said it a million times. "I saw her in concert this evening, like everybody else. That's it. That's all I know."

"But she's local."

"So are thousands of other people. I don't know them all."

The detective—what was her name again? Wyatt? White? Watts—wrote in her little notebook. Why she hadn't just asked the other officers for my statement was beyond me. But I was doing my best to cooperate and not be a pain in the ass. Because I've been told I can be one. By many people.

But I was reaching my limit. A talented young woman was dead, and from what I could see, the cops weren't any closer to figuring it out than they were hours earlier. In fact, they needed a whole new approach, if their communication was as bad as it seemed. And I was tired of trying to communicate.

"Look, lady, I've told you everything I know. Including who I saw Rikki talking to earlier."

Watts blinked. "What do you mean?"

"Mr. Gregg, whatever his first name is."

"You didn't mention him at all."

I hadn't? I'd told my story so many times, I couldn't remember what I'd said. "They were together after the concert, on the stage side of the fence. She stomped on his foot."

The detective gave a surprised laugh, then pretended she was coughing. "Why?"

"Because he was attacking her."

"Attacking her?"

"He'd grabbed her wrist. It was obvious he was hurting her."

"And you saw this how?"

I explained why Nick and I had been held up in the stands, and how I'd just happened to catch the altercation.

"What happened after she…got away?"

"He went the opposite direction. There was another woman there, with an iPad or whatever, so it didn't look like he could go after Rikki."

"Did this Mr. Gregg and the victim have a relationship?"

"How would I know? I assume since she's a singer and he's a recording studio exec there could be something there. But like I said, I've never talked to the girl, and the Greggs and I aren't exactly friends. I don't think they even know my name."

She frowned. "But you know theirs?"

"Well, sure, everybody knows theirs."

"I don't understand."

So I had to explain the whole cheating at the fair thing. She seemed confused. "They don't raise their own cows?"

"Right."

"And that's a problem?"

Obviously, the woman was clueless.

"The whole point of 4-H is for kids to learn about animals, and take on responsibility. If they just buy champions, they haven't done any work, and they take away rewards from the kids who have."

"But what about the kids who had the champions to begin with? At last year's fair?"

"Those kids raised the animals and turned them into champions. They deserved the prize."

She looked at me blankly. "Is this something someone would kill over?"

"I doubt it. People get angry about it, but killing someone? I don't think so. Besides, the Greggs aren't dead."

"True."

I glanced at my watch. Almost two. "Do you know how long ago she died?"

The detective didn't answer.

"Hello?" I waved my hand in front of her face.

"No way to know. We do know she was alive at ten o'clock, because someone saw her heading away from the grandstand."

"Right after I saw her with Gregg."

She nodded. "I suppose so."

I recalled standing in the fairway, seeing Gregg with those thugs. "He was looking for someone later."

"Gregg?"

"It was close to eleven-thirty. He was walking fast past the carnival games with two other guys. They were looking for someone."

"How do you know?"

"He was checking out all the games and vendors, looking through everybody. So were the men." I shuddered, remembering the way the guy's eyes had stunned me.

"Who were they? The ones with him."

"Don't know. I guess you'll have to ask him."

"I will."

I rubbed my temples. "Can I please go home now? I've told you everything I know—" which I'd also told everyone else "—and I'm tired. And I'm sad."

She narrowed her eyes. "Why are you sad?"

Was she kidding? "Because a young woman is dead. Doesn't that make you sad?"

"Well, of course it does, but—"

"Look, Detective, I'm going home."

"I'm not done with—"

"Yes, you are. You are done with me and you're done with Nick."

"Who's Nick?"

Was she shitting me? I looked around. The cops had taken over one of the exhibit halls, closing it off to the exhibitors and visitors, and all of us witnesses were being questioned in different corners of the building. I'm sure everybody with a booth in there was really going to be happy about that in the morning.

But that didn't matter. Nothing mattered except that a talented young woman was dead. My eyes landed on a pathetic huddle in the middle of the room, people I didn't know, probably Rikki's entourage. The group consisted of young women, mostly, all with red eyes and smeared mascara. A couple of guys sat with them, along with a middle-aged woman who stared into space, knees together, feet apart, creating an awkward triangle that wrenched my heart. Rikki's mother? There was no way to know, but no one was treating her like she was special that way.

Across the room, half-hidden behind the regional Relay for Life table, were two men and a woman in power suits. All three were on the phone, and all three appeared ready to explode. When one of them would end a call, he or she would immediately punch in another number and begin talking again. Rikki's agents? Managers? Recording studio executives? But then, Gregg was conspicuously absent. Had he worked with Rikki? If so, I would think he'd be here, for sure. Unless he was the one who had killed her, and had taken off for Brazil.

I let my gaze wander.

The girl who'd found Rikki's body on the manure trailer had been sequestered at the local florist's table, but I couldn't imagine why the cops were keeping her. What more could she say, other than, "I saw the feet, and freaked out"? In other spots teens waited quietly in folding chairs, probably only to end up being questioned about who they'd seen out by the trailer that evening. I supposed it made sense to ask, but who was thinking about loiterers when they were shoveling shit? If it were an attractive teenager hanging around, maybe, but other than that? Everybody else may as well have been invisible, unless they were doing something strange. I didn't think any of the 4-H'ers would have the answers. And I knew for sure that I didn't.

I got up and walked away.

"Hey," Detective Watts said, "you can't just—"

"Watch me."

I spied Nick in the corner of the building, talking to a police officer. Or listening to one. Or else just sleeping. He was wearing a stretched out Dairy Association T-shirt he'd been given by one of the 4-H parents after his had been used for cleaning off Rikki's face. It was better for everyone if his naked torso wasn't open for viewing. Who knew what some crazed stalker woman might do when presented with a living, breathing ivory sculpture. I strode over, and touched his shoulder. The officer stopped whatever he was saying to glance up at me. "Can I help you, Ms.?"

"I'm taking him."

Nick's eyelids cracked open to reveal bloodshot eyes. "Hey, you."

"Hey, yourself. Come on. We're going home."

The officer's head whipped around to the other groups of people, as if checking to see what he'd missed. The detective was striding our way, fire in her eyes, so I hauled Nick to his feet. "Start moving."

He didn't argue.

"Ms. Crown! Stop!"

All heads in the area swiveled our way, and one of the other cops stood up, fingering the gun on his belt.

"Whoa," I said, hands up. "No need for violence."

Watts waved the officer down, and I wasn't sure if her irritation was with me or the gun-happy dude. When he'd relaxed and all the focus had left our little group, she glared at me. "I said I wasn't done with you yet."

"And I said I've given you all I had. Twenty times. And so has Nick."

She eyed him. "So you're Nick?"

He attempted a smile, which even in his state was devastating.

The detective wasn't moved. "I need to talk to you."

He sighed. "Whatever you need."

"Nick—"

"I'm fine. Just…stay with me." He sat back down, hanging onto my hand, and after a moment I yanked a chair over beside him. The officer stayed, and the detective loomed over us.

"From the beginning," she said. "And I especially want to hear about this Mr. Gregg who assaulted our victim."

Nick glanced at me, then started to talk. I crossed my arms and glared at the detective. She may have been in charge, but that didn't mean I had to be nice about it.

Twenty minutes later, in the middle of yet another stupid, repetitive question, there was a commotion at the door, and Daniella Troth burst through, eyes wide, face as pale as Nick's.

"You can't come in here." A cop jumped in front of her.

She peered over his shoulder and scanned the room, skimming over the manure trailer girl, Nick and me, and the line of waiting teens. Her eyes landed on the group in the middle, where Rikki's friends cried. One of the girls jumped up and ran to her, wailing. She flung her arms around Daniella's neck and sobbed. Daniella held onto her tightly, smoothing her hair in such a motherly gesture I wondered if the girl actually was her daughter.

But then other girls jumped up and raced to her, too, and soon she was like a mother hen, so swamped by chicks she could barely stand. The cops gave up trying to separate her from her flock, and stood by, watching. Most of the officers' faces showed sympathy, pain even.

Not so my dear detective. She just looked annoyed.

"Guess other people are sad, too," I said. "Does that make them all suspects?"

She glared at me. "They're girls."

"You're kidding me, right? You think girls can't kill somebody?"

"Oh, I know they can. I just think it's a lot more likely it's someone else this time."

"Like?"

She cocked her eyebrow. "You can't really think I'm going to answer that."

"Nope. Just like we're not going to answer anything else. Come on, Nick. Let's go home."

This time, she didn't stop us.

Chapter Thirteen

Word had obviously gotten out about Rikki's death, because a crowd had gathered outside the exhibit hall. Teenagers, reporters, a drunk guy passed out on a bench. I figured the cops were too busy to get around to hauling him away. Nick and I threaded our way through the people, me leading, pulling him along. We'd almost made it out before they found us.

"Stella?" Zach pushed through the people closest to us. "Is it true?"

Taylor was right there with him, along with Claire, Bobby, and Randy. Taylor's eyes were bloodshot, and her nose had reddened.

"Taylor's mom said something happened to Rikki Raines."

We'd attracted more people, most of whom I didn't know. I jerked my head, and Zach and his group followed us to an unoccupied space next to the junior 4-H building. I wasn't sure what to say. Nick squeezed my hand and gave me a nod.

"Rikki Raines is…dead," I told them. "I'm sorry."

Taylor let out a sob, and leaned into Zach's shoulder. He glanced down at her, then awkwardly put his arm around her. Claire's mouth pinched, and she crossed her arms over her stomach, looking at the ground. The other guys stood silently.

Zach swallowed. "But…what happened?"

"We don't know. She was out behind the calf barn."

"You found her? That's why you were in there?" He meant the exhibit hall, with the cops.

"We heard screaming. We went to help."

"Was she—"

"We don't know how she died, Zach. They didn't tell us anything, and we couldn't see."

Taylor pulled away from Zach. "Is my mom in there?"

"Yes." I thought of how the girls had flocked to her. "How does she know those people, the ones who look like Rikki's friends? Did your mom know Rikki, too?"

Taylor took a shuddering breath. "They all come to her salon, Rikki and her whole group. The salon has a contract with the recording studio. They do all the make-up and hair for their shoots and videos and public appearances and whatever. She got to know Rikki over this past year. I even got to meet her one time. She was so…nice." The tears started again, and Taylor swiped at her face.

Zach stared at me, his expression frightened. It wasn't about Rikki, I didn't think, but what to do with the crying girl on his shoulder. I wasn't going to offer to take her, because God knew I wouldn't be any better. But I knew someone who would.

Nick read my face without a word, and gently extricated Taylor from Zach, murmuring something I couldn't hear. Just like he'd done with Claire's cow Breezy earlier that day.

"Why don't you guys head on back to your trailers," I said. "We'll stay with Taylor till her mom comes out."

I half expected Taylor to freak out at the suggestion, but she was so out of it I'm not sure she heard what we were saying. Besides, Nick knew what he was doing.

Zach and the other boys put up a little token refusal, but Claire seemed relieved.

"Come on, guys," she said. "It's late."

"Calf judging starts tomorrow," I added. "You need sleep."

"You think they'll still go on with it?" Bobby asked. "Won't this mess things up?"

"They can't cancel the whole fair." I didn't think.

Still they hesitated.

"Go on, guys. There's nothing you can do here. They're not going to tell you anything."

In fact, more cops had arrived and had begun dispersing the crowd.

"I guess," Zach finally said. "If you're sure."

"We're sure. We'll see you tomorrow."

Nick had taken Taylor to a bench—the drunk guy had now been removed—so Zach and the other kids left without saying goodbye. I assured Zach I'd let her know where they went. With Daniella taking Friend Consolation Duty, she might be a while. Taylor could always crash in her cousins' trailer while she waited. They were too tired to get up to any shenanigans yet that night. Probably.

When Zach and his friends were gone, I went over to the bench. Taylor sat in the crook of Nick's arm, snuggled up against him like a little puppy. Her face was blank and white, and I don't think she was even aware of where she was.

I stood beside them, watching as the police sent people away. I know "There's nothing to see here" is a cliché, but it was also true. We weren't even in the vicinity of where the body had been found. That was roped off out behind the barn, out of sight from where we were. I wondered if there was a crowd gathered there, too, and how exactly you memorialize a manure trailer.

The reporters were a little harder to dislodge,

and several of them refused to budge. Free speech, and all that. The cops seemed to realize it was a hopeless cause, and left them alone. A helicopter flew over, and I wondered if that, too, was reporters, or if it was law enforcement, searching for the perpetrator, although it seemed a little late for that.

The officers eventually made their way to us, and we explained about Taylor's mom being in the building. They made a call, then let us stay, asking us to just "keep out of the way."

Not an issue. We weren't up for moving.

Almost an hour later—an hour filled with silent tears, blank staring, and sniffles—Daniella Troth exited the building. She was alone, so either Rikki's friends were still inside, or they'd gone out the other side. The reporters were on her immediately, like Queenie on a day-old bone. The cops had pulled some of their manpower, so Daniella was smothered with shouted questions, and microphones stabbed at her face. Two officers did their best to tear the journalists away, but weren't having much effect.

I strode over and forced my way through the reporters. Daniella stared into the camera lights like a raccoon in the headlights of a Mack. I grabbed her arm and backed her up against the building so we weren't surrounded from all sides. I stepped in front of her.

"You." I pointed at one of the cameraman blinding us. "You, and you." All three. "Turn those off."

"Who are you?" A heavily made-up woman I recognized from the evening news pointed a microphone in my face.

I grabbed the microphone away from her and covered the mouthpiece with my hand. "I am the person who's going to make sure this lady isn't hounded by you folks."

The reporter tried to get the microphone, but I held it above my head, and she couldn't reach it. I guess she thought it was undignified to jump.

She put her hands on her hips. "We have a right to know."

"Who am I? I'm surprised you're so interested."

"No, in what's going on."

"Well, then, it's fortunate you have so many people to ask. Just not this lady."

"Who's she?"

"No one you need to know." I aimed meaningful looks at the cameramen.

"You can't make them put down the cameras," Revlon Lady said.

"Oh, can't I?" I handed the microphone to Daniella. "Hold this."

The first cameraman met my eyes as I stepped toward him, but his gaze soon dropped to the tattoo peeking around my neck, and his expression wasn't so confident.

I leaned toward him and spoke quietly. "Look, man, I really don't want to break your camera. Do us both a favor and back off."

He hesitated a few more seconds, then lowered the camera.

"Derek!" the reporter shrieked.

He wouldn't look at her.

I swiveled my head to glare at the other two cameramen. One of them put his down right away, but the second waited a few more beats before complying. I nodded my thanks.

"Come on," I said to Daniella. I walked her in the opposite direction of Nick and Taylor, because the last thing I wanted was to lead the reporter to them. We were almost across the open space when the camera lights went back on. I spun around, but they weren't interested in us anymore. Someone else had exited the building. It was a couple of the girls and the middle-aged woman from the center group.

"Who is that?" I asked.

Daniella sniffed and pulled a tissue from her purse. "Rikki's aunt. She raised her. Those are her cousins. Poor things." She hiccuped.

"You okay?"

"I'm fine," she said, but her nose was as red as her daughter's. "Can we go over to Taylor now?"

Taylor jumped up when we got close, and grabbed her mother around the waist. Daniella hugged her, and whispered into her hair. Taylor nodded, and stepped back, staying close.

"Thank you, Stella, for…that." Daniella gestured at the reporters.

"My pleasure."

"And Nick—I really appreciate you taking care of Taylor."

"Glad to help." He handed her one of his business cards, which bore his cell phone number. "Let us know if there's anything else we can do."

She gazed at the card, then blinked, as if just then realizing what she was holding. "Thank you. I will."

There was so much I wanted to ask her, like how was it she'd gotten to be "mom" to that whole gaggle of girls, why she'd been arguing with Gregg earlier, and just how she stayed looking so beautiful with a Rudolph nose. But even I realized it was not the time for questions. We walked the two of them out to the parking lot, and went our separate ways without speaking again.

Chapter Fourteen

Nick insisted on driving home. There was no talking him out of it. By the time we got there, I was exhausted from staying awake, and he was so pale I was sure he was going to pass out.

Queenie stayed holed up wherever she was, sacked out, I was sure, since it was closing in on three a.m. Nick and I stumbled up the walk and into the living room. I opened the door to the stairs.

"Nick!"

I jerked back, knocking Nick to the side. He caught himself on a chair, and I caught myself on him.

Miranda sat in the dark by the window. She stood up and crossed the room. When she reached us, she poked his chest. "Where have you been? I've been calling and texting and—"

He grabbed her hand and held it. "Miranda, please."

"I know you're mad at me, but that doesn't mean you should go off who knows where and do…whatever."

"We weren't…" He sighed. "Miranda, can this wait till tomorrow?"

"I have a right to know—"

I took a breath, but Nick shut me up with his eyes. Fine. If he wanted to deal with her, he was more than welcome. I stepped into the stairwell, and shut the door behind me. But I stayed at the bottom of the stairs. If she was going to give him a hard time I was going to be there to stop her, whether he wanted me to or not.

"Miranda," he said, his voice muffled but understandable. "I'm thirty years old. I believe I can go where I want."

"With her."

"Yes, with her. She's the one I go places with now."

"As if she cares as much as I do. Look at you. You're a mess. You should've been to bed hours ago. But no, she kept you out doing whoever knows what—"

"Miranda."

"I've told you over and over that she doesn't really care about you as a person—"

"Miranda, stop."

"But—"

"Quiet."

I could hear her intake of breath, it was so loud.

"This has been a terrible night," Nick said. "I don't want to talk about it now. I want to go to bed. I am exhausted and worn out and I'm going to fall over if you don't let me go."

"But…what's wrong? What happened? Did you have an episode?"

"It wasn't me."

"Stella? Something happened to her? She looked fine." Said as if she were disappointed I hadn't dropped dead.

"I'm going to bed now."

"Nick…"

"If you want to know, watch the news."

"Why can't you just—"

"Goodnight, Miranda. I suggest you get some sleep, too. You look like hell."

I barked a laugh, then slapped my hand over my mouth. Whoops.

I didn't wait for the door to open before I ran up the stairs.

Chapter Fifteen

I got through milking on autopilot. Nick had slept right through the alarm, and I'd let him go. He needed the rest. I figured I could take a nap later if I needed to.

I was taking that nap at the kitchen table when someone knocked on the door. I jerked my head up, causing a kink in my neck. Had I really heard something? Yup. There it was again.

I opened the door, rubbing my neck, ready to yell at whatever salesman was showing up that early. By God, if it was one of Miranda's florists or caterers or dressmakers I was going to—

"Willard?" My own local detective stood on the doorstep.

"Stella. You okay?"

"Why wouldn't I be?"

He blinked slowly, his hands in his pockets.

"You're not going away, are you?"

He didn't move.

"Fine. Come on in."

He ducked under the door and followed me to the kitchen, where my cereal had congealed into milky mush. I dumped it into the sink. "I don't make coffee. You dying?"

"I had some already. Thanks."

I poured myself a new bowl of cereal and held up the box of Corn Chex. Willard shook his head and took a seat at the table. When I'd joined him, he said, "Late night."

"You know about it?"

"Some. Want to tell me?"

Surprisingly, I did. I went through the entire ordeal, from hearing the screams to stalking out of the building and telling off the reporters, although I kept that part short and vague. I ended with, "So what's with that detective? Watts? She have a stick up her ass?"

Willard chuckled. "Guess you could say that. She's young, about your age, probably, maybe younger. How old are you again?"

He'd been at my birthday party, so I figured he was just being annoying. "However old she is, she was a jerk. It's no wonder she didn't have a clue what I'd been telling the other cops all evening— none of them probably want to talk to her. What's her deal? She get dropped on her head at birth?"

He leaned back, the chair creaking under his

bulk. "Worse. Dad made detective even younger than she did. Now he's sheriff."

"Sheriff? How come I didn't know that?"

"I don't know. You don't watch the news?"

"No, I mean our Sheriff is Schrock."

"Ah, right. His name is Schrock. Hers is Watts."

"She's married."

"Actually, no. Her folks were never married, and her mom gave her her own surname when she was born."

"So she never really knew her dad."

"No, she did. She just never liked him."

"And now is working for him."

"It's a strange world."

I drank the last of the milk out of my bowl. "Anyway, why are we talking about her?"

"You brought her up. Said she was a jerk."

"Right." I sat back. "So what do you know about last night?"

"That I can tell you?"

"No, that you can dangle in front of my nose and be a butt with."

He laughed. "Probably not a lot more than you already know."

"I don't know anything, except Rikki Raines is dead. I don't even know what killed her." He didn't respond to my hint, so I had to prod him. "Do you know?"

"Not yet. There was nothing obvious."

Which meant no broken neck, or stab wound, or anything else done in a sudden, violent strike. "When they know, will you be able to find out?"

"Most likely."

I rubbed my forehead, in case that might help ease my ferocious headache.

Willard leaned forward, elbows on the table. "Stella. I was wondering something."

I waggled my free hand in a "go ahead" gesture without stopping the rubbing.

"What were you doing on YouTube this morning?"

That stopped the rubbing. "What?"

"There you were, right on my computer screen, threatening innocent reporters and cameramen."

"Innocent?"

"Yeah, you're right. That's pushing it a bit far. But still…" He raised his eyebrows.

Dammit, I should've done more than threaten those people. "I told you. I was trying to help someone."

"Daniella Troth."

"You know her?"

"The sheriff's office does, after last night. She hadn't been on their radar before, but now…"

"They're suspicious of her because I stopped the reporters from harassing her?"

"Who's getting harassed?" Nick stepped up behind me and began kneading my shoulders. God, I loved that man.

"No one." Willard half stood and stuck out his hand. "Good to see you, Nick."

"Likewise." Nick took a brief break in my neck rub to shake Willard's hand, then resumed when I pointed at my shoulders.

Willard sat back down. "I was just telling Stella here that she's a YouTube star."

"Hmpf." My shoulders stiffened.

"The altercation with the reporters last night?" Nick didn't sound surprised.

"Stupid reporters," I mumbled.

Nick squeezed my shoulder, then kept rubbing. A moan rose in my throat, but I remembered just in time that Willard was sitting three feet away, so I kept myself appropriate.

"It wasn't actually the reporters who posted the video," Willard said. "It was a Rikki Raines fan waiting outside the building."

"I thought the cops had chased them all away."

"Yeah, well, you know how that goes. The comments for the video are mostly in support of you, by the way, trashing reporters in general. You even got an interview request and a marriage proposal."

Nick stopped massaging my shoulders again. "Do I need to be worried?"

I patted his hand. "Nah. You're still my first choice. Now keep rubbing."

"Yes, ma'am. So," he said to Willard, "you're here to continue questioning us? Because Detective Watts didn't seem finished. At least not the way she was fingering her handcuffs as Stella spirited me away."

"Daddy issues," I said. "I'll explain later."

Willard laughed. "No, I really did just want to check in. After seeing that YouTube video I wanted to make sure you were all right."

"Very kind of you," Nick said.

I was curious. "How'd you find that YouTube video, anyway? Willard, were you surfing?"

"No." His mouth twitched. "Your favorite police officer saw it and told me about it."

"What favorite—Do you mean Meadows?" An officer in Willard's department who'd rubbed me the wrong way since the day I met him when he didn't believe I was having a life-or-death situation on my farm. He'd sort of redeemed himself later on, but he was still a jerk. "What was he doing looking me up on YouTube?"

"He wasn't looking you up. He was looking up Rikki Raines, and anything that might shed light on her murder."

"On YouTube?"

"People post all kinds of things. You never know what you might find."

"Even if you're Meadows."

"Yes, even then. Anyway, he ran across that video from last night. He, um, was quite… impressed."

"I'm sure." I held up a hand. "We were talking about something before Nick came in. What was it?"

"Harassment," Nick said.

"Right. Daniella. Reporters. Willard said the cops suspected her."

"No, I didn't. I said she was on their radar now."

"How come?"

"Because she knew Rikki Raines. Very well, I guess. Not sure why."

The side door opened, and Lucy came in. She froze in the doorway. "What happened? What did I miss? Why didn't you call me?"

"Relax, Luce, everything's fine. Well, not fine. I mean, it's fine here, it's just not…" My brain stopped working.

"Detective?" she said. "Why are you here?"

"Hello, Lucy." He got up again to shake hands. "Everything here at the farm is going along as smoothly as always, as far as I know."

She cocked an eyebrow.

"Right," Willard said. "That might not be all that reassuring. But really, I'm here about something else entirely. Sorry to frighten you."

She relaxed, but narrowed her eyes at me. "You look terrible."

"Thanks."

"Nick, you look terrible, too."

"Terrible twos," I snickered, then closed my eyes. I really was losing it.

"Have a seat," Nick said. "We'll tell you everything."

I let Nick do the explaining this time. Who knew what would come out of my mouth if I kept talking? Besides, his voice was very soothing.

Some time later, I woke up with a jerk. Someone had placed a pillow under my head, so at least I wasn't sleeping in my cereal bowl. Voices drifted in from the living room. I stumbled over to find the other three looking up at Miranda, who had just slammed the stairwell door, which, of course, had woken me up.

"What's going on?" she said, far too loudly. "Why are all these people in here?"

I groaned, and dropped onto the sofa next to Nick, letting my head fall onto my hands.

Nick patted my back. "Shall I fill her in?" He launched into a quick explanation of the night's events. The story was becoming stale. I'd heard it—and told it—too many times. Almost like it was a movie, instead of real life.

But maybe that was because my head was filled with fuzz.

Miranda's face grew redder and redder as Nick talked, until I thought she was going to explode like a tomato thrown against a country mailbox. Not that I've ever seen that. Or done that.

"Seriously?" she shrieked, interrupting him. "*Seriously?*"

Nick frowned. "What? Are you a Rikki Raines fan? Or…" he looked closely at her. "Not one?"

"No, I'm…she…this summer…him…" She pointed at Willard.

"Me?" Willard said.

"Yes! Can Stella not go two months without a cop checking into her activities?"

"I'm not here as a cop. I'm here as a friend."

"See?" I said to Nick. "Told you I had friends."

"Augh!" Miranda spun around and marched into the kitchen.

Good riddance.

"So what does this mean for today?" Lucy said. "Do you have to go somewhere? Are you actually involved?"

"Not involved," I said, "except for having found the body."

"And annoyed the detective," Nick said.

"And the press," Willard added.

"So, no." I held up my hands. "I have nothing to do with it."

My kitchen phone rang, and Nick smirked. "What do you want to bet that phone call is going to make you a liar?"

I slugged him—gently—and went to answer the phone. "What?" I said into the receiver.

"Stella?" It was Zach, and his voice was about an octave higher than it should have been.

"What's wrong?"

"Melody Gregg's calf is sick, and they're threatening to quarantine the entire barn."

Chapter Sixteen

"What's happening? Watch out for that pothole." I was on the phone with Carla, and directing Miranda, who was driving. She glared at me. I was pretty sure she wanted to give me the finger, the way her hand twitched on the steering wheel, but she didn't. Too bad. It certainly hadn't been my choice to have a chauffeur, but Lucy was busy with a lame cow, Nick had a conference call, Willard was "working," and apparently I wasn't "fit for driving" because I had fallen asleep at the breakfast table. Whatever.

"Not sure what's wrong yet," Carla said. She'd given me the basics when she'd taken the phone from Zach. Basically, the Greggs' calf was foaming at the mouth and rolling its eyes. Not exactly what you want to see in a barn full of animals. "We've got the barn roped off until we figure it out. Hey! Get away from there! Stupid parents. Gotta go, Stella. Get here as soon as you can." She hung up.

"Can't you drive any faster?" I said to Miranda.

"Not around potholes, according to you."

It wasn't my fault the fair didn't have a paved driveway. Or that Miranda drove like an old lady. Or a blind person.

"Hold on," I said. "I'll walk from here." Before she'd entirely stopped I climbed out of the car.

She lurched across the seat. "Where are you going? What am I supposed to do?"

"I don't know. Park. Get something to eat. Look at stuff."

"But—"

I slammed the door. She waited a second, then shot away, enveloping me in dust. Gotta love her.

I made my way to the exhibitors' entrance, and from there to the calf barn. I had to make a detour around the cordoned-off manure trailer—there was now a different one parked across the lot—and was stopped at the door to the barn.

"No visitors," the security guard said, semi-blocking the door with his pole-like frame.

"I'm not a visitor."

He looked me up and down, peering out from under his bangs. "Don't see a badge."

"Oh, for…How old are you? Do they hire teenagers as security now?"

"I'm twenty-one."

"Whatever." I yanked out my phone and called Carla. "Justin Bieber won't let me in."

"One sec."

I tried to see around the guard while I waited, but he shifted position as I did, trying to block my view. Good luck with that, spider legs.

Carla hustled up. "Let her in."

"But—"

I ducked under his arms and through the door, and Carla swept me away. I refrained from sticking my tongue out.

We headed toward the Greggs' calf pen, but were stopped halfway there by Zach and Randy.

Zach grabbed my arm. "What's wrong with the calf? Is it contagious?"

"Haven't seen it yet."

"But what about Barnabas? Should we take him home?"

I put my hand over his, and he relaxed his death grip. "Hey, it will be all right." I knew he was terrified of losing another calf; his experience from the summer before was still fresh in his mind. "Carla's got it under control." I glanced at her. "Right?"

She put her arm around Zach. "Absolutely. We'll know more soon. Give us a few minutes and we'll tell you everything."

I patted Zach's hand, and he let go.

"Come on, man," Randy said. "I think I saw Taylor over by your box."

Zach blinked. "Taylor's here?"

I looked where Randy was pointing and saw the girl hanging out at Zach's stall. Or Austin's, maybe. Austin was taking advantage of Zach's absence to make time with Taylor, letting her pet his calf. Neither Austin nor Taylor seemed especially animated, but I wasn't sure if that was because the chemistry wasn't there, or because of the night's tragic events. Taylor was smiling, and seemed friendly and all, but it didn't have the same blinding effect as the day before. I also wondered how it was she'd gotten admission to the barn, when I'd been kept out, like a criminal. But then I remembered the gender and age of the security guard and figured that answered the question. I wouldn't consider what that meant about me.

Randy jerked his chin toward Austin and Taylor, and Zach's expression changed from just worried, to worried and a little bit jealous. He took off without waiting for Randy.

"Thanks, Bud," I said.

Randy nodded and left.

"So, Carla, what do we have?"

Carla shook her head. "I really don't think it's serious, but I wanted to get your opinion before I made the call."

"Mine? Why? Aren't there any other vets around?"

She snorted. "Too many, but none who are here officially, and all who are waiting for me to fall flat on my face in a cow plop. They want this to be the next plague, or at least Mad Cow Disease, and are already imagining their names on the bylines in *The Veterinary Journal.* But I think what's happening is something a lot simpler."

"What?"

"Nope. I want you to view it fresh."

We were ten feet away from the gaggle of vets and worried 4-H'ers when Gregg saw me. Instead of his tacky clean farmer clothes he was wearing a suit. Maybe even the same one he'd had on the night before at the concert. His eyes were bloodshot and whiskers shaded his chin. The red tie was gone altogether. I guess that's what happens when a girl dies soon after you assault her. I took a moment to consider whether assaulting was all he'd done. And just what his relationship was to the dead singer.

He met my eyes briefly before throwing a tantrum. "What is she doing here? Where's security?"

Gregg's youngest daughter, the one who was supposedly the owner of the calf, stood off to the side, more concerned in picking something off her shoe.

Carla intercepted Gregg before he got close enough I could slug him. "I asked her here."

"You? How dare—"

Carla held up a finger. Not the finger I would have chosen, but it worked to shut him up. While she kept him silent, she looked at me. "Now, please."

I walked up to the pen while the others watched. Gregg wasn't the only one muttering. The other vets weren't exactly thrilled with my presence. Their problem, not mine.

The calf looked fine to me. Bright-eyed, steady on his feet, backed up against the far wall, like any normal calf would do with a million people staring at him. No more of the eye-rolling Carla had mentioned, but that could have been because he wasn't as freaked out as he had been. The only unusual thing I could see was wetness around his mouth, like he'd just taken a really long drink. I leaned toward him, then glanced up at Mrs. Gregg, who stood to the side, hands clenched into fists, which she had pressed against her thighs. "May I go in?"

Gregg sputtered. "No, she can't—"

Mrs. Gregg nodded. Ignoring Mr. Gregg, I slipped through the gate and slowly approached the calf, until I knelt beside him. It wasn't water around his mouth. It was saliva. A lot of it. And it smelled funny. Like…lemons.

I rooted through the calf's feed bin, but there wasn't much there. Not enough to hide what I expected to be the culprit.

I stood up and held out my hand. "Shovel."

Someone placed a shovel in my hands, and I scraped around in the wood chips below the feed bin until I found what I was looking for. I picked it up and held it out.

"What is it?" Gregg grumped.

"Lemon peel."

Carla's eyes sparkled. "Thought so."

The other vets all slumped as one entity. There went their Pulitzers, or whatever vets get for writing articles no one else can understand. They drifted away, as did the other 4-H'ers and their parents. They understood what had happened, and realized whatever danger they'd imagined was completely overstated.

"So what if it's a lemon peel?" Gregg said when they'd all left. "What's going to happen to the calf?"

"Nothing's going to happen to it," Carla said.

"But it was foaming," Mrs. Gregg said. "It was sick."

"No, it wasn't." I gave the calf one last pat and walked out the gate. "Somehow a lemon peel got into its feed. It chewed on it, because that's what calves do. Lemons make them foam at the mouth."

"But its eyes, they were all—" Gregg demonstrated, rolling his eyes like a crazy person.

"You would, too, if you suddenly had a lemon in your mouth."

His nostrils flared. "How did a lemon get in its feed?"

"How would I know?" But I had an idea.

"Dad," the Gregg girl said, "can I go now?"

Such concern. Enough to make your heart harden.

Gregg jerked his chin, and the girl was off in a heartbeat. Gregg glared at me, like the whole thing was my fault, then spun on his heel and stalked off. Mrs. Gregg watched him go, turned toward Carla, then hurried after her husband. Gotta love the family dynamics. And the gratitude.

But forget them. "You done with me, Carla?"

She sighed. "All done. Thanks for being the voice of reason."

"Hey, anytime."

"Carla?" One of the other vets from her practice hustled up. "I was over in the rabbit building with Susie—" his daughter "—when I heard what was going on. You need help?" He glared at one of the other vets, who was still hanging around the edge of the barn.

Carla patted his shoulder. "I got it, Don. But thanks."

"Stella," he said to me.

I nodded.

He leaned on the stall. "So, this the calf?"

"Yup. He's fine." Carla explained about the lemon.

"Stupid pranks," Don muttered. "But good job. So, if you don't need me?"

"We're good."

He waved and was gone again, back to his daughter and her rabbits.

"So, the quarantine?" I said, returning to the important stuff.

Carla gave a double thumbs up. "Completely lifted."

"Thank you. I'll let Zach know."

"Thanks so much for coming. I didn't want those other vets getting involved, and I hated to bother Don…" Her shoulders slumped, and the stress of the past hour showed in her face.

"Carla, I'm always here for you. You know that."

"I do. It's just…this job is not turning out to be as fun as I thought."

"Carla—"

"I'll be fine." She gave me a quick hug, then yanked out her phone, which was ringing yet again. She answered, waving goodbye as she gathered her toolbox and strode away.

I found Zach talking to Taylor at his stall.

Taylor had abandoned Austin, who was now perched on his straw bale with Randy, doing something with a phone. Zach and Taylor leaned over the fence, patting Barnabas.

"Zach," I said.

He spun around so fast I thought he'd fall over. "Is Barnabas going to be okay? All the calves?"

Now there was someone who cared about the animals.

"They'll be fine."

Austin and Randy joined us.

"But what's wrong with their calf?" Austin asked. "Are they quarantining the barn? Or canceling our judging?"

"Nope, it was just a prank. Someone put lemon peels in his food."

Austin laughed, and ran a hand through his hair. "Thank God."

Taylor's nose wrinkled. "What?"

Zach explained what happened.

"But why would he eat a lemon peel? Wouldn't it be sour?"

"If it's dry enough he wouldn't notice. Might even think it's a treat at first."

"So someone did it on purpose?"

"That would be my guess. Don't know how it would get in his food, otherwise."

"Who would do that?" Taylor asked, her voice strained.

"Yeah," Austin said. "Who?"

"That's easy," I said. "Someone who wants the Greggs to lose the championship."

Chapter Seventeen

I stepped outside and called Nick—on my cell phone, which he'd insisted I bring with me—to let him know all was well.

"Who plays pranks on calves?" he said.

I repeated what I'd told the kids. "There are a lot of people here who resent the Greggs. Kids who have a lot invested in their own animals and don't want the Greggs to win undeserved prizes."

"So they take it out on the calf?"

"Lemon peels aren't going to hurt him. Just make him look bad. They probably figured if they could get him disqualified, all the better for everyone else."

"It's still not right."

"Of course not. I'm just hoping it stops there."

We enjoyed silence for a moment before he said, "So, you heading home?"

"As soon as I find Miranda."

"Just text her."

"Don't know if she'll answer when she sees it's me."

He laughed.

"I really didn't mean that to be funny."

"Yeah, well, it was. She'll answer. I can't imagine she wants to spend any more time at the county fair than she has to."

"Maybe she's still sitting in the car."

"Too hot."

"Not if she left it running." Which I wouldn't put past her. It struck me that she would have had to pay to get into the fair if she'd actually attempted it, since I hadn't taken her in the exhibitors' entrance. Whoops. But then, she was so freaked out about Nick giving me money to keep our home in the black, why should I help her any? "Or else she left me here, and she's on her way home."

"She wouldn't do that."

I wasn't so sure. "I'll be home soon. I hope."

"See you then. Love you."

"You, too."

I hated texting. The only time I ever did it was when I needed to get in touch with Zach or Mallory, or one of the other Granger teens. Carla had tried to get me into it, but I shut that down real quick. If somebody wanted to tell me something, they'd get a much more timely response if they just called and let me talk to them. Typing stuff out with my thumbs was a waste of time and energy. This whole texting thing had, of course, been another source of contention with Miranda, who wanted to text me price quotes and photos and all sorts of crap about weddings. She finally realized she wasn't getting answers because I wasn't sending them—not because I wasn't receiving her texts. Yet another reason for her to hate me.

I opened my Contacts and pushed the call button. The phone rang once. Twice. I knew that on Miranda's end it was playing that annoying song, the one where the woman is singing about needing a man to make her complete—I know, that could be a million of them—but at least all I could hear was the tone. After a few more rings, the call went into her voicemail—"Hello! You've reached Miranda! Leave a message!"

No! I didn't want to!

I hung up. She'd see my missed call, and maybe she would deign to call me back.

So. Hmm. What to do? I thought of checking out the dairy barn, to see what Claire was up to, but I really didn't want to run into the Greggs again. I had no desire to go anywhere near the hall where the cops were camped out, and the carnival rides made me want to throw up just looking at them. I made my way toward the food tent. I could always eat.

"Ms. Crown?"

Oh, great. "Detective Watts." She wasn't looking any too happy. Whether that was because of me or because she'd just gotten a whiff of the pig barn I wasn't sure. Either way, I wished I'd managed to take off before she found me.

She fingered her handcuffs. "You interfered with a police investigation."

"Really? How?"

"I saw you on YouTube harassing the press."

"Oh, are reporters a part of the police department now?"

"You said you were going home. Instead, you waited outside the building."

"So? Is that a crime?"

"The police dispersed the crowd. You stayed anyway, and caused problems."

"I caused problems? I'd say it was that pushy reporter who caused the problems. If you folks had done your job right I wouldn't have had to step in."

"Threatening the press isn't our job."

"I was protecting an innocent citizen. Somehow I thought that was the whole point of the police department."

Her nostrils flared. "Why were you still there?"

"We were taking care of someone."

"Yes, the daughter of a—" She stopped and

glared at me, like I'd almost made her say something she wasn't supposed to.

"Of a what? Suspect in Rikki Raines' death?"

"She is not...are you friends with Daniella Troth? Because I wouldn't have thought so."

I bit off the retort I wanted to make. And I didn't hit her. Instead, I said, "Do your superiors know where you are?"

Her mouth opened and closed, like a stupid fish, and then she closed her eyes and took a deep breath. When she opened her eyes she said, "Look, Ms. Crown, I'm not sure how or why we got off on the wrong foot, but all I really want is to find out who killed Rikki Raines. I just..." She shook her head.

"What?"

"We were both tired last night. You'd talked to a lot of people, and so had I. I'm not experienced at this. You can see how old I am. It's not exactly—"

"—easy to compete in a man's world."

She gave a small smile. "Or, more specifically, my dad's world."

"The sheriff."

"Yeah."

"Was he here last night? I didn't see him."

"Would you believe he's out of state? The biggest case here in...ever...and he's out in Colorado at some training conference." She gave a laugh that was more like a hiccup.

"He coming back?"

"I'm sure he is. Wouldn't want to miss out. Besides, I'm sure he's in touch with all the higher-ups."

"Reporting on you?"

She made a face. "Among others."

"I guess that is his job, right?"

"I suppose." She looked somewhere past my left ear. "So, are we good?"

"We're okay."

"I'm glad. Talk to you later." She angled away.

"Hey, Watts," I called after her.

She turned, eyebrows raised.

"Good luck."

She saluted with a finger and strode away.

I bought a pulled pork sandwich and a lemon shake-up at the school boosters tent and sat in the back corner, where the canvas flap was open and I could feel a breeze. The place was bustling with customers, and the high school and parent volunteers working the counter smiled through their sweat. Not exactly high on my to-do list on summer days, to run the fries basket.

I was about halfway through the sandwich when Austin sat down across from me.

"Hey," I said.

"Hey." He had a double cheeseburger, fries,

deep-fried pickles, a thirty-two-ounce Powerade, and a piece of cake. He could compete with Carla, the way he was going. The problem with Carla was, she didn't have the hollow legs.

"No one else hungry?" I said.

Austin shrugged, and picked at his food. "I'm older than most of them anymore, so I don't know, it feels kind of weird to hang out with them. They're off doing other stuff, I guess. Getting ready for judging."

"Taylor's their age. You seem to like her okay."

"Yeah, but she's hot."

At least he was honest.

"Scare you this morning?"

He picked up his sandwich, then set it down without taking a bite. "You mean about the sick calf? Sure. But we were all the way across the room, and we've only been there a day. I didn't think Halladay could get sick that quick."

So he didn't know everything, even though he was a teenager, and a farmer. Just goes to show what wishful thinking can do. "I'm glad it turned out to be nothing. I understand why someone would want to do that to the Greggs, but I hope they don't try anything worse. It could hurt the calf. Or disqualify the whole barn."

Austin stuck a fry in his ketchup and swirled it around. "Do they know who did it?"

"Don't think so. Not anything to go on when there's only a chewed-up lemon peel as evidence, and since nothing really bad happened I can't imagine they'll put much time and effort into it. Especially with all the other stuff that happened last night."

He was quiet for a moment as he scraped icing off his cake with his plastic fork. "You mean, the whole Rikki Raines thing? Yeah, that's…pretty sick."

"Did you go to the concert? I didn't see you."

He set his fork down. "I was there. I just hung out on the edge. I could see fine."

I sat back, sipping on my lemonade. "How come you're the only senior in 4-H? What happened to everyone else your age?"

He wiped his mouth with his sleeve. "They lost interest, I guess. But I want to go to ag school, and this is as much of an application priority as anything. I'm the president of the club, and I've been in it forever, since I was, I don't know, third grade, when we were allowed to start. I'll get good references from the leaders, and my project this year was to help out one of the local vets, which was cool."

"How do you think Halladay will do this afternoon?"

"Good, I hope. He's one of the best calves I've

ever had. Got lucky for my last year. Sometimes you get a calf and you think he's going to be great, and it turns out he's a loser, and sometimes it's the other way around. Halladay's been great since he was born."

I knew what he meant. Some milkers were that way. They start out as beautiful heifers, bright-eyed and perfect, then somewhere along the way their milk dries up, or they produce half what the others do, or they can't get pregnant. Sometimes there's no rhyme or reason, and no tests or check-ups can tell us what the deal is. Then, as much as we hate it, we have to give up on them. As Ma Granger would say, "It's just the way God made 'em." Unfortunately for cows, it's a little different than when you say that about a person. People don't go to the slaughterhouse if they don't fit our business model.

"You and Halladay ready for judging today?"

"I guess." He set down the fry he was holding, and pushed back his chair. He hadn't eaten a thing. He must have been much more nervous about judging than he admitted. "I'd better get back. My sister's on cow plop duty while I get something to eat. She'll be ticked if I don't relieve her soon."

I remembered cow plop duty. You had your calf as clean as you could get him, and you didn't want him getting any fresh manure on those pristine hooves. So whenever there was a cow plop, it had to disappear, fast. "See you around."

He jerked his chin at me, and left, dumping his entire lunch in the trash. Watching him go, I noticed Bryan standing at the front of the tent, tray in hand, shoulders stiff, eyes darting from table to table. It was like he'd traveled back in time to the high school cafeteria, where the weird kid with the NASCAR obsession wouldn't exactly have been the prom king. Or would even go to prom.

I held still, hoping if I played possum I'd luck out and he wouldn't see me or the empty chairs beside me. But since hope and luck have a way of abandoning me in times of social awkwardness, his eyes landed right on me. I could tell by the way his Adam's apple bobbed up and down, and the color drained from his face.

Oh, for heaven's sake.

I waved to the chair opposite me. I didn't attempt to smile, because he would've seen through that. I could show kindness to my best friend's boyfriend by simply offering him a seat, right? I didn't have to throw in a hostess personality with it.

He blinked, scanned the room again—a little desperately, I thought—then shuffled over. "This seat taken?"

I pushed it out with my foot. "By you."

"Um. Thanks." He set his tray down, paused

for a moment, then perched on the edge of the folding chair. His food consisted of a bowl of chicken noodle soup, two packets of crackers, and a bottle of water.

"Making up for Carla?" I said.

"Huh?"

"Nevermind."

He picked up his spoon, then set it down. Then picked it up again. And looked at his bowl.

"What's wrong?" For Pete's sake, was I really so terrifying the man couldn't even eat soup?

He set the spoon down again. And took a deep breath. And let it out.

"Bryan."

"It's Carla," he blurted. "I think…I think…"

Oh, Lord, I was going to strangle him. "You think what?" That she was going to dump him? No way that could be it. I wasn't that lucky.

"I think someone's trying to get her license taken away."

Chapter Eighteen

"Her veterinary license?" I had to assume he meant that, and not her driver's license. Because who would care about whether or not she could drive?

"Yes." He poked at his soup with his spoon.

"How? Why would you think that?"

He finally gave up on his food and set the spoon down very deliberately, beside the bowl. "She got some threats last night."

I sat up. "From who?"

"Don't know. They were texts. She wouldn't show them to me at first, but when one of them made her cry I grabbed her phone. It said—" he shook his head "—that she didn't know what she was doing, and they'd prove it today, or something like that."

Hmm. One of those vets at the Greggs' stall, maybe?

"What did she say?"

"That I shouldn't take it so seriously."

Of course she would tell him that. He obviously didn't agree, or he wouldn't look so upset. Okay, so score one for Bryan.

"You going to hang out with her today?"

For a second I thought he was going to cry, too, and I wished I hadn't asked. "I offered, but she said she's so busy, and she doesn't want me to feel like I have to, so I should just do my own thing for a while. It was obvious I'd just be in the way."

"Bryan, when a woman says you should go 'do your own thing,' she doesn't really mean it."

He frowned. "Carla would not lie."

"Of course she wouldn't. But what she meant was that she would love for you to be with her, but she won't be able to pay attention to just you. She's afraid you'd be bored, and she doesn't want to put you through that."

"So it's not that she doesn't want me around?"

Hardly. Not the way she was looking at him the night before. "Bryan, if I were you, I'd find out where she is and go there. Do what you can to help her today, and just…be glad to be with her, even if tending sick animals isn't the most thrilling activity in the world. That's all she wants." He stared at me blankly, and I was afraid something had short-circuited. "Bryan?"

He blinked. "Yeah. Thanks. I think…I think I'll do that. You're…that was…nice of you." He got up and walked away, leaving me with his tray of uneaten soup.

"Stella?"

Holy crap, I was Grand Central Station.

Daniella Troth eased into the chair Bryan had just vacated. She looked terrible. Well, terrible for her, which was a normal day for anyone else.

I pulled Bryan's tray to the side so she wouldn't have to smell it. "I'm surprised to see you."

"Yeah, well." She sighed and rested her elbows on the table. "Taylor has to be here because of the Lovely Miss competition, so I really have no choice. I mean, I guess I could have brought her here and gone home, but I already took off work until after the pageant on Wednesday night, so I might as well stick around. Sorry, I'm babbling."

"No, that's fine." I finished my lemon shake-up, then wished I hadn't. I was still thirsty. I looked around for one of the kids cleaning up tables and waved her over. "Can you get me another one of these? And one for her, too." Daniella, I meant.

The girl's forehead wrinkled. "Well, I'm not really—"

"Here." I pulled out a few dollars and stuck them in her hand. "Two. Thanks."

She hesitated, but I smiled, and she went away, apparently still not sure how fetching lemonade was in her job description. She'd figure it out.

"Rikki was such a nice girl," Daniella said, as if the lemonade interruption had never happened. "I just can't believe…" She pressed her fingers against her lips.

"Do they have any idea what happened yet?"

She shook her head. "They said they couldn't tell. That it didn't look like anything was wrong with her."

Exactly what Willard had said.

Daniella slumped. "It doesn't make any sense. None of it does."

"Gregg records her, right? I mean, he puts out her records."

"What? Oh, right. Yes, he does. He likes to make such a big deal about how he 'took a chance' on her." Anger flashed across her face, then disappeared. "She was a sweet country girl who got noticed, and he wanted to make her just another one of his harem."

"His harem?"

"Sorry." She made a face. "That's what we call them over at the salon. You know, we want to think the best of everyone, but the truth is, some of those girls…" She picked at a perfect fingernail. "They'll do anything to achieve their dreams. What they don't understand is that when they do those things the rest of it all becomes meaningless. Or… tainted."

"But Rikki wasn't like that?"

"Not yet. Oh, I know that sounds awful, but I've seen it happen so many times, with all the business we get from the studio." She smiled sadly. "I had hopes for Rikki, though. She'd toughed it out this long. She had a supportive group of friends from home, a strong family. A wonderful aunt who raised her. I really thought she would make it, and keep her own identity. I don't know." For a moment I saw how old Daniella really was. She was still beautiful, but also aged.

"I saw her arguing with Gregg last night," I said. I had seen Daniella arguing with him, too, of course, but I wasn't going to mention that. "After the concert."

"Where? At the barn? Near the…trailer?"

I could tell by the way she said it that she meant the manure trailer. It's hard for city people to understand that cow poop is just part of the life. We farmers don't even think about it, except for in extreme cases. Cows make it, we shovel it. That's about as simple as it gets.

"No, they were still in the arena, by the stage."

"So she was wearing her concert clothes?"

"Yeah." It struck me then that Rikki hadn't been in those clothes when I'd dug her out of the manure pile. If she had been, I would have recognized her immediately from her white boots. Even

covered in cow crap those would have been familiar. Instead, she'd been wearing stuff I would have
expected at the calf barn. Jeans and work boots. I
tried to remember what shirt she'd been wearing,
but it had been so filthy I hadn't even thought to
check. Plus, I was busy trying to get her face cleared
so she could breathe. Until I realized she was dead.
"Where did she go after the concert? Why had she
changed clothes?"

"No one knows."

Someone did. It couldn't really be a coincidence
that the most famous person at the fairgrounds had
been murdered and hidden on the trailer tons of
people used every day.

"Any idea what she and Gregg were arguing
about?"

She shook her head. "I couldn't be sure, but
I wonder if—"

"Here." The high school girl set two lemonades
on the table.

I took the straws she handed me. "Thanks."

"Um, anything else?"

"Nope. This is great."

She hesitated.

"What? You want a tip?"

"No. Aren't you the one who found Rikki
Raines? And you're on YouTube. With her." Her
eyes widened as she recognized Daniella. Her

mouth flopped open, and she ran back into the kitchen.

"Time to make our escape," I said.

Daniella seemed in a daze, so I grabbed her and our drinks and shoved her out the tent flap. We were gone before the girl got back with whatever rubbernecking friends she'd gone after.

When we were a safe distance away, I pulled Daniella into the coolness of the home crafts building. "What were you saying?"

"About what?"

"What Gregg and Rikki might have been fighting about."

"Oh, I don't know if I should—"

"It wasn't a friendly argument. He was really angry, and I guess she was, too, but he grabbed her. I was about to go help until someone else came up and distracted him. Rikki got away, and he wasn't able to follow."

Daniella closed her eyes, and for a second I thought she was going to pass out. I grabbed an empty chair from behind one of the tables—"Yes, knitting booth lady, I will bring it back,"—and sat Daniella on it.

"Here, take a sip." I handed her one of the lemon shake-ups.

She took a drink, then let out a deep, shuddering breath.

"Their argument?" I prompted.

She hesitated, then said, "He wanted her to take part in this marketing thing, and she didn't want to."

"What kind of thing?"

"She'd already said yes to one big thing this summer, and other places were starting to call. Magazines, cable shows, you know. She was afraid of filling up too much of her time. Plus, the thing Gregg wanted her to do wasn't something she felt good about."

"What was it?"

Daniella shook her head. "Really, Stella, I don't feel comfortable talking about it. I'm sorry."

"Okay, how about this? What was the thing she'd already said yes to for this summer? Can you tell me that, at least?"

"Oh, sure, that wasn't a secret. She was spending all her spare time being one of the judges for the Lovely Miss Pennsylvania pageant."

"The one one your daughter is in?"

"Yes. She's been judging all summer. She seems…seemed…to be enjoying it." Her eyes filled with tears. "Rikki would come into the salon before the pageants, sometimes, to get a manicure or touch up her hair." Her mouth twitched. "She may have been a down-home girl, but she still wanted to look her best, especially when all the contestants would be dressed to perfection. Plus, the girls in the competition like to think their judges know what they're talking about."

The girls—and their mothers—also became fanatical about winning. I thought about that crazy Summer girl and her fake boobs and lips. *What mother allows her sixteen-year-old daughter to mutilate herself that way?*

Not Daniella.

"Taylor seemed to like Rikki," I said.

"Oh, she did. She got to know Rikki a little at the salon. After school sometimes Taylor will come by until I'm done with work, and she happened to be there one time when Rikki was getting her nails done. Rikki was very sweet with her, and Taylor became an instant fan. She was so thrilled that Rikki was one of the judges. I don't know how she's going to respond to all this."

"Stella!" Miranda strode up and planted herself in front of me, fists on her hips. "Where have you been? I've been texting you forever. I even called."

"Sorry. Didn't hear it. I suppose you're ready to go."

Her eyes flicked to Daniella, who had recovered from our conversation so quickly she was back to looking perfect. Miranda's face betrayed her confusion. "Are you a friend of Stella's?" The tone of her voice made it clear she couldn't imagine how that could be.

"Daniella Troth." Daniella stood up and shook Miranda's hand. "A pleasure to meet you…"

"Miranda Hathaway. I'm Stella's…her boy-friend's sister."

"Fiancé," I said. "Nick is my fiancé."

Miranda rolled her eyes.

Daniella gripped Miranda's hand with both of hers. "You're Nick's sister? He's such a sweet-heart. He was absolutely wonderful with Taylor last night."

"What do you mean?" Understanding lit Miranda's face. "Wait a minute. You're that lady. The one on YouTube with Stella. Your daughter's in the Lovely Miss Pennsylvania pageant."

Daniella smiled. "That's right."

Miranda grabbed Daniella's hands, her eyes gleaming. "And, you own a salon!"

Heaven help us.

Chapter Nineteen

Twenty minutes later, during which I heard more words about cosmetics and nails and hair and facials and jewelry than I ever wanted to, or could possibly understand, Miranda had extracted Daniella's cell phone number, work hours, and a discount for an appointment at the salon later that week, once Daniella got back to work. Miranda was still going strong—happy to have found a woman who spoke her language—but Daniella's façade of strength was beginning to slip.

"Miranda," I said, interrupting some list of scents, or colors, or something else involving girly words like sandalwood and jasmine nectar.

I distracted her, but just enough for her to change subjects. "So you do hair and makeup for all of the Philadelphia recording artists?"

"Not all. Just the ones who record on the Sunburst label. And some individuals."

"But that's got to be so crazy having all of

those stars come in there! What are they like? Are they amazing?"

Daniella smiled, but her eyes looked weary. "They're just people, Miranda."

"But—"

"Miranda," I said. "We need to go."

"Stella, I'm not—"

"Daniella has responsibilities. Her daughter, remember? The Lovely Miss pageant?"

"Oh, right." She went pink. "I'm sorry, Daniella."

"Not a problem. It's been fun talking with you. I'll see you at the salon when you come in, if I don't see you before."

Miranda smiled. "Can't wait."

"Stella," Daniella said. "Thank you." Her gratitude weighed so heavy I knew she actually meant, "Please take this insanely energetic woman far away and let me go free."

"Anytime. See you around."

"You'll be at the pageant tomorrow?"

"Oh. Well…"

"Of course we'll come!" Miranda said. "You can count on us." She threaded her arm through mine. "Right, Stella?"

Daniella smiled at me, her eyes knowing. "Whatever works with your schedule. I'll see you later."

Miranda kept a hold of my arm until Daniella

was gone, then turned on me. "When were you going to tell me about her?"

"What's to tell?"

"For heaven's sake. The woman is the answer to our problems."

"What problems?"

"Your wedding problems!"

I refrained from punching her in the throat, and strode away.

"Stella!" She ran to catch up with me. "What is wrong with you?"

I swung around so quickly she bashed into me. I pushed her off. "What's wrong with me? I'll tell you what's wrong with me. I was up until God-knows-when talking to cops and taking care of that woman and her grieving daughter, I found a murdered girl in a shit pile, my best friend has someone out to get her in trouble, Zach's calf is in a place where people are playing possibly danger-ous pranks on animals, and we don't have wedding problems. You're the one who called Nick my boy-friend, instead of fiancé. Apparently you're the one with the wedding problem."

I stared her down until she dropped her eyes, then continued marching toward the parking lot.

"That's your phone," she said, jogging along.

"What is?"

"That sound. Oh, my gosh, you still use that generic salsa beat?"

I slid out my phone. Yup, it was ringing, and it was Zach. "What's up?"

"You didn't answer my texts."

"Sorry. You know me and this stupid phone. Everything okay?"

"I think so. You still here? Can you come over?"

"Sure. I'll be right there." I hung up and saw I had other missed calls. Nobody I knew, because they just showed up as phone numbers, instead of names. Erase. I changed course, heading toward the calf barn.

"Now what?" Miranda trotted along.

"Zach."

"What about him?"

I didn't answer, because I didn't know. He was waiting outside the barn, at the far corner, and he wasn't alone. Taylor was by his side—huge surprise—and another girl I didn't know. Taylor shot me a quick smile, but overall she gave off sadness, and almost…fear.

Zach waved us to the side of the barn, out of sight of the main path.

"What's going on?" I stepped closer to him.

He glanced at Miranda. "What's she doing here?"

She stiffened. "Excuse me—"

"She's my ride."

"Oh. All right."

"You want her to go away?"

"I don't know. You trust her?"

"Standing right here, folks," Miranda said.

"Um, who is she?" Taylor said.

Miranda bristled. "Who are you?"

"Taylor Troth."

Miranda blinked. "Daniella's daughter?"

"That's right. And you are?"

"Miranda Hathaway. So pleased to meet you." She held her hand out. Taylor shook it, but swiveled her eyes toward me.

I sighed. "My fiancé's sister. I don't trust her when it comes to planning my wedding, or even liking me. But when it comes to life and death, I guess I have to trust her, seeing how she already saved me once."

Miranda nodded sharply, like she herself had proved the point.

Zach shuffled his feet. "Well, all right, then." He glanced around, like he was afraid we were being watched.

"Zach, you're scaring me."

"Sorry." He gestured toward the girl I didn't know. "This is Laura Tiffin. She's got a calf here, too. She's in my class at school."

I checked her out. She was shorter than Taylor by several inches, and her blond hair was that flyaway kind that always looks messy, or like she got shocked by lightning. Her eyes were a faded blue, her lips pale, and next to Taylor she looked entirely insubstantial and flighty. Like a scared rabbit. "Tiffin? Do I know you?"

She flicked her eyes at Zach, and he nodded at her.

"You probably know my folks." She named them. Another dairy family. No one I knew well, but it was a familiar farm.

"Okay." I was done with niceties. "Why do you all look so weird?"

"Tell her, Laura." Zach crossed his arms.

"Well…" She moved back, so she was against the barn. "I was here last night, right? After the concert. I was checking on Bunny. My calf."

"Bunny?" Miranda said, laughing.

Fitting, seeing as how I was thinking of the girl as a rabbit, herself.

"Bunnicula, actually," she said. She didn't care what Miranda thought. That was obvious.

Join the club.

"Anyway Bunny had been skittish all day since I brought him, and I wanted to make sure he was okay, you know? So, anyway, hardly anybody was here, and I didn't really feel like going back to the trailer, and he was still jumpy, so I just sat in the stall with him. It was really quiet, you know, just the calves moving around and breathing and stuff, since the public wasn't allowed in yet, and everybody else was out." She hesitated.

"And?" Miranda said.

I glared at her. "Give her a second. She's obviously spooked."

"By a smelly barn?"

Seriously, I was going to brain her if she didn't shut up.

"Nevermind her," I told Laura. "Take your time."

She glanced at Zach again, and Taylor touched her arm.

"So I was sitting there, sort of half asleep or whatever, and somebody came in."

"To your stall?"

"No, they went right past me and down the row. Like around to where the Greggs' calf is."

Oh. *Oh.*

"Who was it?"

"I wasn't paying attention, and I didn't really feel like talking to anybody, so I just sort of stayed quiet and still. But then they were whispering, and I heard one of them giggle, and she said, 'You're sure this won't hurt him?' and the other one, he said it wouldn't."

Holy cow. "They were putting the lemon in the calf's food."

"That's what I figure now, but I didn't know it then."

"You should have told somebody," Miranda said. "Why didn't you? Did you at least tell them today?"

"I told Zach." Her voice shook. "As soon as I heard what happened."

"Nevermind Miranda," I said. "She apparently thinks this is a Class A felony." Which it might have been, actually. I wasn't sure. But the calf was fine now, so I doubted the cops were going to get involved any more than they already had been. They had bigger things to worry about. "What happened next?"

"Okay, well, I was afraid they were going to do something really mean, so I peeked around Bunny and saw them. A guy and a girl, like I thought from the voices. But it was dark so I couldn't tell who it was." She swallowed. "And then…then they came back down the row, so I ducked into my stall and hid behind Bunny." She hugged herself.

"And?" Miranda said.

I pushed her back. "Will you shut up?"

She gasped, then got all pouty.

"Go on," I said to Laura. "Did you not

mention seeing them because you knew the girl, and you didn't want to get her in trouble?"

Laura's lip trembled. "I couldn't see the guy, because he walked by on the far side of the row, and like I said, it was sort of dark."

I tried to keep my voice calm. "But what about the girl?"

A tear rolled from Laura's eyes. "It was Rikki Raines."

Chapter Twenty

"Rikki Raines?" Holy crap, Laura might have been the last person to see Rikki alive. Other than the guy she'd been with, of course.

"What time was this?"

"I guess around elevenish or whatever, because some of the lights had been turned out, but lots of people were still out doing rides and stuff. They hadn't made their last visits to their calves. You know, they usually do that after one, when the rides close."

That would fit the timeframe, when Nick and I got to the barn. Rikki had probably been stuffed on the manure trailer shortly after Laura saw her. Maybe the guy had been the one to put her there.

"You don't have any idea who the guy was?"

Laura shrugged. "I didn't see him, and they were talking real quiet, so I couldn't recognize his voice. I'm sorry." Her voice trembled, and she chewed her lip. Taylor put her arm around the girl's shoulders.

I tipped my head sideways, and Zach met me several feet away.

"You realize she has to tell the cops this. And they're going to wonder why she's just now mentioning it."

"I know. I just thought, if she told you first, it might make her feel more ready to tell somebody who matters."

"Thanks. I appreciate the affirmation." My sarcasm went right over his head. "But still, why didn't she tell somebody this morning?"

I thought it was a valid question. We went back to the others. "Laura." I kept my voice quiet. "Why didn't you tell anyone till now?"

She squirmed. "I was afraid they'd think I had something to do with it."

A common worry when dealing with crimes. I should know.

Laura continued. "But I would never put something in a calf's food."

I blinked. "The calf. Right, of course you wouldn't. But what I mean is, why didn't you tell anyone you saw Rikki?"

She shuddered. "Oh, I know, yeah, that's way more…" Her chin trembled. "I was afraid they'd think I did that, too."

I looked at the tiny girl. The only way she

could ever kill someone was by accident. "You didn't, right? Do anything to Rikki?"

"Stella!" Zach practically jumped me.

"No! No, I would never…" Laura hugged herself and sniffed.

"Of course you wouldn't. I just wanted to make a point. Look at you. They're not going to think you did it."

"I don't know about that," Miranda said. "She withheld evidence for almost twelve hours now."

"Miranda—"

"Fine. I get it, okay? I'm just saying the cops might not be so understanding."

I hated to say it, but Miranda was right. "You need to go tell the cops. Right now."

Zach frowned and pulled me aside again. "Judging begins this afternoon. What if they don't let us go in time? We'll both miss our event."

"I'm sorry, Zach, but this has to take precedence. A woman is dead, and Laura has important information."

"But—"

"How about if I take her over to talk to Detective Watts? You stay with Barnabas and get ready. That way you're not at risk for being late, too."

"I don't know. Laura's kind of scared."

I smiled. "I can be non-scary if I want to. And I think Watts can, too." Our little meeting this morning had showed me another side of the detective. One that was still young and vulnerable. That could be an asset in this situation.

He narrowed his eyes. "You sure?"

I slugged his arm—in a non-scary way—and we went back to the girls. Zach explained what needed to happen. Laura regarded me with something less than absolute trust.

"I'll go, too," Taylor said. "You won't be alone."

I decided not to argue that she wouldn't have been alone with me. I wasn't someone who mattered, anyway, so there was no point in trying to make a point.

Laura thought it over, and finally nodded.

"You sure?" Zach said.

I thought that was pushing it, so I said, "Come on, Laura. We'll take care of you."

"What about me?" Miranda said.

"You need me to take care of you?"

"No, Stella, I mean what am I supposed to do?"

"About what?"

"Being here!"

"I don't know. Look around. Watch some judging. Check out the rabbits. Eat some deep-fried pickles."

"Eww!"

"Or go home. I can give Nick a call when I'm ready."

"Fine. Unless you need me. I can stay." She said this half grudgingly, half hopeful, eyeing Taylor, like if she got in good with the daughter, that would further cement her new bond with Daniella, the salon goddess.

"No, go on home. I'll be in touch."

"If you're sure…"

"Go."

After a few more token "I can stays," she finally left.

"Okay," I said. "Laura, let's go see if we can find the detective."

Watts wasn't at the building when we arrived, but one of the cops said he'd call her, and sat us in some chairs in the corner.

"Do you think she's going to be mad?" Laura shrank into her seat. Now she looked more like a scared mouse than a rabbit.

"Just tell her your story," I said. "If she's mad, I'll deal with her."

Taylor squinted at me. "How?"

"She and I have come to an…understanding."

I expected her to ask what I meant, but her attention was across the room. Gregg had come in with an older man in uniform. The sheriff, Watts' dad. So he'd made it home already, sooner than Watts had thought. I bet she was thrilled.

"What's he doing here?" Taylor said.

"He's the sheriff."

"No, I mean Mr. Gregg. Do you think they're questioning him, as maybe the killer?" She sounded both hopeful and disgusted. I could relate. I wanted to both beat him up and chase him off, so the whole dual desires thing was familiar.

From the way he was being greeted by the sheriff and other officers, I doubted he was a suspect. Potential killers weren't usually invited into the fold with bad coffee and donuts. And Gregg had one of each in his hands. He didn't look very interested in the food, though. His hair was wild, and I wasn't sure what kind of look he was going for that day with his dress pants and "farmer" shirt. It was almost like he'd gotten dressed in the dark. Or a daze. Sort of how you might behave if you'd killed someone and were feeling guilty. Or, to be fair, if one of your upcoming stars had gotten murdered the night before.

I studied Taylor. "Do you know him?"

"Not really."

"But you don't like him."

"I've met him before, but he wouldn't remember me. That's how he is." She shrugged. "I hear a lot about him from my mom, and from the other girls, you know, Rikki's friends."

"What do they say?"

She squirmed. "That he makes girls…do stuff."

Exactly what Daniella had told me. I watched as the creep talked with the police officers. When it looked like he'd had enough small talk, the sheriff guided him to a more private area. What would the sheriff have to tell him? Or maybe the sheriff really was questioning him? That would be more believable. If I believed that politics and power never made people look away from obvious issues, like the fact that Gregg had been fighting with Rikki the same night she got killed.

"There she is." I stood up to get Watts' attention, and she came over. "I see your dad made it."

"Yup. Wouldn't want to miss the chance to be a hero."

"But a hero for who?"

She glanced over at her dad and Gregg, and by the set of her shoulders I could tell she understood me. And I could also see she wasn't sure which side her father would end up on, if he had to choose. She pulled up a chair, studying the girls. "So, what's this big news you have to tell me?"

Laura looked up at me, and I nodded. "Go ahead. She'll listen. And she won't get mad." I said this last part to Watts, of course. She gave me a funny look, but I think she got the point.

"Well," Laura said, "it was late last night…"

She told her story. I could see the war in Watts to either freak out and yell at the poor girl for not coming forward sooner, or to be the calm, cool, mother/big sister figure and gather information through non-threatening questions. Fortunately, the less frightening version came out, and Watts didn't burst a blood vessel or anything. That I could see.

"Amanda."

Her questioning jerked to a stop, but otherwise, she didn't move.

I'd watched the sheriff walk across the room and hadn't been sure whether to break Watts' rhythm of questions to warn her of her dad's arrival, or let it take its course. I hadn't decided what to do until it was too late. Which I guess was making a decision not to tell her.

Watts still didn't look at him. "I'm in the middle of something."

"I can see that, but this is important."

"So's what I'm doing."

He waited until she very carefully closed her iPad and stood up.

"Thank you," he said. "If I could just have a minute of your time."

They stepped away. My hearing wasn't good enough to catch words, but it wasn't hard to tell that Watts was pretty ticked off at being interrupted.

"You're doing great," Taylor said to Laura.

Laura shuddered. "Do you think she believes me?"

"Of course she does."

Laura didn't ask me, but then, I was just an adult who didn't matter. What did I know?

Watts came back, looking shaken.

I sat up. "What's wrong?"

"Nothing."

"Liar."

She glared at me. "Nothing I can tell you. How's that?" She sat and focused on Laura. "Still no idea who the guy was you saw Rikki with last night?"

Laura shook her head. "I'm sorry."

"What about anyone else in the barn? Did you see anyone? Hear anyone?"

"I told you, I was sort of asleep before they came in, and then I was hiding so they wouldn't see me. So I didn't see anybody else, either."

"Okay." Watts let out a slow breath. "Let's go through it all again."

I glanced at my watch. Time was creeping toward Laura's event. If we didn't get out of there soon, she wouldn't have time to get Bunny ready. I slid out my phone and texted Zach. It took me a year, but I did it.

could someone check on bunny

I only had to wait a few seconds before receiving an answer:

bobby and claire got it covered

Awesome. It made sense, since their judging wasn't until tomorrow, and they knew what was needed to get Bunny presentable. All that would be left would be for Laura to get changed and present her calf at the ring on time.

"You again?"

It took me a moment to realize Laura had stopped talking and everyone in our little group was looking up. Gregg had broken away from his fan club, and was steamrolling my way, murder in his eyes.

Chapter Twenty-one

Gregg stopped a few feet away, staring at me, looking even wilder than he had when he'd first arrived. I slowly closed my phone, not wanting to spook him, but chose not to say anything. He obviously wanted a fight, and it wouldn't be the smartest thing for me to slug him with all of our county's finest standing around watching.

"Why are you here?" He wasn't going to let it go. He obviously lacked my maturity. "Are you a suspect? Or just butting into things that aren't your business?"

"I'm not a—"

"Mr. Gregg." Watts stood up and moved inbetween me and the idiot. "Ms. Crown is merely helping with our inquiries."

"Oh, so it's like that, is it? You are a suspect?" He took a step toward me, Watts mirroring his move.

"Mr. Gregg, please. I'm conducting an interview. If you could please move along, I would appreciate it. This doesn't concern you."

"Of course it concerns me. One of my most promising young protégés is dead, and this woman is in the middle of it."

Oh, for Pete's sake. Protégé? Really? The word "conquest" came to mind much easier than protégé. "I'm not in the middle of anything," I said. Which wasn't exactly true, seeing how I'd found the body, and had brought one of the last people to see her alive to talk to the cops. But who was counting? "I'm just being a good citizen. And you know what good citizens do? They report things they see. Like seeing someone have an argument with Rikki only hours before she shows up dead. Would you know anything about that?"

He went white, then red. Like a barber shop pole. He even looked like he might start spinning around. "What are you—Who is she to—"

"David? Anything wrong?" The sheriff—Watts' dad—came up behind Gregg.

"That woman." He pointed a shaking finger at me. "I want her arrested."

"For what?"

"Killing Rikki Raines."

The sheriff looked at Watts, who was rolling her eyes like a teenager. "She's not even a suspect, Da—Sheriff."

He walked over to me, holding out his hand. "Sheriff Nathaniel Schrock."

I stood up to meet him. "Stella Crown."

"Ah, the young lady who found our victim."

"What?" Gregg was so loud the rest of the room went silent.

The sheriff hesitated for a second, then said, "It's okay, everybody. Nothing to see here."

Gradually, the voices started up again.

Gregg's voice shook, but at least he wasn't screaming anymore. "Are you telling me this…this woman found Rikki?"

Watts nodded. "She did."

Gregg really was going to explode. I wondered how messy it would be. Eh. I'd seen worse.

"David, come on. Doesn't one of your girls have an event coming up?"

Gregg blinked, like he wasn't sure what the sheriff was talking about.

"Remember?" I said. "One of the events you bought for your daughters?"

Gregg made a move toward me, but the sheriff stepped in front of him, while Watts gave me the evil eye. I know. I needed to shut up.

Schrock pulled a schedule out of his pocket, along with a pair of glasses that he perched on the end of his nose. "There, see? Calf judging. Your youngest is in it. It starts in a half hour."

Laura jerked her head up. "Half hour?"

I held my hand out toward her, like I would a frightened animal. "Watts?" I kept my voice low.

She swiveled her eyes toward me.

"We gotta go. Laura's in an event. That same one your dad's talking about."

Sheriff Schrock led Gregg away, Gregg looking back over his shoulder at me, until finally they were out of hearing range, with several other people between us.

"Thanks for coming in, Laura," Watts said. "Next time, though, it would be better to come right away, all right? Now, here." She gave each of us a card. "Call me if you think of anything else."

Taylor pocketed the card. "We can go?"

"Yes. Thank you. Stella, you have a second?"

I jerked my head at the girls, and they took off. "What?"

Watts glanced the direction her dad had gone, then scooted her chair closer. "Do you know the woman who is the official veterinarian for this year's fair? I figured you might, since you're a farmer."

"Yeah. Her name's Carla Beaumont. Why?"

Watts' stylus hovered above her iPad. "What do you know about her?"

My hackles rose. It had only been an hour since Bryan had said someone was out to get my best friend. Was that "someone" the police?

"We have a theory about what killed Rikki

Raines," Watts said. She hesitated, as if deciding whether or not to share. She probably shouldn't. But I wasn't going to tell her that.

"We think it might have been poison," she finally said. "Administered with a syringe."

"So?"

"Stella, think about what Dr. Beaumont would have here, at the fair. Syringes. Medicine. All being carried around with her. Lots of it deadly to humans."

I laughed. "Are you for real? Tons of people have syringes at the fair. I give my animals injections all the time for worms or whatever. Not a new thing."

"This wasn't a worm medicine."

My mind raced back to a few months ago, when someone had stolen meds from the back of Carla's truck. "Ketamine?"

"We don't know for sure. They're still running tests." She glanced at her notes. "But it was something that caused paralysis, and we know Dr. Beaumont would have those things in her box. For surgery, and other things."

"Was it Ace?"

"What's that?"

"Acepromazine. A tranquilizer." Vets used it as a sedative before operations, or even to help with car sickness in dogs. It had actually started out being used on humans, and still was some-times used as an anti-psychotic drug. It shouldn't be deadly, not unless…"How much medicine was she given?"

"Enough of whatever it was that her throat swelled to the point she couldn't breathe, or swallow. She basically suffocated."

My stomach dropped. Poor Rikki.

"She never had a chance," Watts said. "And the worst thing is she would have known what was happening, but couldn't do anything about it." She shook her head, and I saw the sympathy in the slump of her shoulders. It was nice to see a cop care about the victim, especially after she'd been questioning my own emotions the night before.

But wait. She was saying Carla had something to do with it.

"Watts, Carla would never do something like that."

"I'm not accusing her. Yet. But it does look suspicious."

"Because she's a vet? What does that have to do with Rikki Raines? Carla didn't even know her."

Watts' eyebrows rose. "And you know this how?"

"We talk. If she knew Rikki Raines, I would have heard about it."

"Just how well do you know Dr. Beaumont?"

Should I tell her? "Carla's my best friend. Or one of them, anyway. I've known her forever."

"So I can't trust you to see the truth."

"Truth? What truth? All I see is stupid suspicion."

"It's a syringe. And a good possibility of veterinary medicine."

"Oh, come on. There's no way for you to know that about the medicine unless you have a detailed report. Do you?"

No response.

"Plus, anybody could get a syringe. And how do you know it's a vet's syringe, anyway? Syringes all look the same."

She blinked. "Do they?"

"Well, sure. Except for the honking huge needles, I would think. And as for the medicine, you said it yourself she has it here at the fair. Anybody could have taken it."

"Really? She's that careless with her box?"

"She's not…Listen, Watts. She couldn't have done it. I was with her while Rikki was getting murdered."

She went all skeptical.

"And not just me. My fiancé. Her boyfriend. We were doing the whole fairway games and unhealthy food thing. We met her after the concert and went from there. And it was for a while before Rikki was killed, because Laura saw Rikki after that."

Watts tapped on her iPad. "What time are you saying you met her?"

"I'm not just saying it. It happened. And it would have been, I don't know. Ten-thirty. Eleven. Way before Rikki died. And listen, I'm sure the carnies wouldn't remember us, but the kids saw us over by the double Ferris wheel. That was right before Nick and I went back to the calf barn and found Rikki dead. Carla was with us the whole time. You can look it up in your notes. I told you that last night, the same as I told all the other cops."

She frowned. "But—"

"So you can't pin the murder on Carla. It didn't happen."

"But it could be her medicine."

"Possibly. If someone broke into her stuff."

She let out a huge sigh and sank back into her chair.

"Sorry to blow your lead, Watts, but I'm not going to let you destroy my friend just so you can look good to Daddy."

"That is not—"

"What made you think of her, anyway?"

She wouldn't meet my eyes.

"Let me guess. Anonymous tip?"

"We have to take every one seriously."

"Whatever." I stood. "I gotta go. And look, I really do hope you find who killed Rikki, but you're wrong on this one."

I left her hunched over her iPad, tapping uselessly on the screen.

Chapter Twenty-two

I stopped outside the building and called Willard. When he answered, I told him what had just happened. "Can you find out what they know? Is this official?"

"I haven't heard anything," he said. "I'll check it out."

I thanked him, then caught up with the girls at Laura's stall after trying to call Carla. I wasn't going to let her be ambushed by Watts without warning. Even if there was no way Watts could reorganize the timeline to implicate Carla, she still might try to pin the stolen meds on her. That would tear Carla apart, if it were true. Carla didn't answer, so I texted her, telling her briefly that Watts might be around asking stupid questions. I did a quick sweep through the dairy barn on my way to the calf barn, but didn't see her anywhere. I hoped she would see my message sooner rather than later.

"Stella!" Taylor was still at Laura's stall. "Laura just left."

"Come on. Let's get a seat."

Taylor and I hoofed it to the arena just as the bucket calves were being judged. This is the youngest class, born only months before the fair, between March fifteen and May thirty. They were still in their adorable knobby-kneed stage, not as awkward as newborns, of course, but still fresh and innocent. The 4-H'ers were knobby-kneed, too. Younger than Zach, since they had to be between eight and thirteen to show this class. They looked as cute as their calves, wearing their white clothes, their nervousness showing in their stiffness and obvious discomfort about where to stand and how to hold the halter ropes. The older kids were fairly experienced, in most cases, but the eight-year-olds still had a lot of learning to do.

Bobby and Claire had found seats across the arena, Bobby very bright in an eye-splitting neon shirt, but there was no room with them, so Taylor and I squeezed into some free seats on the bleachers. Only then did I allow myself to relax. My sore foot, which I'd been on way too much that morning, let itself be known, but I didn't care. I was just glad to be where I wanted to be for the first time that day. I would have hated to miss Zach's market judging event, and poor Laura would have been devastated if her opportunity to show her calf had been lost. No matter that what we'd just done was necessary, missing her event would have tarnished Laura's 4-H experience forever—what hadn't already been tarnished.

The final six bucket calves were lined up in the front of the ring now, and the judge was looking them each over, marking a tablet, stepping closer for a look at this or that. He seemed agreeable enough, talking with the kids, asking questions we couldn't hear, and nodding or smiling at their responses. Twice he had calves change places, until he seemed satisfied with his arrangement.

He visited the table to the side of the ring, and a ring man accompanied him back to the center, carrying ribbons. Using the handheld microphone, he praised the class for their care and quality of their calves, and congratulated them all on a job well done. The group in the back line realized by now that they wouldn't be ribbon winners this year, and their disappointment showed in their hunched shoulders and forlorn expressions. The younger few were still excited, watching everything with wide eyes, but the older ones understood it was over.

The judge handed out the ribbons, from sixth to first place, and took a moment to acknowledge the attributes of the champion. The girl holding the halter appeared ready to burst with pride and joy, and practically danced her way out of the ring when it was all over.

"We're next?" Taylor said.

We. She and Zach were already a "we"? Or was she lumping herself in with me? Were she and I a "we"? Not my usual speed for bonding.

"Zach and Laura will show in this next group," I said, "along with Austin and Randy."

"And them."

I followed Taylor's gaze to the bleachers on the other side of the ring. Mrs. Gregg perched on the edge of the first row, with her two older girls beside her. One of them was texting, and the other one was practically sitting on the lap of the guy next to her. He didn't seem to be protesting.

Mr. Gregg slid into aisle space beside Mrs. G, but didn't sit. His arms were crossed, and while he'd smoothed down his hair, his face still bore the expression I'd last seen in the cop building. Pissed off and freaked out. I guess that's what happens when you get called out for being an asshole, and you don't have any defense. Especially when you're used to people pandering to you because they want something. His wife didn't look overjoyed to see him. In fact, she didn't even acknowledge his presence. Couldn't blame her.

"You think they'll win?" Taylor's pretty face bore a frown.

"Unfortunately, there's a good chance of it."

"Cheaters."

"Hey, there. Room for us?" Nick stood beside me, Miranda with him, showing what some might consider to be an expression of curiosity. I knew she was just trying not to smell anything.

I nudged Taylor with my hip, and she scooted down, making room.

Nick sat beside me, slipping his arm behind me, grabbing the edge of the bench. "You okay?"

"It's been a long morning. I'll explain later. Your day?"

"Productive."

"Well, at least that's one of us. What are you doing here?"

"Didn't want to miss Zach's event. He's practically my nephew, you know."

We smiled at each other, until I fully realized who'd come with him. "What about her?"

He gave me his innocent look. "She wants to spend quality time with me, while she can."

I tried not to show my skepticism.

"Here they come!" Taylor chirped.

The first of Zach's group paraded into the ring, and we all sat up straighter, watching for our friends. Austin was the first we saw, with Zach entering a few calves behind him. He looked very handsome in his whites, which Taylor appreciated, if the way she clutched her program meant anything. Laura showed up several calves later, with Randy directly behind her.

The calves were all beautiful, their coats glossy and combed to perfection. Barnabas, in particular, had never looked better. Zach had worked wonders with our ordinary, non-genetically planned calf. Zach led from Barnabas' left side, his right hand holding the halter rope, his left his show stick. They filed into their spot, and Zach used his stick to gently prod Barnabas' feet into straight, square positioning. He then rubbed the stick on Barnabas' belly, to ease any nerves he might be suffering. I didn't see any nerves, though. Barnabas looked like he might as well be standing in his stall back at home. Sleeping.

Austin's Halladay fared just as well, and I remembered the pride in Austin's voice as he described his "lucky" calf. Austin wore his whites well, although he looked awfully pale. Probably because he didn't eat a bite of that lunch he'd bought. Even with the vampire impression, I couldn't help but notice the difference a couple of years made. Where Zach was gangly and just growing into his nose, Austin had matured to the point he looked like a man. It was time for him to be done with 4-H and move on to other things. He was ready.

He needed to be ready, because Melody Gregg's calf was gorgeous. Melody's showmanship wasn't up to Austin's standard, but that didn't matter in this category, where the judges were looking at the calves themselves. Her champion looked every bit of one, from his high, straight back, to his straight, strong legs, and wide, even hips. He walked right along with her, not minding her unsure—and lazy—hold on his halter, and when it came his turn to take his place in line, he placed his feet like a veteran, which he was. I wondered what Gregg had paid for him, and whether it was worth it to him. Maybe that depended on whether he won or not. Or maybe just whether or not Melody was a pouty mess when it was all over.

Randy's calf gave him a little trouble, jumping around, but it looked like it just wanted to play, not that it was scared. He tried rubbing its stomach, but eventually gave up and took a firmer grip on the halter rope. The calf would calm soon, and as I said, this wasn't the showmanship portion of judging, so it didn't matter as much as it could. Randy, being the kind of kid he was, would be able to weather it.

Laura and her calf were another story. The girl was obviously still feeling anxious from the past hour with the detective, as well as from her realization of what she might have witnessed, and that had transferred to her calf, who skittered sideways, colliding with Randy and his calf. Randy jumped, yelping and hopping on one foot. Ouch. Even with a yearling, that was a lot of weight when it landed on your tender bones. My foot throbbed with a sympathetic pain. Laura pulled her calf away, apologizing to Randy, then walked Bunny forward, out of the line. She circled around again to the back of the group, re-positioning herself and her calf in their assigned spot, next to Randy. Bunny's eyes rolled, and he balked, turning his hind end in a half circle, with Laura's grip on his halter rope as the center point. Randy and his calf avoided contact this time.

"Why doesn't someone help her?" Taylor asked me.

"They can't. It's all on Laura. At least this event is about the calf, and not about Laura's performance. The next one is the one on their showmanship, so this would have been a disaster for her and for Randy." I was proud of Randy for how he'd recovered from the incident. Looking at him, I'd never know anything had even happened. He'd turned his back on Laura and her calf, focused totally on his own thing. His calf was calm now, standing squarely, eyes forward.

Taylor gripped her knees so hard I thought she might cut off circulation to her feet, but I liked that she felt so much compassion for a girl she'd just met. Zach, I was sure, would have been worried, too, if he'd been in the stands, but he had his own little guy to think about, and was so focused on keeping him happy and still I don't think he'd even seen what happened.

The judge began walking up and down the line, studying the calves, viewing their heads and faces. He then walked behind them, checking them out from the rear. I knew he was looking at the structure of their hips and hind legs. These male babies wouldn't be having their own calves, of course, but their bloodlines would determine future generations of dairy cows, so the judge wanted to see straight, wide bones, and excellent symmetry.

When the judge returned to the front of the line, the ring men had the kids begin walking around the arena. Soon the whole lot of them were parading in a circle, with the judge taking a look at the calves' feet, and the way their bodies moved as they walked. Laura's calf had calmed down, probably because of Laura's own demeanor, and by getting some action going, instead of standing in a static line. Seeing that Laura and Bunny would be okay, I switched my focus to the others.

Zach was doing great, Barnabas meandering along in his usual carefree style, like he wouldn't want to be anywhere else. He was almost too casual, flirting with the crowd, like he should have been participating in the Lovely Miss Pennsylvania pageant, instead. I couldn't help but laugh, and pointed him out to Nick.

Austin's calf was living up to expectations, striding purposefully, head high, following Austin's lead exactly. He really was a beautiful calf, and seeing him in the ring showed him off. I hadn't really taken the time to check him out in his stall, and realized I'd overlooked his star potential. He would make a fine stud someday, with his beautiful dairy characteristics.

Randy's calf, the other one from my farm, walked along smoothly enough, but while he was a fine calf, he certainly wasn't of the same caliber as Austin's. Randy could maybe end up in the top ten, but I couldn't see him placing any higher than fifth or sixth.

Melody Gregg's calf…well, he was perfect. She, on the other hand, looked like she'd rather be somewhere clean, preferably without livestock.

"Who is *that*?" Miranda's shocked voice pierced the air.

I followed her gaze across the ring, and it didn't take me long to see Summer, in all her plastic glory, surrounded by a posse of fans, including her mother, a couple of less flamboyant girls, and her boobs, which were large enough to count as people.

I laughed. "That's Nick's new girlfriend."

His arm tensed behind me. "Stella…"

"Oh, stop it, Nick, she knows I'm kidding."

"Seriously," Miranda said, "who is she?"

I glanced at Taylor, who was watching Zach with such concentration I didn't think she heard our conversation. Ah, to be so young and tunnel-visioned.

"Her name is Summer. She's a contestant in the Lovely Miss Pennsylvania pageant. We met her and her lovely mother yesterday, when the girl tried to abduct Nick by stuffing him into her cleavage."

"Does she look…like that up close?"

"Worse. And I'm fairly certain the only real thing about her is maybe her earlobes. And those are disguised by earrings."

"You mean—"

"Nose, lips, hair, boobs. As far as I could tell without touching her—" I shuddered "—it's all been altered."

"Is that legal?"

"If your mother condones it, I guess. And if you know the right people."

"Or the wrong ones."

"Exactly. Summer thought Nick was pretty special. Gave him his very own pretty-please invitation to come to the pageant."

"And how did you respond to this invitation, Nick?"

Nick looked very pointedly at the calves in the ring. "Not participating in this conversation."

"Why not?"

"It's creepy."

The judge began reorganizing the calves, until he had them in the order he preferred. Zach and Barnabas stood at what looked like a respectable fifth place, Laura at ninth, and Randy further down the line. Too bad, but that's the way it went when you took charge of a calf at birth and had no idea what to expect. Good care and loving can only go so far.

The only two places the judge seemed unsure of were the ones on the top end of the line. Austin's Halladay, and Melody Gregg's calf. At this point, Melody's calf stood in the Grand Champion slot, with Austin's in Reserve. Austin stood straight, his shoulders high, eyes following the judge as he moved. Melody watched the judge, too, but with a more casual air, as if she already knew she had it won. Made me want to smack some sense into her. Or feed her some lemons. Obviously, I wouldn't do either. But it was fun to fantasize about.

The judge was taking his time, walking around the calves, leaning over for better angles, holding out his hands as a primitive measuring tool. He stood in front of the calves, hand on his chin, head swiveling back and forth.

"Come on," Taylor said. "Come on, come on, come on…"

Finally, the judge stepped back and nodded, gesturing to the officials that he had the order the way he wanted it. Crap.

Austin's shoulders remained high, but now his chin thrust out, and I could see his eyes blazing even from that distance. Reserve Champion was amazing, but not when you lost Grand Champion to a girl who hadn't touched her calf more than a few times, and then, only when she had to. And when her dad had bought her the win.

The older Gregg girls were already up and moving away, followed by the guy who'd been sitting next to them. Mrs. Gregg was smiling and clapping, obviously glad their money paid off. Gregg himself looked smug, and just as smackable as his daughter. Only difference was, with him I could see myself actually following through with the daydream.

Chapter Twenty-three

Taylor skipped ahead as we made our way back to the barn, and was already waiting at Zach's stall when we arrived. He and Barnabas showed up several minutes later, brandishing their pink ribbon.

"Ooh, Zachy! Fifth place!" Taylor hugged him, and he hugged her back, careful not to squish his prize.

"Yes, Zachy," I said. "Great job."

He smiled and bumped my fist. "It's your ribbon, too."

"Nah. I mean, thanks, but you did all the work."

"Yeah, I know, but I wanted to make you feel included."

"Great job, Zach." Nick shook Zach's hand, before Taylor could claim him again.

"Come on, boy." Zach led Barnabas forward, and the calf good-naturedly entered his stall and nosed around for the water bucket.

Miranda stepped back, closer to Austin's stall, and tried to avoid contact with Zach or his calf. She glanced at her watch, and I wondered why she had even come back to the fair if she hated it so much. "Quality time" was only worth it if you made it that way.

"Way to go, Barnabas." I patted his back after the gate shut. "You're a good boy."

He shook his head and snuffled.

"So," I said to Zach, "you displaying the ribbon? Or keeping it safe somewhere?"

"Putting it up, for sure." He scootched past Barnabas and attached the ribbon to the boards. "Looks good, doesn't it?"

Taylor clapped. "It's great!"

Nick grinned. "The pink matches Mallory's poster."

Zach shook his head. "You're killing me, man."

"Speak of the devil," Miranda said.

Mallory and Brady pushed through the crowd of returning calves and exhibitors. "Hey, bro, good job."

"Thanks, Mal."

"Where were you guys?" I asked. "I didn't see you over there."

"We were in the back, behind some epically nasty girl. I swear nothing about her was real."

I glanced at Nick. "Was she, um…"

"Disgusting?" Mallory said. "Yes."

"What did you think, Brady?"

His ears went pink. "She was, uh, interesting."

Nick coughed, "Leave it," into his hand, and I figured I'd save Brady any further embarrassment. "Randy okay?" I asked Zach.

He shrugged. "He's fine. I don't think he really expected much. He did all right. At least he wasn't last."

Austin arrived at his stall, and led Halladay inside. He didn't bring an entourage with him. Just his calf and his light purple banner, which I knew would say Reserve Champion.

"What about that boy who lost out on Grand Champion?" Miranda said. Her back was to Austin, and, not surprisingly, she didn't recognize our wide eyes, or even the finger I slashed across my throat. "Isn't he a friend of yours, Zach?" she yammered on. "That had to suck, losing to that girl."

"It did."

Miranda spun around at the sound of Austin's voice. "Oh. Sorry."

"I'm sorry, too, Austin," Mallory said. She knew him from school, where they were in the same grade. "You should've won. Your calf is awesome."

"Thanks, Mal." He rolled up his banner and stuck it in the footlocker he kept at the end of the stall. I didn't blame him for not hanging it up.

He'd been hoping for the dark purple one, and it had to bite to lose to a girl he knew didn't deserve it. Maybe later in the week he'd feel more like displaying what was, in reality, quite an achievement.

"You still have the showmanship event, right?" Taylor said. "Isn't that what you told me?"

"Yeah, but this is the one I really wanted."

No response to that.

Taylor's phone broke the awkward silence with a cheerful bird tweet. She checked it, and made a sad face. "I gotta go. Rehearsal for tomorrow night. You are all coming, right?"

Everyone made the appropriate noises, except for me. I wasn't yet so taken with the girl I was willing to sit through that kind of torture. Especially if it meant I had to see more of Summer. Literally. Wasn't there a swimsuit segment with pageants? I didn't think I could take it. Taylor left after extracting a promise from Zach that he'd still be around when she was done for the day.

Mallory was next to go. "Brady and I are heading over to watch that dog show they're putting on in the domestic pets building. Anybody want to come?"

Nobody did, so the two of them took off. Bobby and Claire came by then, to offer their congratulations to Zach, and their consolation to

Austin. Claire hung back, as usual, checking out the crowd. Probably looking for Taylor, poor kid. When it was clear her competition was absent, she moved closer to Zach. "You did really great."

He smiled at her. "Thanks. Barnabas was awesome."

"Yeah." She reached in and petted the calf, who gazed up at her with adoring eyes. "You were good, too, though. You'll do great in the showman-ship competition on Thursday."

"Thanks. Barnabas makes it easy."

"Stupid Greggs," Bobby said. "Too bad that lemon didn't get into the calf's food later in the day, huh, Austin?"

Austin's head snapped up. "What?"

"You know. The lemon, the one that made him drool all over. Too bad whoever did it didn't wait till later today. Then he might not have been in the judging at all."

"Then none of the calves might have been in it," I reminded him. "The whole barn could have been quarantined."

"Oh. Right. Well, anyway, our judging's tomorrow. We'll try to kick the Gregg girls' butts for you."

Austin turned away. "Yeah, you do that." Not like he cared. It wouldn't change anything for his results. And Bobby didn't really have the cow to back up his words. Claire, however, had a chance. It was big of her not to mention it just then.

"Hey," I said. "Were any of you in here last night late?"

"Like how late?" Bobby said.

"I don't know. Eleven-thirty. Midnight."

"We were out on the rides. We saw you, remember? We were on the Ferris wheel."

"Right. How about you, Austin?"

He didn't answer, his head down as he scooped some droppings from Halladay's wood chips.

"Why are you wondering?" Claire said.

Bobby rolled his eyes. "Duh. That's when Rikki Raines was getting dumped in our manure trailer."

Zach winced. "Geez, Bobby."

"Sorry. I didn't mean...whatever."

Claire frowned. "You think we had something to do with it?"

"No." I gave a little laugh. "I do not think you did anything to Rikki Raines. I just thought, if you were here, maybe you saw something. Or someone."

"But there are always people around here. How would we know if something was different?"

"I heard it was pretty quiet right around then, actually."

"Says who?"

"Laura," Zach said. "She—"

"—was taking care of Bunny," I said, cutting him off. "She said it was so quiet she fell asleep."

Zach gave me a funny look, and I shook my head.

"Well, like we said, we weren't here." Claire glanced at her phone. "And now I have to go get in line for milking."

"It's not near time," Bobby said.

"It is if you don't want to wait a year." She hesitated, then walked off without him. "It's your time you'll be wasting."

"Oh, for—Hang on, I'm coming! See ya, Zach." He trotted off after his sister.

"Not the brightest bulb, is he?" Miranda said.

"He's a nice kid."

"You would say that."

"Yes, I would, because it's true. Weren't you going home?"

Nick slid his hand along the inside of my elbow. "Weren't you?"

"I was planning on it."

"Um," said Zach, "do you need me for anything?"

All three of us looked at him.

"Like what?" I said.

"I dunno. I'm just hungry, is all."

"So go eat."

"All right. Uh, thanks."

"See ya. And congrats again."

"So," Miranda said when he was gone. "Can we please go now?"

"You know, you could have stayed home."

"I wanted to spend time with my brother. Is that so wrong?"

I really was going to strangle the woman one of these days. If Nick wasn't such a hottie—and a huge piece of my heart—I would be glad to send her packing, never to be seen again.

Nick tilted his head toward the door. "So, you ready then?"

"You two go on ahead, and I'll be right there. Wait for me outside?"

His curiosity was plain, but he just said, "All right. Come on, Miranda."

She made a face. "We have to wait for her again?"

"I'm sure she has a good reason."

I did, but it wasn't one I liked. It was one of suspicion. And I hoped to God I was wrong.

She huffed, and strode toward the door.

"I'll just be a minute," I told Nick.

As he left, I stepped over to Austin's stall. "Tough competition today."

He kept cleaning.

"Austin."

Finally, he stopped, and leaned on his pitchfork. "What?"

"You were here last night by yourself, weren't you?"

"No."

"During the concert. Everybody else was gone. You stayed behind."

"I told you I was there. I just stood in the back."

"That's right. What song was she singing when you got there?"

He frowned. "What is this? Why are you asking?"

"Austin, what song?"

"I don't remember. "Rainestorm," maybe."

Okay, so he'd gotten there only a few minutes late. But then, what I was considering wouldn't take long. "How long did you stay?"

"Till the end."

"You heard all the songs? The encore?"

He went back to his work.

"Austin?"

He threw a cow plop into the corner. "What?"

"What was the encore?"

"Oh, for—" He stabbed his pitchfork into the straw. "'Forever Your Country Girl.' Okay? Are we done now?"

"And after the concert?"

"What do you mean?"

"Were you out here again?"

"Of course I was. I checked in on Halladay."

"Were you alone?"

He froze, his eyes darting everywhere but my face, and my heart rose into my throat. Was his guilt even worse than I thought? Had he done something even more terrible?

"Austin? Someone saw you." Okay, so it was a little white lie. Or gray, maybe. "And they saw Rikki Raines."

He stared at me, his eyes wide and shining. "I didn't hurt her," he finally said, his voice low. "I would never hurt her. I loved her. I've loved her since second grade, when I hit her in the face with a kickball, and she told me it wasn't my fault. You have to believe me. I didn't do it. I—" His voice hitched, and he swiped at tears. "She loved me, too. She said so."

"Austin. Wait a minute. You were friends with Rikki Raines?"

He shook his head. "Not just friends."

"You were her *boyfriend*?"

His head shot up. "Is that so hard to believe? I'm not good enough for her, is that it? Stupid farmer kid? Is that what you think?"

"Oh, for Pete's sake, Austin. Look at me. Look who you're talking to. You think I look down on you because you're a farmer? What am I? Huh?

What's Zach? What are most of the people I love? Farmers. Mechanics. Good, blue-collar folks. So don't give me that crap."

He sniffed again, and wouldn't look at me.

"Austin, how could you be her boyfriend, and no one knew?"

He was quiet for a few moments. "Have you seen the papers? Those stupid 'newspapers' that tell the gossip from the entertainment world? It's all about famous people's personal lives. Their boyfriends, girlfriends, people they hate, people who hate them. There's no such thing as private anymore. Rikki doesn't…didn't want that. She wanted us to just be us. Not us and the world."

I couldn't blame her. Not after everything I'd seen about her and that other singer, what was her name, Valerie Springfield, and the guy who supposedly drove a wedge between them. "What about that other guy? The actor from that zombie show?"

He snorted. "She couldn't stand him. They were at a premiere once and somebody took their picture, totally made it into something it never was."

"So she and that other singer? There wasn't really a rivalry?"

"Oh, sure there was. Valerie Springfield hated Rikki, at least that's what Rikki heard. Valerie thought Rikki was keeping her from moving up the food chain. That there could only be one star from rural Pennsylvania. Stupid, of course. Why would Rikki care? They weren't even at the same label."

"Did Valerie hate Rikki enough to kill her?"

He breathed through his mouth, his brain obviously on overload. "I never said that. I don't know her. Just what Rikki told me, and she thought the whole thing was ridiculous. And lame. I just know I loved Rikki. And I would never, ever hurt her. Not even a little."

I stepped closer to him, speaking so no one else could hear. "I don't for a second think you did. But I do think you hurt someone else. You and Rikki put the lemon in the calf's food, didn't you?"

He sniffed, and wiped his nose with his sleeve. "It was just supposed to—"

"—be a joke? It's never a joke when you hurt an animal."

"It didn't hurt him. He's fine."

"But it could have kept him out of the competition."

"So? He didn't deserve to be in the competition, anyway. I mean, she didn't. Those stupid Greggs deserve everything that's coming to them."

"Everything? You mean there's more?"

"No! I just…" He closed his eyes briefly, and when they opened again, he didn't look scared anymore. He just looked pissed. "That family thinks they own the world. The fair. Rikki's career. It's about time someone told them different."

"Austin." I looked at the boy—for at that moment he was definitely a boy, and not a man—and pushed down the anger rising in my gut. "You've put me in a horrible position. You know what this kind of thing means. You know what I should do. What I'm supposed to do, if I follow the rules."

His nostrils flared, and another round of tears gathered in his eyes. Not pissed anymore—now he was terrified. "The lemon wasn't going to hurt him."

"Austin, you sabotaged another person's animal. You should be expelled from the fair."

"Please." He sniffed and wiped his nose with his sleeve. "Please, Stella, I didn't mean…and now Rikki's dead. And the calf won, anyway, right? So it didn't change a thing. It didn't hurt anything."

"Didn't it?"

"What? What did it do? She still won!"

Dammit, what was I supposed to do? Turn him in, and he'd lose everything. Scholarships, respect, perhaps even his clean criminal record. Did he deserve that? But if I let him go, I was an accessory to a crime. I was an adult, not living up to the rules and regulations expected of us. Especially someone who was sponsoring an animal. Someone who spent her life protecting and caring for animals.

"Stella." Austin sank onto a straw bale. "It was dumb. I know it was dumb. And wrong. I won't... I'm sorry."

I clenched my jaw, already kicking myself for what I was about to do. But, holy crap. How could I destroy the future of this kid? Even if he was a moron. "Listen. If I let this go, which is the stupidest thing I'll have done in a very long time, you have to promise me—swear on Halladay, or your mother, or whatever keeps you up at night—that you will never, ever do anything like this again. If you so much as consider sabotaging another animal, I'll be all over you like flies on my manure pit. You understand me? You do something like this, and it's not just you who will be in trouble. It will be my ass, too, because I turned my back on it this time."

Austin nodded, not looking at me. His Adam's apple bobbed up and down, and he clenched his hands so hard he probably left nail marks on the backs of his hands. "I know. I'm...I won't ever. I promise. I swear. Please. You have to believe me. I'm telling the truth."

Idiot kid. It was a little late for that.

"But that's not it."

"There's more?"

"Of course there's more! You could have been

one of the last people to see Rikki alive. You were with her just before she was killed."

He dropped his face into his hands and sobbed. "I never should have left her. She said she would be okay…"

I sat next to him and put my hand on his back. He stiffened.

"Austin, what happened?"

He wiped his nose again. "I got a text, asking me to come by the fair office."

"At midnight?"

"I know, it was crazy. But I didn't want to take any chances and miss something. So Rikki said she'd sneak over to our trailer. My folks never stay here, so there wouldn't be anyone to see her. She couldn't come to the fair office with me, because, well, there would be too many people around. I thought she'd be fine." He sobbed again, and I squeezed his shoulder.

"So you got to the office, and then what?"

"Nobody there had texted me. It was just the one old guy there, and he didn't know anything. So I went back to my trailer, and Rikki wasn't there. I tried texting her, but she didn't answer, so I thought maybe she got spooked, and took off. I just texted her that I'd call her tomorrow. I mean, today. Of course I never heard back."

I drummed my fingers on his back. "Do you still have the text you got from the fair office?"

"No." He got out his phone and scrolled down. "It was just a number, because I don't have the office in my contacts, and there was no reason to keep it."

I wished he had, because it very easily could have been someone luring him away from Rikki. Someone who had access to his phone number. But I'm not sure he'd put that together yet.

"Austin, I know this is hard. Really hard. But you need to tell the cops, not about the lemon, that's small stuff compared to Rikki. But you need to go. Today. Now. Tell them about the bogus text, and about being with Rikki that night."

He sniffed, but didn't respond.

"I'll give you a little time, but if you don't go, I am going to tell them this. It's too important to let go. You want me to go with you?"

He held so still I thought he was ignoring me altogether, or just was too far into his head to hear me. But then he shook his head, so subtly I almost didn't catch it. "I'll go," he whispered. "By myself."

I waited a few more seconds, then quietly walked away.

Chapter Twenty-four

"Everything okay?" Nick met me outside the barn.

"No, not really. I need to check in with Carla now." She'd never replied to my text warning her about Watts, and I was worried she hadn't seen it, and had been blind-sided.

"All right. Do you know where she is?"

I loved that he didn't question me about why I needed to see her, or why I had steam coming out of my ears. "I'll find her." I pulled out my phone, which was getting more use that day than it had in the past several months. Speed dial three, behind only Nick and Lucy. Lucy…I should probably check in with her at some point.

"Hey," Carla said. I could hear voices in the background, and what was probably an electric fan.

"Where are you? We need to talk."

"So talk."

Hmm. Had Watts already cornered her and accused her of killing Rikki Raines? "If this is a bad time—"

"I'm in the rabbit barn. Come on over." She hung up. All was not merry in Carla Land.

"Are we going, too?" Miranda said, when I informed them where I was headed. "More animals?"

"They're rabbits," I said. "Cute. Fluffy. Babies."

Nick nudged her. "Come on, Sis. It'll be fun."

She sighed. "Fine."

We made a quick stop to get Miranda a corn on the cob on a stick, and found Carla talking with a young girl who was holding an adorable, charcoal-colored lop-eared bunny. Too bad Tess wasn't there. She would have gone ballistic. Bryan waited a few feet away, sitting on Carla's vet box, the one Watts thought had been burgled for the Acepromazine. Or where Carla had stashed her murder weapons. Bryan made a face at me which could have meant, "Thank God you're here," or "Watch out, she's in the mood to kill somebody." Which wouldn't be good for her future, if Watts got wind of it.

The girl soon put the rabbit back into its cage, and Carla turned toward Bryan. He gestured at me, and she dropped onto a straw bale right next to him, blowing hair off her forehead. "Hey. Sorry I was short with you on the phone. It's just…this day." Her chin trembled, and she looked down at her knees.

Bryan put his arm around her shoulders and

squeezed, but gazed at me with a helpless please-do-something sort of expression.

I jerked my head for him to move, and took his place beside her. "Can you folks give us a minute?"

Nick immediately guided Miranda to a cage where a pair of rabbits looked like they were made entirely of exploded fuzz. Bryan shifted from one foot to another, then shuffled after Nick.

I knocked Carla's knee with my own. "Want to talk about it?"

She took a shuddering breath. "You won't believe it."

"I think I will. Have you checked your phone lately?"

She jumped, like I'd prodded her. "Crap, I turned the sound off a while ago, because I couldn't concentrate on anything. I'd be in the middle of checking an animal, or talking to someone, and the dumb thing would go off. Then I was just telling a kid I thought his pig was going to have to be taken home when the stupid phone rang, and it was a terrible time for an interruption. I forgot to turn it back on, and then—oh." She held out the phone with my text on the screen. "So you know about the detective."

"I know what she thinks. What did she tell you?"

"Other than that I need to watch my step, and

give her a detailed timeline of my whereabouts, and not leave town?"

"She didn't really say that."

A grin flickered across her mouth. "No, but she might as well have. But get this, you know how I've been saying these 4-H'ers and their parents are running me ragged? They just might be my alibi."

"I thought I was your alibi."

"Well, yeah, but then you left, remember? I was checking on a goat late last night, right while you were finding Rikki Raines' body on the manure trailer. That kid and her parents will vouch for me."

"I think Watts knows you're out of the picture as the actual murderer."

"Yeah." She glanced at the box under me. "But I might be a partner in crime."

"No. Just because someone stole your stuff—if that even happened—it does not mean you're responsible. It means someone took something that wasn't theirs and used it in a way you never would."

"But if I'd locked the box up better—"

"It was locked?"

"Well, sure. I would never leave it open. Too much dangerous equipment in there. Obviously."

"Did it look like someone had gotten in? Is the lock messed up?"

"Not that I noticed." She leaned down to look between my knees at the keyhole. "There are scratches on there, but they could have happened anytime. It's not like I'm always watching for someone to steal my stuff. The only other time I got robbed was when my truck got mashed, and that was obviously different. I don't like thinking somebody's always out to get me."

"Of course not. You have all that goodwill toward men I'll never have."

She chuckled. "Toward women, too."

I knocked her with my shoulder. "So now what? What did Watts really say?"

"She wanted to know if I'd noticed anything weird, or if I was missing something. But I hadn't had a chance to go over inventory since Sunday. These kids and their animals. What is up with them needing a vet all the time?" She grinned, and some of her usual spark made its way back into her eyes. "So we went through the box. It's impossible to tell if I'm missing a syringe—I've got a container of a hundred, and I'd have to go back through records to find out how many I've used since I stocked up. Plus, there's no way to tie the syringe to me, necessarily. It's not like they each have a serial number, or anything. It was the same brand, we think, but they're like, everywhere."

"What about the Ace?"

Her face darkened again. "I'm not missing any of that, according to my records, but I could be wrong, I guess. I'm not a perfect organizer every second of the day. God, how did this happen?"

"Hey, remember what I said? Not your fault. You're here to do a job. Tranqs are part of it. Other people need to keep their hands off."

"Yeah, I guess."

We sat for a few moments, and then I said, "Bryan thinks somebody's out to get you."

A flash of irritation raced across her face, but I wasn't sure if it was directed toward Bryan, or toward the "somebody." "He's sweet. But I'm fine."

"Carla, could it be the other vets? The ones who wanted this job?"

"Why would they want it? It sure hasn't been fun so far. And no, I can't see someone trying to get me unlicensed over a week-long stint at the county fair. It's not that great an honor. I'm finding that out fast."

"So who else? Anyone unhappy with results lately? Someone have a prize animal you've had to put down, or anything?"

"It's been a very tame month. I've thought about it. I can't come up with anybody who would be mad at me for any reason."

"So maybe Bryan's just imagining things."

"I sure hope so, but I don't know. It was the whole lemon peel thing that really got him worried.

He figures somebody did it just to see if I could figure it out."

Damn that Austin. He had no idea how his stupid actions would affect people other than the Greggs. I knew I'd regret keeping my mouth shut.

"He's wrong," I said.

"Who is?"

"Bryan. About the lemon peel. It had nothing to do with making you look bad."

"How do you know?"

"Just…trust me on this."

She frowned. "Is there something I should know?"

"No." I stood. "Anyway, I thought it was the texts that got Bryan all riled up."

Her face darkened. "He told you about those?"

"Sure. He's worried."

"And smothering me."

"Carla, he loves you. He wants to protect you." Wow. Was I really defending him? I must have been suffering from a lack of sleep. Or something. "So who sent the texts? And what did they say?"

"Don't know who they were from. It was just a number. And they just said stupid things about me becoming a laughingstock, or being proven incompetent, or something."

"Do you still have the texts?"

"Why?"

"I want to see the number."

She gave me a suspicious look, but got out her phone. Of course I didn't recognize the number. I don't even know why I looked. I wished I had the number of the person who'd texted Austin, pretending to be the fair office, so we could compare them.

"What?" Carla said.

"Nothing."

She was still looking at me funny. "What are you not telling me?"

"Nothing. Please, don't ask anymore."

She stared at me for a few more long moments, then shook her head. "Fine. You can tell me when it's convenient for you."

"Carla…"

"No, no, I'm sorry. It's just been such a crappy day so far. And now I need to help a hysterical mother who is sure her son's pig is on its deathbed, but he's headed off to be in the parade. The kid, not the pig. You going?"

"I don't think you need me to come. Isn't Bryan going with you?"

"I meant the parade."

"Oh, I guess. I told Zach I'd be there to wave. I also told him not to take my eye out with a Tootsie Roll."

"Wear safety goggles. Okay, I'm off. Thanks for the pep talk."

"Anytime."

Bryan must have been watching, because as soon as Carla stood, he hustled over to grab her box.

Nick came over, too, and we watched them leave. He brushed some straw off my back. "Everything okay now?"

"It's better. But still not perfect."

"Nothing ever is."

"Speaking of not being perfect, where's Miranda?"

He grinned. "She's fallen in love."

"She found Mr. Right in the rabbit barn?"

"Sure did. Come meet him."

I trudged after Nick, knowing whoever this guy was, I was going to hate him.

But I was wrong.

How can you hate a little guy named Pouncer, who weighs thirteen pounds and is covered with fuzzy, black and white spots?

Chapter Twenty-five

I needed pie. Nick needed to sit. Miranda needed…
a brain transplant. The booster food tent could offer
two out of the three, so we headed there as soon as
Miranda was done with her rabbit love fest. There
was no point going home anymore, because we'd
have to turn right back around if we were going to
make it to the parade. So food was the answer. But
as soon as we sat down with two pieces of cherry
pie and a Diet Coke—Miranda was such a party
pooper—I was sorry we'd come in.

"Hello, again!"

The three of us gazed up at the mother of the
hideous Summer, me with regret, Nick with something approaching fear, and Miranda with distaste.
At least she and I had that in common. And at least
the monster daughter was nowhere in sight.

"So, have you cleared your schedule?" The
woman gazed straight at Nick, of course, like he had
completely overpowered her with his gorgeousness.
Which, perhaps, he had.

Miranda's nose wrinkled. "Cleared his schedule for what? You do know he's engaged."

The miraculous thing here was that she said that last sentence without a stutter or even a hint of disgust.

The woman batted her eyes, which wasn't quite as terrifying as when her daughter did it, but was bad enough. "He knows what I'm talking about."

From his blank expression I could tell she was wrong.

"The Lovely Miss Pennsylvania pageant," I told him.

Understanding brought life back to his face. "Oh. Um. I really wasn't—"

"You simply must come. Summer would be so thrilled to see you in the audience." Her body language suggested that she herself wouldn't be sorry, either. Sometimes I didn't mind the whole Nick-as-chick-magnet thing, but this woman was beyond creepy, being totally oblivious to me, sitting right beside him.

Miranda's eyes were like tractor tires, probably because she was waiting for me to deck the woman. But I gripped my plastic fork, breathed deeply, and tried not to imagine plunging the utensil deep into the woman's throat. Probably wouldn't work, anyway, plastic not being the best weapon known to a crossed woman.

Nick smiled, back in control. "I'll see what I can do, Mrs...."

"Moss. But it's just Ms. And you can call me Sherry."

"I see." His eyes flicked toward me. "I'll have to see what my fiancée is thinking of for tomorrow evening."

Her adoring gaze went sour for a second, before the fake smile came back, which she aimed at me. "Surely you don't want to miss out on such an exciting event. My daughter is going to do very well, I know, and I would hate for anyone to miss it."

"I really—"

"—don't," Miranda said. "Or, she doesn't. Want to miss it, I mean. We'll be there. Thank you for the invitation."

Ms. Moss turned her smile on Miranda, where it faltered. Try to hook one guy, and suddenly she's got two women to deal with. Not in her plans, I didn't think. "Well, that's...wonderful." She blinked, like she was resetting her program, then dove into her purse and pulled out a photo of Frankenstein Summer.

Miranda gaped at it. "This? Is your daughter?"

"Yes. Isn't she lovely?"

Miranda choked and coughed, like she'd just

swallowed her Diet Coke the wrong way. I whacked her back, to make the idea convincing.

"But that's the girl we saw at the calf judging. She's—" She put her hand over her mouth, like she couldn't stand to say any more about it.

Summer's mom was oblivious to the whole freak out going on in Miranda's head. She was more interested in beaming at Nick. "I'm so glad you'll come. It will be a pleasure to see you there, Mr.…"

"Nick. Just call me Nick."

"Oh, yes. Nick."

I swallowed. Just hearing her say his name in that breathless way made me want to go take a shower. Or at least spray myself down over at the dairy barn.

Finally, the woman swayed away, looking back over her shoulder to see if Nick was watching. He wasn't. But I was. She spun around and hustled away.

"Nick," Miranda said, "you are way too nice to women like her. It's disgusting."

"Sorry. Don't mean to be disgusting."

"No, you're not disgusting. She's disgusting. Tell him, Stella."

"Actually, I found the entire thing disgusting."

"And how can she possibly think her hideous daughter has any chance of winning the pageant? I'm sure the judges would rather pick a girl off the street than have that monstrosity representing Lovely Miss. I know I would."

It was a valid question. Did Summer's mom really not see the joke her daughter had become? And how did she get into the pageant in the first place? Were there no guidelines? No criteria for being at least fifty percent human?

I knew just who we could ask, if we cared that much. Taylor. Or her mom. But I really didn't care enough to even think about it another second. "So, what do we do now? You guys want to go? I'm ready to ditch this place."

Miranda checked her phone. "But isn't the parade soon? And isn't Daniella's daughter going to be on a float?"

"Yeah, I guess. Zach's going to be on the dairy one, with the other kids in his 4-H club, and I did tell him I'd watch. Not that he really cares." I dropped my forehead onto Nick's shoulder. "Can't we just go home? I'm tired of being here."

"We should ask Taylor," Miranda said.

I rolled my head to look at her. "If we should go home?"

"No, dummy, how that Summer girl got into the Lovely Miss pageant."

"We can't really go home," Nick said. "Not if you want to keep your promise and see the parade.

It starts in an hour. And then the combine demo's after that."

"So?"

"You're not really going to make me miss that, are you? My one chance at seeing farm equipment destroy each other?"

I leaned back. "Really? That's on your bucket list?"

"It has been ever since I heard about it last week."

"Fine." I relaxed into my chair. "What are we going to do for an hour?"

"Ask Taylor about the pageant," Miranda said again, echoing the thoughts I'd had a minute before and had forgotten already.

"Why do you care so much?"

"Because that girl—not Taylor, I mean the surgically enhanced one—should never have gotten into the competition, and I want to know how it happened. Come on, we've been doing everything for you today. Can't we do something for me?"

Nick, being no help at all, was watching me with amusement. "What do you say?"

"Whatever."

Miranda clapped. "So where do you think Taylor is?"

"Don't know."

"But you can find out. Who has she been hanging around ever since meeting him yesterday?"

Right. I sighed and texted Zach.

is taylor with u?

He buzzed me back almost immediately.

yes

where ru?

west parking lot getting ready 4 parade

"All right. If we want to catch him, we've gotta go now."

Miranda was up and halfway to the exit before I'd even sat all the way up in my chair.

"Come on, Love," Nick said, holding out his hand and grinning. "Let's go do something for Miranda."

I let him help me up. I could think of something I wanted to do *to* Miranda. Would that count?

Chapter Twenty-six

Holy crap it was hot. Six in the evening and it felt like high noon. I half expected someone to stroll out onto the street with six-shooters and a ten-gallon hat. I edged back, away from the curb, into the sliver of shade provided by the arts and crafts building. Sweat rolled down my back—and my front—and I tried to remember why parades in the middle of the summer were supposed to be fun.

We hadn't had any luck getting to Zach or Taylor, because only those involved in the parade were allowed behind the barricades by the time we got there. Our investigation into the inner workings of the pageant would have to wait. Darn. And here it was so important.

Lucy, Tess, and Lenny had joined us for the parade. Lenny was large enough to act as a shade tree, but his family had staked that spot out before the rest of us could make a claim, so we just had to sweat it out.

"Ooo, look Tess, I can see a firetruck!"

No, it wasn't anyone's mom who was so excited. Not a little kid. Miranda. It was like she'd never seen a parade before.

"I've never seen a parade!" she squealed.

"Seriously?"

She clasped her hands at her throat, staring down the street. "Well, like the Macy's one on TV, and whatever, but not in real life. Unless you count the one we saw in that dinky little town near home, where there was only one firetruck and the mayor. That doesn't count."

I looked at Nick. "Really? No parades?"

He shrugged. "Not in our family's activity plan, I guess. Or our town's. I don't know why."

I caught Lucy's eye, and she shrugged, like it was a mystery to her, too.

"Eee!" Miranda shrieked. "I hear a band!"

Oh, thank God. The firetruck was also blowing its horn, deafening everyone within the square mile and drowning out whatever Miranda said next. Soon the flag corps strode by, beginning a long line of what would be a show-and-tell of regional emergency fleets, high school marching bands, floats with the different 4-H clubs, horses, tractors, classic cars, and the Kiwanas guys on their miniature motorcycles. I'd seen it all before, so I took the opportunity to check out who was watching the parade around us.

The Grangers had their usual spot down at the end of the fairgrounds, but it was so crowded I couldn't imagine trying to squeeze my whole troop in there, so we had searched out this spot and found it without too much difficulty. Pretty much everybody on our stretch of road was involved with the fair somehow. Other people chose to stay in their own front yards or along the sidewalk downtown, where the parade began. Still yet another group wanted to be sure of prime seats for the combine demo, and were already marking their spots in the grandstand.

Claire and Bobby's folks, Amy Kaufmann and her husband, had set up across the street, and I gave them a wave. Also in our section were Randy's parents and siblings, Laura's folks, and several other families from the church I sometimes attended with the Grangers. The kids held their bags at the ready, waiting for the first float to throw candy. Tess was right there with them. I was surprised Miranda hadn't snatched some poor kid's bag out of his hands so she could grab the first bubble gum to be tossed out.

A marching band blew by, then some adorable miniature horses, followed by the first of the 4-H floats. The rabbit club. The kids on the float—mostly girls—waved and smiled and threw candy, almost whacking Miranda before she realized what was happening. When she did, she jumped up and down and clapped. Yay.

While horns aoogahed and kids (and Miranda) screamed, "Here! Throw some here!" I observed the on-lookers. Most of the crowd watched with small children on their shoulders or at their feet, but a smaller portion stood back, like me, wondering just how they'd been talked into doing this again. But then, I knew why. Zach. Randy. All those kids. This was one place where all were equal. All were given recognition for the hard work they'd put in during the year, regardless of how worthy their animal was, or where they'd end up when judging was over. It was great to see them out there, having fun, acting as a team rather than competitors.

I sucked down a water bottle and took a few steps to toss it in the recycling bin at the corner of the building. After I threw it in I glanced up and spied Daniella just down the way. She stood by herself, hand shading her eyes as she looked up the street, waiting for the Lovely Miss Pennsylvania float, which would be appearing at some point.

"Hey!" I called. "Daniella!"

She turned, but before I could catch her attention, someone else got it. Mrs. Gregg. She scurried up and touched Daniella's elbow, and the two women got into a conversation I would have described as intense, if Daniella hadn't kept watching down the street. Mrs. Gregg wore her city farmer clothes, but her Yes-I-belong attitude had disappeared. Now she looked out of place and out of sorts. She spoke with lots of hand gestures, while Daniella nodded and watched for Taylor's float, until Mrs. Gregg finally grabbed Daniella's arm and forced her to pay attention. Daniella gave one last glance toward the road, then turned her whole body toward Mrs. Gregg.

I wondered what they were talking about, but it wasn't really my business, and I wasn't worried about Daniella being able to take care of herself with Mrs. Gregg, so I turned to go, and smacked right into Austin. I mean really smacked him. I stumbled backward and kicked over the recycling bucket, while Austin bashed another guy, knocking him several steps.

"Sorry," he said to the guy. The guy frowned, but didn't stop.

"You okay?" I asked Austin, helping him up.

"Fine. You?" He picked up the recycling bucket and dropped in a couple bottles that had spilled out.

"Peachy. Where are you in such a rush to?"

"Me? You're the one who's like a tanker truck.

I'm lucky I'm alive." He grinned, but the grin didn't meet his eyes.

"Austin? What's wrong? You still pissed about today?"

His eyes flashed. "I'm fine. I'm over it. Sorry I ran into you."

"Austin, have you talked to the cops about last night?"

He saw something over my shoulder. "Gotta go. See ya."

He weaved his way through the crowd, done with me. But I wasn't done with him. I looked over at Nick, but he was waving to Zach's float, which was going by, Zach and Randy throwing more than one person's share of candy toward our group. Tess scampered onto the street to pick up the bubble gum and Tootsie Rolls. Miranda jumped out with her, scooping up a handful and dumping it in Tess' bag. Dammit, I was going to miss Zach's float, or I was going to lose Austin, and I hadn't liked the look in his eyes. Austin's head was still bobbing along, and Zach would survive if I didn't acknowledge the float, so I took off after the kid who worried me the most.

Austin wasn't here for the parade, that was obvious. Hands in his pockets, he trudged ahead, not watching where he was going, or anything going on around him. No wonder he'd slammed into me. But he'd seen something behind me that made him say he had to take off. What had he seen?

I looked ahead, but didn't see any people I knew. The junior fair building? Food? No. Something far more interesting.

Austin was headed right to the building where the police had set up shop to investigate Rikki Raines' murder. Thank God. He was going to do the right thing.

My phone rang, and I checked the screen. Willard. "Hey, what did you find out?"

"Hello, to you, too."

"Willard—"

"So here's the thing. No official report on what killed Rikki Raines. I could get confirmation that she'd been paralyzed by something, causing her to suffocate, but toxicology hasn't had a chance to analyze the medicine yet. This did just happen late last night, and no matter what television says, there's no way to get results that quickly."

"So Watts really is going by an anonymous tip. Or a guess."

"That's right."

If I could have, I would have strangled Watts right there.

"But guesses—theories—are what we go by a lot of the time," Willard said. "And if we don't act on our instincts, we sometimes miss things."

"So that makes it all right for her to accuse and terrify Carla?"

"Of course not. There are smoother ways to go about these things. But as we've talked about before, she's young, and—"

"—and she wants to impress Daddy."

"There is that."

I thanked Willard, extracted a promise that he'd let me know as soon as he heard anything more specific, and went back to my family.

Chapter Twenty-seven

The grandstand was crowded when we arrived, and I didn't see anyone we knew to squeeze in with. Lucy and Lenny had taken Tess and gone home, and I was beginning to wish we'd gone with them.

The combines were already lining up outside the arena, and it was obvious that plenty of people in the bleachers had begun their drinking some time before. I hoped the drivers of the combines had waited to start on their booze until after the demo, but I wouldn't have bet anybody on it.

A tanker truck was spraying down the mud pit, creating a soggy, sticky mess, and firefighters stood ready outside the arena, which was lined with tires inside metal side rails. An ambulance had its place off to the side, and already a young guy sat in a folding chair, receiving attention, holding a rag to his forehead. Tow trucks and front end loaders waited for their turns to pull dead combines from the pit, and beyond all that, straw bales made seats for those people who needed to be close for one reason or another.

Nick shielded his eyes and scanned the people in the thick, restless crowd. "You sure you want to risk it?"

"Eh, what are they going to do?"

"Puke on us," Miranda muttered.

I led the others across the front and up the far stairs, finding us enough space for two people, which we made to fit three. Normally I don't mind being that close to Nick, but not when it was closing in on a hundred degrees and his sister was practically my Siamese twin.

Miranda's face told plenty about the situation. Just by looking at her, you could know that we were surrounded by large, sweaty people with beer logos on their stretched-out t-shirts, and plastic cups of the same drink sloshing around everywhere.

"Why are we here again?" she said.

A loud click came over the sound system, and then a voice said, "Please rise for the singing of the national anthem."

We smooshed our way to a standing position, as crammed together as the cows when they're rushing into the barn for milking, or pushing to get to the hay when we feed them outside. Only the cows smelled better.

Some family with large smiles and cowboy

hats sang the song, and we sat down again while the first heat of combines chugged into the arena.

"Now what?" Miranda said.

"Just watch."

It was like a combine rainbow in the mudpit— a green one named SwampRat; a white and black one painted like a cow with a sign saying; "Show us your teats!"; an orange one called Smashing Pumpkin; a yellow one dubbed Sunshine; and a red one emblazoned "Rotten Tomato." Each went to its specified starting spot, a fluorescent orange flag waving from a dowel rod attached to the side of the cab. The flag would be their token of surrender, should the driver snap it off. It took a while for the drivers to get positioned, because the machines weren't exactly speedy, and they needed to back into their starting spots. Finally, they were poised, and the official shot off the starter pistol.

The red and orange combines flew right out of their spaces, well, if five miles an hour is flying, and headed for each other in a way that made me think they were probably friends—or enemies. The cow one and the yellow one waited just long enough to go after the first ones, and the green one spun in the mud, smoking and jerking, either stuck or fried. The cow smashed into the back of the red combine, pushing it into the orange one, and the driver's head whipped back and forth.

"That can't be good for them," Nick yelled, trying to be heard over the noise.

"They're twenty-year-olds," I yelled back. "Do you think they care?"

The green one got bashed by the yellow, who was backing up to take another shot at the green one's back tires, the weakest spot on the machine. But before Sunshine could make the run, the driver of the green one ripped off his flag, so Sunshine had to stop, which made it a prime target for the red beast, who banged into it so hard I was surprised the driver didn't go flying out. Thank God for seatbelts and helmets.

They kept on bashing and crashing into each other until only the red combine remained running and was declared the winner of the heat. The tow trucks and front end loaders took ten minutes to pull out the losers, and the next heat entered the ring.

"GO GET 'EM, STINKBOMB!" a woman behind us shrieked.

Miranda jerked forward so hard she hit the guy in front of us, who turned around and leered. "Want to do that again, little lady? I wouldn't mind." He patted her hip.

Miranda was obviously speechless, so I answered for her. "Back off, sleazeball."

"Hey, she's the one feeling me up."

I leaned forward, meeting his watery eyes. "Back. Off."

He did.

"You let the teenagers come here?" Miranda said, when she got her voice back.

"They're all down there." I pointed to a special section, marked off for the 4-H'ers. "Booze-free zone."

"Wish we were with them."

I was beginning to wish that, too. I searched the young faces, but couldn't find any of the kids I knew, until I finally spied Bobby's neon green shirt. Once I saw that, I could make out Zach, Taylor, Claire, Randy, and Laura—who was apparently now part of their crowd. Zach and Taylor sat beside each other, with Laura beside Taylor, while the other three sat directly behind them. Poor Claire. She had the perfect sight lines for what she really didn't want to see.

Being a teenager really did suck sometimes. I remembered. But then, being twenty-nine had really sucked as well, so I figured they'd better get used to it.

Four more heats of combines destroyed each other, and while the winners made repairs, pick up trucks took the stage.

Miranda dropped her head into her hands. "I thought it was over."

I patted her knee. I would have preferred to pat her back, but I couldn't move that far.

The pick ups went through the same routine as the combines, but the demo went a lot faster, since they were smaller vehicles. They smashed and banged, backing into each other to preserve the engine compartment, as well as the driver, and then we sat through a brief intermission while firefighters put out a fire in an old Ford.

"Poor trucks," Nick said.

I shrugged. "They've lived a long life."

"But to end up this way…"

"Hey, the drivers love them. For now."

The firefighters left, and the trucks went at it again, one of them getting hung up on a side rail, stuck while another truck just whacked and whacked it. Finally every truck but one had died, and the winning driver climbed out of the driver's window, pulled off the helmet, and shook her hair free. The crowd went silent for a split second, then went crazy. Who'd known it was a woman out there?

The area cleared out again, and the championship for the combines was finally ready to begin. By now, the air was filled with gas and diesel smell, dust, blue smoke, and the lovely odor of burning tires, thanks to their constant spinning in the mud. Miranda had turned a pale shade of green, and I was beginning to feel a little worried she was going to heave on the gross guy in front of her. That wouldn't turn out well.

She pressed her hand over her mouth, and swallowed. "This is supposed to be fun?"

I sighed again. Heavily. "Why did you come, again? Wait, I know. To spend time with your brother."

"And to try to understand you better. Which is getting harder and harder as time goes by."

The starting shot was given, and the combines went at it.

"Destroy him, Stinkbomb!" the woman behind us screamed, and clobbered Miranda's back with her knee.

"Will you watch it?" Miranda snapped.

The woman didn't hear her, instead screaming for Stinkbomb to "Crush his back axle, you moron!"

I smiled at Miranda. "You don't find this fun?"

In answer, she took her index fingers and stuck them in her ears.

"No sense of culture," I said to Nick.

He grinned, and then his brow crinkled. "Is that your phone?"

I pulled it out. It was ringing. "How on earth did you hear that?"

"Super powers. Who is it?"

"Don't know. It's just a number." I stuck the phone back in my pocket.

"You're not going to answer it?"

"I don't answer if I don't know who it is. If it's important, they'll leave a message."

"Are you sure?"

The red combine crashed into a camouflage one, and the woman behind us—along with a good portion of the crowd—went crazy.

"You get 'em, Stinky!" the woman screamed.

"I guess it's important," Nick said.

"What is?"

"Your phone call. Someone just left you a voice mail. I heard the ding."

I pulled the phone out again. Nick was right. I considered where I was sitting, in the berserker woman zone, but also considered how hard it would be to make my way out of the grandstand. Lesser of two evils. I dialed voice mail and covered my other ear.

"Stella?" Bryan's voice came over the line. "Where are you? Are you still at the fair? I don't know what to—If you're here, please come to the dairy barn. It's bad. Carla's bad. Please, I'm not sure how to—" The message cut off.

"Gotta go." I stood.

Miranda glanced up, hope in her eyes. "Are we leaving?"

"I am."

"Well, then, I'm coming, too."

Nick stood up. "What's wrong?"

"Move it!" the crazy lady screamed. "Get the fuck down!"

Miranda blinked, then put her fists on her hips. Good lord, she was going to take on the crazy woman. Just as Miranda opened her mouth, I jerked her away, and the crowd closed in behind us. Miranda might not like the woman's foul language, but no way would she win that fight. We picked our way down the stands. When we were clear of the crowd, we moved faster.

"Why did you yank me away like that?" Miranda said, plucking at my arm. "That woman had no right to—"

"That woman would have kicked your ass."

Miranda stopped with the plucking.

"Where are we going?" Nick said.

"Dairy barn. Carla's in trouble." I kicked it up to a jog, leaving the two of them behind.

They knew where to find me.

Chapter Twenty-eight

I burst into the barn, expecting a crowd, but saw only a small group. They were standing at the Greggs' stalls, and Gregg himself was yelling and poking a finger in Carla's face. His head looked like it might explode any second, but that was exactly how I felt watching him assault Carla.

I strode over and pushed his hand away, stepping between the two of them, wondering why Bryan hadn't done that already. Mrs. Gregg stood behind her husband, her face all blotchy from crying. Her eyes were rimmed with red, and she swiped at her face with her hand. The older two girls were there, too, expressions blank, mouths open.

Gregg's yelling stopped when I moved in, and his face went some kind of nuclear color. "You? Get out of the way before I—"

"Make me."

"Stella…" Carla grabbed the back of my shirt.

I held out a hand to shut Gregg up and turned to Carla. "You okay?"

"Come here. Please." She pulled me away from the group. Her face was so pale I was afraid she was going to either faint or throw up, so I led her to a straw bale and had her sit. Bryan was nowhere to be seen, and I wondered why he'd disappeared. He'd been there a few minutes ago, when he called me. At least I think he had.

"What's going on?"

She slumped against the stall behind her. "The Greggs' cows. They're sick, both of them. And I don't know what's wrong."

"Tell me the symptoms."

She took a shuddering breath. "Dizzy, at least they keep swaying into the sides of the stalls. Fever. Rolling eyes. It could be anything. Drugs. Sickness. I just don't know."

The bags under Carla's bloodshot eyes were on their way to becoming serious luggage, and her shoulders slumped so low she threatened to slide right off the bale. All of her usual confidence and pep was gone.

"When did this start?"

"A few hours ago. I got the call just before the parade that the cows were acting strangely. It's gotten worse fast."

"So, not lemons this time."

She shook her head so miserably I was afraid she was going to join Mrs. Gregg and start crying.

"That first night, she called me and I told her she was imagining things. What if she wasn't? What if I did miss something?"

I guess we couldn't rule it out.

I sat beside her. "Okay, what have you done so far?"

"All the usual things. Temperature, looking in the eyes, everything I could do without hauling them off to the office. Bryan just ran some body fluids to the lab. We evacuated the surrounding stalls, even though it would be too late if there really is something wrong, and I called my partners. One of them should be here soon. Oh, God, I feel like such an idiot."

"Did you check their feed?"

"There's nothing left in their stalls. No hay. No grain. They've eaten every crumb."

Or somebody had cleaned it up.

A commotion over at the cows caught my attention. Someone new had arrived. Carla's head shot up hopefully, but the new arrival wasn't one of her partners. It was one of the nasty vets who had shown up the day before, during the whole lemon fiasco. He went directly to Gregg, who began talking loudly and pointedly.

"She can't figure out what's wrong. It has to be something simple, right?" He glanced at us, making sure we saw that he had called in someone else.

"I'll stop him," I said, rising.

"No." Carla's hand shot out to grab my elbow. "Let him examine the animals. Maybe he'll catch something I didn't. We have to remember it's about the animals. We can't let something happen to them just because some people can't deal with me."

"But Gregg thinks he can just call in some other vet. And that vet thinks he can come into your territory."

"Let him. You know how I said this job wasn't as fun as I thought it would be? He can have it."

"But your reputation—"

"—is fine. Two days—because that's what it's been, can you believe it?—can't ruin my career."

I wasn't so sure about that. Not with Gregg and his connections involved.

Nick and Miranda joined us, and Carla's eyes barely lit up at the sight of Nick in his well-fitting jeans. Not a good sign.

"Stay with her," I told them.

I wandered toward the cows, trying to stay out of Gregg's sight lines, but that was impossible. He was completely aware of me, and his eye was twitching. His nostrils were just flaring when his flunky vet stepped back to confer with him. Whatever he was saying, it wasn't good, because Gregg grabbed the closest thing to him—a bucket—and flung it across the room, barely missing a 4-H'er who had bent over to pick something up.

"Stella? What's happening?" Don, one of Carla's partners, the one who had been on hand the day before after the lemon fiasco, spoke quietly beside me.

"Something bad, I guess. Gregg's throwing a fit. You gonna take a look?"

"In a second." He went to sit with Carla, where they had probably about the same conversation she and I had had.

"I don't believe this!" Gregg yelled. "Somebody is out to get us!"

He met my eyes for a few seconds, then stomped away, the vet scuttling after him. Mrs. Gregg stood as if frozen, while her two older girls hovered in the background, obviously not sure whether they should care about what was happening, or go do something more fun. One of them jumped, pulled her phone from her pocket, and began texting away. The other turned to the guy beside her. A different guy from the one at calf judging earlier.

Spectators began drifting away. The only ones staying were people who had cows in the barn, and were worried about them being affected. I went closer to the stalls now that Gregg was gone. Mrs. Gregg looked too out of it to notice, and I wasn't sure if she would even care. The cows seemed disoriented, off balance, and their eyes had a glassy sheen. Almost like they'd been hypnotized. Or were in pain.

Don followed me over to the stall. "What do you think? You see anything like this before?"

"Actually…" A memory was coming back to me. I'd had an intern one summer, stupidest kid I'd seen for a long time, but I was doing a favor for his parents and giving him some pointers. He'd found some bad hay I'd thrown out back for the garbage, and figured it just hadn't been put away properly. He fed it to some unfortunate cows, and they'd all looked just like this, like they were either drunk or suffering incredibly bad hangovers.

I put my hand on the closest cow's side and leaned on it. The cow moaned and inched sideways. Stomachache. I met Don's eyes briefly, then went to the trough, where the hay would have been placed earlier. It was empty, as they had said, but I leaned in and smelled it, catching a whiff of rotten odor.

"Bad grain?" Dan said.

I stood up. "Could it be that simple?" I turned to Mrs. Gregg. "Who's been feeding these cows?"

She blinked. "What?"

"Feed. Who's been giving it to them?"

"My daughters, of course. They're their cows."

Uh-huh. I looked at those very daughters,

whose interest in their sick cows had lowered even further, so much so that one of them was walking away.

"What is it?" Mrs. Gregg said.

I returned to Carla and knelt in front of her and Nick. "Did you find any smidgen of grain to send to the lab?"

"Just crumbs. Along with a sample of the water."

"Maybe crumbs will be enough."

"You think it was the grain?"

"It would explain how the cows are acting, and would be incredibly simple to do. No needles, no hard-to-find drugs. Just rotten sileage. Or even hay."

She closed her eyes and sighed. "But why?"

"I think we know why," I said.

She shook her head. "The cows weren't the ones cheating."

"Of course not. But feeding those idiot girls rotten sileage wouldn't knock them out of the competition."

She didn't smile. "Okay. It was to get back at the family for how they play the game. But that still doesn't tell us who. Who would do such a thing?"

A sick feeling rumbled in my stomach. I really hoped I didn't know the answer to that.

Chapter Twenty-nine

Austin was nowhere to be found in or around the calf barn, and he wasn't hanging out at the food tent. The combine demo had ended by that time, and he wasn't at the grandstand. We ran into Mallory and Brady—who had been there to cheer on Brady's buddy Smashmaster—and they hadn't seen Austin, either.

"Why are we looking for him?" Nick said.

"He hates the Greggs."

"Yeah, but so do lots of other people."

I stopped walking and pulled him to the side of the fairway. Miranda came along, because she was still stuck to us, like flypaper. "Now, look. You cannot tell anyone else what I'm about to tell you. That means you, too, Miranda."

She frowned. "What am I, a snitch?"

"You'd better not be."

"She's fine," Nick said. "What is it?"

I explained Laura's revelation about what she'd

seen the night before, and Austin's story about being with Rikki and placing the lemon in the calf's trough. "I did see him going to the cops' building during the parade, so at least he listened to me on that account."

Miranda gasped. "Maybe he killed her, and he was going to confess."

"I don't think so."

"Why, because he's one of your farmer clique?"

"We don't have a clique."

"Right. That's why you don't think he did… wait a minute, you don't think he killed Rikki, but you do think he messed with the Gregg's dairy cows?"

"He brought the lemons."

"But just because he did the lemons doesn't mean he did this, too. He promised not to, didn't he?"

"I know, but not everyone keeps promises, and he could easily have tampered with the Greggs' grain before heading over to see the cops, while everyone else was at the parade. The 4-H'ers were all out of the barn, gone to ride on the floats."

"Okay, hang on." Nick held up his hands, referee-like. "We don't have to make this a huge discussion, like everything else with you two. We're just trying to find Austin, right? So Stella can talk to him?"

"More like interrogate him," Miranda muttered.

"I won't…it's not like I want it to be him."

"Will you two just—" Nick dropped his hands. "Come out to the car when you're ready to go home. I'll be trying not to punch something."

Miranda and I watched him stalk away.

"Well?" I said. "Aren't you going with him?"

"Um…I don't think so. He just slipped into his annoyed zone. When he gets like this I leave him alone."

Annoyed zone. With us. With me. I really was being a pain in the ass, wasn't I, when it came to Miranda?

"So come on, then," I said. "Let's go find Austin. To talk to him gently."

She eyed me suspiciously. "You want me to come with you?"

"Where else would you go?"

"Fine."

"Fine."

We'd already checked the grandstand and the food tent, and we knew he wasn't in the barn. I had Miranda stick her head in the cops' building, because I didn't want to get harassed about what I was doing there, and if I had more to add to my statement, but he wasn't there, either.

"Why don't you just call him?" Miranda asked.

"Because I don't generally collect teenage boys' numbers."

"You have Zach's."

"Because he's family."

"He's not your fam—"

"Wait. I know where we should check."

Miranda caught up with me. "What I was going to say is, Zach would know his number."

"Maybe. Ask him."

"I don't have Zach's contact information!"

"Then here." I thrust my phone at her. "Text him."

"But…" She stumbled after me, texting while we speed-walked. I hoped she wouldn't run into anything, including me.

She was done by the time we reached Austin's trailer. Everything was dark. I pointed to the side of the trailer. "Wait there."

"But—"

"He's not going to talk if you're here."

She gave a huge sigh, then stomped into the shadows. Good riddance. Although I was going to have to adjust my attitude to get back in Nick's good graces. Crap. I liked being rude to Miranda.

"Hello?" I knocked on the door. No response. I tried the door, but it was locked, so I knocked again. Something clanked inside, and the door opened. Austin's mother stood there in pajamas, not exactly happy to be awake. I was surprised she was even there. According to Austin his folks weren't spending the week with him.

"Sorry to disturb you," I said. "Is Austin in?"

She peered up into the narrow bed above the driver's seat, and nodded. "You need him?"

"Please."

"This isn't about Rikki again, is it? He's talked to enough people about that today."

The cops. "I know. This isn't about that. I promise."

"Then what?"

"Can I please just talk to him? It won't take long."

Her mouth pinched, but she must have seen something in my face, or remembered that Austin was eighteen and able to make his own decisions. "Just a sec. I'll ask if he wants to come out."

She disappeared back into the trailer, closing the door, and I heard mumbling, then a thump, like something dropping from the ceiling.

Austin came to the door in shorts and a T-shirt, squinting. "What?"

"Can I talk to you a minute?"

"I guess." His mother stood in the background, making no secret of listening.

"Outside?"

He glanced back at his mom, then stepped

out, shutting the door behind him. He took a few steps away, out of hearing range, and crossed his arms. "What do you want?"

I searched for signs of guilt, but saw only cranky teenager. "Do you know anything about what's going on in the dairy barn right now?"

He made a confused face. "You know I don't have a dairy cow. Why would I know anything about whatever it is?"

I would have bet anything he was telling the truth. "Who else hates the Greggs enough to sabotage their cows?"

His eyes widened. "I didn't do any—"

"I know. I believe you." Because I did. He didn't look like someone who'd broken a promise, or who had harmed a second and third animal that day. My conscience eased. I hadn't realized just how worried I was that I'd let him off the hook, and he'd done it again, with a more serious consequence. "But someone else got to their dairy cows. Any ideas?"

"How about everybody in the barn?"

"That's helpful."

"Well, it's the best I can do. I'm hardly over there. Ask Claire or Bobby. Maybe they saw something, or know more about the people in that class." He clenched his jaw. "You really thought I did it, didn't you?"

"You did the lemons last night, so…" I shrugged. "You do something stupid like that once, you're going to have to pay the consequences of someone like me not quite trusting you anymore."

He looked at the ground. "Yeah. I know."

"What's your mom doing here?"

He shrugged. "I called her. Asked her if she could come."

An eighteen-year-old, who realized he still needed his mother. My heart melted even more. "All right. Go back to bed."

He shuffled around a little, then crept back into the trailer. I could hear his mom's voice before the door shut, asking what was going on now.

Chapter Thirty

None of us spoke on the way home. Miranda was driving, so she was concentrating on that, which was best for all of us. Nick sat alone in the back seat—his choice—and my foot was throbbing like it had been stepped on by a cow. Oh, right. It had been.

Stupid me, when we got home I took the time to check my answering machine, which was blinking. And stupid me again, I pushed the button. Detective Watts. The bank. Watts again. Another cop. All of which had taken the advice Miranda had put on the recording, and called me on my cell phone. But that didn't make their messages any less annoying than they'd been on my voice mail. They might have even been worse, since I was exhausted, and worried, and just a little freaked out by the whole harming-cows-thing. Plus, it made me mad again that the cops would think I'd have more information than what I'd given them the night before. I'd found the girl. That was it. Nothing else. I punched the erase button. I'd deal with the answering machine recording when I wasn't half asleep.

I fell into bed, barely even saying goodnight to Nick. He was asleep within seconds, it seemed, and I expected to follow him to dreamland. But I didn't. My brain decided it was time to work. And my foot decided that painkillers were not enough to stem the pain. Damn foot. Damn brain. I tried counting cows, but that just made me think of the fair, and I didn't want to think of the fair. I wanted to think of Harleys and fresh air and grilled hamburgers. Not fried ones, like at the fair.

The fair.

Sigh.

So I might as well go with it—what about the fair was keeping me awake? Dead country singer, whose manure-crusted face kept popping into my head? Misguided teen, whose prank was both illegal and idiotic, about which I'd broken how many rules by not reporting him? Sick dairy cows, harmed by some unknown assailant? My best friend, supposedly sabotaged by a jealous colleague? The cops, who wouldn't leave me alone, because I was the one to pull the poor dead girl from the shit pile?

Life was so much easier when all I had to

worry about was my future sister-in-law's wedding planning.

I rolled onto my side and propped my foot up on a wad of blankets. Nick lay on his back, his profile beautiful in the faint moonlight coming through the translucent curtains. All I wanted was to run away with this man and not come back until all the questions were answered. Was that so much to ask?

Apparently, yes.

Okay, so connections. Rikki sang for Gregg, the CEO of Sunburst Studios. Daniella ran the salon where Sunburst sent all of their artists for cosmetic expertise, and knew Rikki. Daniella's niece and nephew had cows in the same class as Gregg's daughters. Mrs. Gregg and Daniella were talking at the parade. Gregg and his goons had been looking for someone the night before when I'd been on the fairway, shortly before the screaming girl had discovered Rikki's body. Austin knew Rikki from childhood, and he'd been seen with her the night before, when the two of them had been busy feeding the Greggs' calf lemons.

But there were tons of other people at the fair. Who's to say Gregg or Daniella or Austin, or even the thugs, had anything to do with Rikki's death? In fact, if Gregg was looking for her, didn't that pretty much mean he didn't know where she was, which should bring me to the conclusion that he hadn't killed her? And I couldn't make the leap from feeding a calf citrus fruits to killing a friend, or even a girlfriend.

Oh, for crying out loud, I was never going to sleep.

Moving as carefully as possible, I rolled out of bed and limped downstairs. Nick's laptop lay on the coffee table, and I powered it up. When I pulled up the browser, I took note of what he'd been looking at. Flowers. Caterers. Wedding licenses. Okay, so Miranda had gotten ahold of the laptop. That was clear. Further down the history were things that made more sense for Nick. Realtor sites. Weather in Virginia. Stock prices.

I clicked in the search bar and typed in Rikki Raines. Of course all of the first hits, several of the first pages, in fact, were about her death. Mostly entertainment news sorts of places, ET, Perez Hilton, *People*. Lots of photos of her onstage, talking with fans, hanging out with her producer… David Gregg. I studied the pictures, trying to see if there was anything to gain from them, but mostly what I saw was Gregg's plastic smile and Rikki's real one. In most of the photos they were surrounded by other celebrities, or people I didn't recognize, who must have been fans, since the photos had been tagged on people's Facebook pages.

Bloggers had been busy guessing who had killed her, and why: crazed stalker types, who believed she would love them if she only gave them a chance; girls who thought she stole their boyfriends; even Valerie Springfield, that other singer Austin had talked about, because she wanted the zombie show guy all to herself. Nobody had mentioned Gregg, or his wife, or anybody else who made sense. And Austin was nowhere to be found, which spoke to how well he and Rikki had kept their secret.

I was shocked to see a hit on the YouTube video I'd starred in the night before. I checked to see if there was a way to delete it, but since I hadn't posted it, there was nothing I could do except watch it and wish I'd had the sense to break that person's phone—or arm—before he'd had a chance to publish.

There didn't seem to be anything else to learn about Rikki, except that she was expected to be a contender in the Grammy Awards' Best New Artist category. A shame that someone so talented, and from all accounts so real, sweet, and filled with integrity, had been taken before she could reach her potential.

I still wasn't tired, so I looked up the fair's schedule, making sure I wasn't forgetting anything for the next day. Nope. Main thing I wanted to see was the dairy judging, and that would take place in the afternoon, which meant I could spend some time at the farm. A welcome change after the past two stressful days. A little time away, and I felt like I'd become completely disconnected. I guess it hadn't helped that I'd dealt with not just a murdered girl, but sick cows and a best friend who was maybe being set up for a fall.

A photo on the page's constantly changing headline caught my eye. There was Claire, smiling for the camera, her face next to her gorgeous cow's. I clicked on the photo and was taken back to YouTube, where Claire had made a video, probably for a 4-H project, about how to prepare your dairy cow for showing at the fair. She went through the whole process of combing, brushing, washing, shining, trimming, and everything you do to make your cow as beautiful as she can be. Her cow, September Breeze, didn't need that much help. She really was a gorgeous specimen.

I yawned, finally, and decided I was ready to sleep. Or to at least try. I closed the laptop and made my way upstairs. With any luck, I wouldn't dream about anything except sleeping.

Chapter Thirty-one

I didn't get a whole night's sleep, but what I got was heavy, so I felt pretty good when I woke up at five-thirty to milk the herd. The smells, the sounds, the feel of their leathery udders, all of it reminded me what was important in my life, what was real. The dust sent up from the grain, the scrape of my boots, the sight of contented cows chewing their cuds, it was all good. And thanks to my generous fiancé, I didn't have to worry about losing it anytime soon.

Once milking was done, but before I let the cows loose, I took a moment to wrap my arms around Tinkerbell's neck and breathe in her oily, musky scent. She turned her huge head toward me, and I nuzzled her. Life was sweet.

"Miss us?" Lucy stood in the aisle, smiling.

"Don't get any ideas, Luce. I'm not going to hug you, too."

She laughed. "Wouldn't dream of it."

I gave Tinkerbell a pat and walked around to

unhook the girls from their chains. Lucy took the other side. I spoke over the sounds of departing cows. "You're early today."

"Wasn't sure how things turned out for you last night, or how late you got home. I wanted to make sure you were all right."

"Thanks, but I'm okay."

She was quiet for a few seconds. "Want to tell me about it?"

No question. "Yes."

So while we scraped the stalls, limed the walkways, and got the place ready for evening milking, I went over everything that had happened since I'd seen her the morning before. There had been no time to talk at the parade, and it felt good to put some order to it all. I told her about Watts accusing Carla of having something to do with Rikki Raines' death, the anonymous theory about what might have killed her, and how the official results weren't even back yet. I talked about Miranda, and how I didn't think I could survive a lifetime of having her as a sister-in-law. I even told her about Austin, and how guilty I felt for not turning him in.

"He's a kid," Lucy said, when we'd finished, and were sitting on some straw bales, drinking some water. "He made a mistake."

"A criminal one."

"Yeah. But you do believe him, right? That he

wouldn't harm any more animals? That he didn't do the Greggs' dairy cows?"

"I do. But still—"

"You made the decision, Stella. You need to stand by it, or go to the authorities today, no matter the consequences. I guess you need to decide which way you can live with it."

I wiped my forehead, already sweating at eight o'clock in the morning. "I know. I don't want to destroy his future. And I really don't think he'll do anything that stupid again."

"Then let it go. You've got other things to worry about."

"Great. Thanks."

"Sure thing. What are your plans for today?"

"Stay here till after lunch. Then I want to go in for dairy judging. Claire Kaufmann's cow is gorgeous, and I want to see how she does. If I had to guess, she's got judging wrapped up now that the Greggs' cows are out of the running."

Oh, God. She wouldn't have done anything to those cows, would she? Not Claire. I thought back to the night before. Had she been in the crowd of people in the barn? I couldn't remember seeing her, or Bobby, or even their mom. But then, she wouldn't want to be hanging around looking guilty, would she, if she'd done anything? And I'd been preoccupied. I might not have noticed her presence.

"What's wrong?" Lucy said. "You look like you just swallowed a frog."

I told her my worries.

Lucy frowned. "Now you're just seeing conspiracies."

"If Austin could do it…"

"It doesn't mean that another good kid would stoop to the same thing. Or a worse thing. And Claire is a good kid, right?"

"The best. But then, I thought Austin was, too."

Lucy shook her head, and got up. "You're here for the morning?"

"That's the plan."

"Then come on, I've got some two-person jobs you can help with. You need to get your mind off all this stuff for awhile, and rejoin us normal people."

So for the next several hours Lucy and I made repairs, went over inventory, trimmed some hooves, and basically worked side-by-side. And I was happy. Or at least content.

Queenie was part of the morning, too, and I made a fuss over her, feeling guilty at how absent I'd been the past two days.

"She doesn't hold it against you," Lucy assured me. "It's been so hot she's just been shacked up in the barn, panting a lot."

I knew she was right. But I felt bad, anyway.

At noon we left Queenie in her shaded nest, and joined Nick and Miranda for an Italian hoagie lunch. Then, unfortunately, it was time to head back to the fair.

Chapter Thirty-two

The closer we got to the fairgrounds, the more my anxiety came back about whether Claire had been the one to poison the Greggs' cows. Would she really go to such lengths, in order for her animal to come out as the champion? I didn't know. And I hated even thinking about it.

Miranda had tagged along again, claiming to want to "get to know you better," but I really think she wanted to make sure Nick wouldn't commit any more money to me or my farm. Because Miranda just didn't like me enough for anything else. She sat in the back seat, texting away—to how many people, I had no idea. The way she was going, she might have been texting her entire town. Or state.

We got to the arena in time to have our pick of seats. Claire and Bobby's mom were already there, sitting with Daniella, who I remembered was her sister. Amy's stiff posture spoke of nerves. I knew from talking to her before how high her hopes were that Claire would do well. Bobby's cow was okay, too, but not of champion quality. Not like Breezy.

Zach and his posse were sitting in the front row of the bleachers. Taylor had the seat right beside him, of course. At least she wasn't sitting in his lap, like the Gregg girl had been doing with that guy yesterday. Taylor talked to the other kids, as well as Zach, and smiled, and laughed, and Zach gazed at her like an adoring, half-brained puppy.

A voice came over the microphone announcing the start of the dairy judging, and my stomach turned flips. *What would I do if Claire won? Would I confront her about her possible crime? Let it go? Ask her mom? Pretend it never happened?*

Nick bumped my shoulder with his. "What's wrong?"

I shook my head, not wanting to voice my fears. I'd hoped the Guernsey class would go first, to get it over with, but the Holsteins were at the top of the line. Then the Ayrshires. And finally the Guernseys. I gripped my seat, holding my breath as the kids walked their cows in and around. There was no contest. I mean, sure, there were some other nice animals, but Claire's September Breeze was far and away the nicest. Her color, her frame, her udder…you couldn't ask for a better example of perfection. Not unless you had the Greggs' cows in the ring with her.

The judge didn't take long to pronounce the winners, and Claire walked off with the champion ribbon, leaving me with questions and an acidic stomach. I slid off the bleachers.

Nick's eyebrows rose. "Don't want to stay for the rest?"

"Something I need to do. I'll be back."

Miranda stood up. "I don't want to stay."

I caught Nick's eye, pleading with him to keep her with him.

"Miranda and I will meet you after you're done. How about in the rabbit building?"

Miranda clapped. "I can see my bunny again?"

I left them, and made my way to the dairy barn. I was waiting at Claire's stall when she arrived almost a half hour later. Her usually open, pleasant face—except for when she was fighting jealousy over her cousin's hold on Zach—was closed down. Angry.

"Posing for pictures of the champion?" I said.

She rolled her eyes. "Like it means anything. Or these do." She threw her champion banner and ribbon onto her storage box.

"They don't? I can think of a lot of people who would love to have them. Including your brother."

She snorted. "Like Bobby's cow could beat Breezy." She got Breezy settled in the stall and slammed the door. "The two cows—count 'em, two—who could have challenged Breezy, and they're out of the competition. I mean, I hate those Gregg girls and their stupid champions, but seriously, I wanted to beat them. Not win by default because some stupid person poisoned their cows."

Something deep inside me relaxed at her words, and I suddenly couldn't believe I'd ever thought she could harm the Greggs' cows. "Hey, it still means something. She's gorgeous, and perfect. She would've beat them."

"Yeah, well, now we'll never know."

"You'll go on to State, right? You'll face some good competition there."

"I guess." She patted Breezy's neck. "You're a good girl. None of it is your fault. I'm not mad at you."

"She is a good girl," I said, "and not just because she has good genes. You've put a lot of work into raising her. It shows. It matters."

She leaned her forehead on Breezy's. "Does it?"

"You know it does. Don't trash this accomplishment. I mean it."

She turned her face, so her cheek rested on Breezy's head. "I sound like a jerk, don't I?"

I smiled. "I wasn't going to say it in those words. But, yeah."

Amy ran up and grabbed Claire in a huge hug. "I knew you could do it! I'm so proud of you!"

"It wasn't—" Claire's eyes flicked up to mine, and she gave a little smile. "Thanks, Mom."

Daniella came next, moving at a more dignified pace, as befitted her gorgeousness, and offered Claire a hug, as well. Claire took it with good grace.

"Taylor wanted me to pass on her congratulations," Daniella said. "She'll tell you herself, later."

I looked around, spotting Zach and Bobby at the end of the aisle, making their way toward us, sans Taylor. "Where is she? I saw her at the arena."

"The Lovely Miss pageant is today."

Oh, crap. I'd forgotten all about it. I tried to look non-committal and bland, so no one would ask if I was going.

"She stayed until Claire won," Daniella continue, "then ran to get ready. She held out as long as she could. I hope she made it on time, but she wanted to be there to see her cousin win."

Claire considered this, then shrugged. "That was nice."

Amy checked her watch. "The pageant is in about an hour. You're going, right?"

For a horrible second, I thought she was talking to me, then realized she was asking her daughter. I inched away, finally far enough from the others that I turned and ran.

That had been too close.

Way, way too close.

Chapter Thirty-three

"It's not fair," Miranda said. "All week we've been doing everything you want to do, and nothing I want to do."

"Then why didn't you want to just stay home? I could've gladly done that, and then we both would've been happy."

She glowered at me.

"It can't be that bad," Nick said. "Can it? How bad can a pageant for teenagers be?"

"Nick, Summer is going to be there."

He winced. "Right."

"You two are the biggest babies," Miranda said. "You can't spend an hour or two supporting Taylor and Daniella, and all of the other accomplished young women, because you're afraid of one teenage girl?"

"She's half silicone," I said.

"And the other half, air," Nick added.

"With a smidge of chemicals in places I don't want to think about."

"So?" Miranda frowned. "It's not like she's a killer robot or anything."

Nick made a face. "Are you sure? I think she's a Stepford daughter. Except scarier."

She grabbed his arm and pulled. "We. Are. Going. I promised Daniella."

He looked back at me pleadingly. "You're not letting her kidnap me?"

I wanted to. I was chicken that way.

"He'll be surrounded by beautiful young women," Miranda said. "You want to risk that?"

"They're just girls," I reminded her.

"But their mothers aren't. And they're also… beautiful."

That was stretching it. Summer's mom was certainly not in that category. I would assume most of the other pageant moms were all about artificial enhancement, as well. But Taylor's mother, well, she *was* the category if you were talking about beautiful and nice and perfect. And who knew how many others of those there might be?

"Fine. I'll go, just to protect Nick's honor. But I'm not going to watch."

Miranda smiled and strode ahead.

"My honor?" Nick said.

"Sorry. It was the first thing that came to mind."

"I'm not sorry. I'd like to see you protect my honor. Could be entertaining."

I slugged his shoulder, and we trudged after Miranda.

The pageant was being held on the smaller stage rather than the main grandstand. I guess they weren't expecting a huge crowd, especially since they were competing against the lawn-mower race, and, well, you can imagine how popular that would be. We got seats about halfway back, on the aisle, which was great, so I could make a run for it, if I had to. The stage was set up with deep red curtains, and a huge chandelier hung from the rafters. I hoped it was fake, because if it was really made of glass and fell, it would kill whoever it landed on.

Daniella was already there, seated in the second row with Amy, Claire—who made no secret that she'd rather be anywhere else, Bobby, Randy, and, of course, Zach. That poor guy had been kicked so hard by Cupid, his ass was going to be one gigantic bruise when he fell back to Earth. Or, wait. Cupid shoots people, right? Whatever. Daniella saw us arrive and waved. Miranda about fell over returning the greeting, so I kept my response minimal.

"You sure they're sisters?" Nick murmured.

I could see his confusion. Where Daniella was fashionable, classy, and perfect, Amy was merely…

sweet. Amy looked absolutely fine, of course, but Daniella, next to her sister, was like a full-fledged chocolate-fudge milk shake compared to a non-fat, lactose-free, vanilla smoothie. Edible, but not something you'd walk a hot mile for. I would have felt sorry for Amy, but she didn't look like she did. She was smiling and laughing and sharing secrets with Daniella. A farmer comfortable in her own skin, rather than pining after her sister's. I liked that.

All around us were more people who seemed like they belonged there, rather than in the dairy barn. Parents of the contestants. Sponsors. Lots of people in clothes too clean to have been worn around the fair. Who knew if they'd even been on any other part of the grounds, or if they'd shot in solely for this one event? I couldn't exactly see women in tight, shiny dresses and high heels taking advantage of the pony rides. Or daring to eat something that might have a fraction of grease involved.

My eyes snagged on Summer's mom, and I whipped my head back around so fast I about gave myself whiplash.

Nick followed my line of sight. "Ah. The lovely Ms. Moss."

"Sherry," I reminded him. "She wants you to call her by her first name because you're so close."

I took a chance and looked again. Today

Sherry wore a dress that should have been on an eighteen-year-old—if anyone—and her hair looked freshly colored, now so bright it was a toss-up whether it was supposed to be blond or that white old people grow into if they're lucky. Her lipstick was at war with the hair in the brightness contest, and I averted my gaze before my retinas went bad.

"Know who took Rikki's place?" Nick indicated the young woman at what I presumed was the judge's table.

"No idea." She looked the part, though. Gorgeous. Young. Fashionable. All smiles.

Beside her were two other judges, one a tall, black-haired woman with skin so pale I thought maybe someone had drained her blood without telling her. The other was a man, African-American, gorgeous in that way Lenny Kravitz was in the *Hunger Games* movies. Almost unreal. In a sparkly way.

Music began playing, the crowd hushed, and yet another well put together woman strode onto the stage. She wore a shiny black dress, off the shoulder, ending just above her knee. Wait…was she competing? She looked a little old.

"Isn't she gorgeous?" Miranda exhaled.

Yup. It was official. I really didn't belong in that crowd.

"Welcome to today's pageant, ladies and

gentlemen," the woman said, revealing two rows of impossibly perfect teeth. "My name is Madison Wilkins, from the local NBC affiliate, and I am honored to be with you all for this very exciting day."

Polite applause. I checked around the room and discovered a cameraman in the back corner.

"We've all been waiting for this event for a long time. Today will decide which young woman will have the amazing opportunity to represent this county in the Lovely Miss Pennsylvania pageant, spreading her goodwill and virtue throughout our glorious state. What an honor. What an experience."

What a load of crap.

"Before we get to our main event—"

Uh-oh.

"—I would like to take this opportunity to thank all of those who have given so much of their time in support of this wonderful organization. But especially I would like to recognize our judges, who by the end of the summer will have spent at least fifteen days judging the contestants in our region, and who will move on to judge at the final event. Mr. Terence Williams, CEO of TW Designs, stand, please, will you Terence?"

The audience clapped politely.

"Mrs. Bridget Trapp, former Lovely Miss Pennsylvania."

The tall, deathly pale woman rose, and the audience clapped some more.

"And, finally, our newest judge, Valerie Springfield, who was kind enough to step up to fill dear Rikki Raines' shoes. Valerie is another up-and-coming vocal artist from Lancaster, and we are so glad she can be here with us."

An awkward silence, followed by even more awkward applause.

Valerie Springfield? Wait. Austin had told me about her. She was the one who had been in the papers as having a war with Rikki over some actor. The war that had ultimately convinced Rikki to keep her relationship with Austin a secret. She allegedly also thought Rikki was keeping her from becoming a star. Can you say, "motivation for murder"?

"Of course we are so sad to be missing our friend and sweet judge, Rikki Raines," the emcee continued, "and we pray that her killer will be brought to justice in record time. Let us please observe a moment of silence in honor of our fallen friend."

A deathly quiet, during which only two children screamed or said, "What's happening, Mommy?" and "Pretty lights!"

"And now," the woman said, "for a pre-pageant

surprise! Please welcome the finalists of our region's Junior Lovely Miss Pennsylvania pageant!"

Wild applause.

"Junior?" I choked.

"Sure," Miranda said. "They'll show off the younger girls first. It'll be adorable."

Ho. Ly. Crap.

A parade of little kids, all primped and dressed up and made up like they were twenty-five, trounced across the stage, singing and dancing and generally making me want to heave. What was wrong with parents who would do this to their children? They should be doing Tess-type things, wrestling with Queenie, playing with kittens, and running barefoot in the grass, with their hair in tangles. Not prancing around like little prom queens.

To keep myself sane, I glanced around the room. Lots of parents and grandparents, a few teens, organizers, and…Gregg. What was he doing here? He stood in the back, flanked by the same two goons I'd seen with him the other night, before Nick and I found Rikki. He was wearing his suit again, instead of the farmer clothes. His arms were crossed, and he was scowling. Until the emcee lady approached him. Then he was all smiles. They shook hands, and she gestured toward the judges' table. Of course. Gregg had supplied Rikki's replacement. The other "up-and-coming" vocal artist. I wondered just what she'd done to catch his eye, since according to Austin she recorded under a different label.

I took a better look at her. Valerie Springfield. Not as homegrown-looking as Rikki had been. Her face looked almost sculpted, with perfect skin that could only come from a bottle. Her clothes fit a little too snugly, and her eyes held a hard shine not present in Rikki Raines' photos. She sat back in her chair, legs crossed, expression unreadable as she watched the eight-year-olds pretend they were more worldly than they were. Or, at least, than they should have been.

How much of a rival had she been for Rikki? Enough that she would kill Rikki to take her place? Not at the pageant, nobody cared that much about these things, did they? But at the record label. Or in the life of that zombie actor.

I glanced at Gregg again, hoping to get another clue from him. But he wasn't paying attention to Valerie, or the goings-on up on the stage. Instead, when the emcee's focus left him, his eyes darted around the room, until they landed on Daniella. She didn't see him, or the way his eyes burned as they rested on her. I was glad Mrs. Gregg wasn't there to see the display. His attention eventually shifted to the stage, and finally to the judge's table, where he watched Valerie watching the girls.

The juniors finally finished with a group song and dance number, and the audience responded enthusiastically. Valerie responded by shifting in her seat and pulling out her phone. After viewing it, she glanced up and back, locking eyes with Gregg. He gave her a blank look, and she nodded, so subtly I wouldn't have noticed if I hadn't been watching so closely. She turned back toward the stage, gripping her pen so tightly I thought it might break and spurt ink all over her too-tight shirt.

"Wasn't that lovely?" The emcee was back up on the stage. "Let's have another round of applause for our region's Junior Lovely Miss Pennsylvania finalists!"

Gregg took the opportunity to duck out of the building, which didn't go unnoticed by Valerie. Her shoulders relaxed, and the pen became no longer in danger of its plastic life.

"We will take just a short break now to get ready for our Lovely Miss Pennsylvania pageant. Feel free to stand up and stretch, but don't go far! Our distinguished young women will be ready for your attention in five minutes!"

The other two judges stood, and the tall woman strode away, while the man's attention was captured by a round and well-dressed woman who shook his hand vigorously. Valerie stayed in her seat, her mouth tight as she doodled on a paper in front of her.

Her phone lay on the table. What had Gregg texted to her? Was he giving her judging instructions? How could I get a look?

A mother behind us tapped Nick on the shoulder. "Excuse me, but are you here as a scout? You just have to be in the modeling business."

He smiled. "Thank you, but no, I'm just here for a friend."

Her face fell. "You mean one of the girls?"

"Yes, ma'am. Is your daughter in the pageant?"

"Oh, yes, she is. You'll see her. She'll be the second one. But you won't need me to tell you. She's the prettiest, and her talent with the baton is simply amazing, so I hope you—"

"Excuse me," I said, wrapping my hand around Nick's arm. "But he needs a minute." The pushy lady had given me an idea. I pulled him into the aisle, away from the woman's ears. "You want to help me with something?"

"Sure. What can I do?"

I smiled and patted his rump. "Just be your gorgeous self, Babe. I want you at your most distracting."

He glanced down at his jeans and T-shirt. "Not exactly model material."

"Monster Mom thought you were. And I'm

sure the lovely up-and-coming Valerie Springfield will think the same. Miranda? Hey."

She dragged her eyes from the stage, where pedestals were being lined up, for the finalists, I presumed. "What?"

"Can we get your help?"

She sighed. "As long as I don't have to leave."

"Nope. In fact you can sit right there."

"Okay. I guess. What do you want me to do?"

Chapter Thirty-four

"Pardon me." Nick approached Valerie while I scooted around behind her. I could tell the instant she saw him, because her posture became suddenly straighter. It was like attraction vibes were going off like fireworks. Or bombs.

"Hi," she said. I guess even up-and-coming stars get speechless when faced with utter perfection.

He smiled, which wasn't exactly fair, putting that much wattage into it. "Hi. My name's Nick. I was wondering…my sister's a fan. Would you be willing to come say hello? She's kind of shy, and I can't convince her to come over and talk to you herself."

I know, it was a stretch. But why else would Miranda not have come along with her brother?

"I'd be happy to." Valerie oozed up from her seat—Nick had the jelly-legs effect—and took his arm. I didn't attack her, for the good of the cause.

Nick glanced back at me as they left, and I

eased over to the table and slid her phone right off, into my hand. No one noticed. I hid myself in the corner, my back to the room, and touched the phone's screen. The phone hadn't gone back to sleep yet, so I was able to get right to the icons without inputting a password, which was a huge relief. I would have been totally screwed if I'd had to deal with that. But the icons. Holy crap, there were so many of them. What they all meant was a mystery. My phone is as basic as they come, no touch screen or fancy apps, so I had no idea which picture to push. I tried several before touching what should have been the obvious envelope icon, which I only then noticed, and the recent texts lined up on the screen. There had been several in the past few minutes—ah, the thrilling life of a young person—but Gregg's wasn't there, at least not by name. I scanned the list: Ashley, Marco, Mom, Sunny, Silver, Bee, and the list went on. Had she already erased it?

I looked at the first text, which was a mishmash of misspelled words and punctuation. I wasn't even sure what it meant. This Ashley person had to be one of her friends. Marco's text was a plea to meet him that night at a club called the Roxxy, which I recognized as the name of a Philadelphia dance club I wouldn't be caught dead in. Mom wanted to know if Valerie was coming home that weekend.

Sunny said—Wait. Sunny. As in Sunburst Studios? I'd found him. The text, which had been sent four minutes earlier and completely fit our timeline, said simply, "Do your job."

Her job? Other than being a country star? It seemed he'd stopped in at the pageant solely to give Valerie this message, because he hadn't even stayed for the event itself. What was Valerie's job? To rig the judging? To make sure a certain person won? Could she have that much sway, especially without making it completely obvious what she'd done?

The microphone squealed, and the emcee said, "If you could please find your seats, ladies and gentlemen."

With a start, I realized Valerie would be coming back to the table. In fact, she already was back, and searching for her phone. Nick still stood next to her, watching me with wide eyes. Crap. I closed out the text screen, hoping she wouldn't notice the phone had been used. I crept back toward her, the phone in my hand. The phone buzzing in my hand. Another text. I glanced at it, but the message was not from Sunny, so I didn't bother reading it.

When I got close, Nick touched Valerie's shoulder. She looked up at him, her concern over her phone vanishing for a moment as she gazed with adoration into his beautiful eyes, and I slid the phone back onto the table and walked away.

Seconds after I returned to my seat, Nick was beside me.

"Too close," he said. "You get what you need?"

"Did it work?" Miranda said, before I could respond.

"I got something. Not sure what it was."

"Shh!" The lady in front of us turned around and glared.

"Sorry," Nick said, and gave me a mock afraid face when she wasn't looking.

Peppy music started, and the Lovely Miss contestants took their pre-arranged places on the risers, all looking young and energetic and unrealistically beautiful in their "casual dress," which ranged from sundresses to designer jeans and frilly shirts to bermuda shorts and tank tops. Well, they all looked beautiful except Summer, who should have been in a freak show instead of with that group, with her tight and revealing off-the-shoulder translucent yellow shirt. If you could call it a shirt with that little material. I wasn't sure whether to take cover, in case those silicone basketballs broke loose, or to shield Nick's eyes with opaque safety goggles. No need for that, actually, since he was looking at his knees.

Taylor didn't look like the rest of the others, either, most of whom wore more makeup than an international Cover Girl convention. Out of all of them, Taylor looked like a real, naturally attractive teenage girl. Which of course meant she wouldn't win. Not if the rest of the lineup was any indication of what judges looked for. Unless…

What stake did Gregg have in this pageant? What was his connection, other than Rikki, and now Valerie? It would be Taylor. Or, if not her, Daniella. I had no way of knowing if anyone else had anything to do with him, or Sunburst Studios, or even his cheating cows. Not that the cows were cheating. I don't think they were smart enough. Anyway, assuming Taylor was the connection here, what if Valerie's "job" was to make sure she won? Or didn't win?

I glanced over at Daniella, but there was no indication of whether or not she had a clue of a cheating conspiracy. It was hard to believe she did. She didn't seem to have much invested in this pageant—other than the investment of raising a daughter—so I couldn't imagine she would break rules to have Taylor win. She'd said the whole idea was Taylor's, so she was supporting it for that reason only. But with mothers and daughters came loyalty, and that whole helicopter, hovering, want-my-child-to-be-happy thing. Lucy had somehow seemed to avoid that with Tess, so far, but I figured she was the exception. And look at Daniella. She was gorgeous. Nice. Perfect. Who did that? Nobody was like that for real.

Everything in the room went quiet as the emcee raised her hands. "Welcome again to our pageant. We are thrilled to introduce you to our contestants. Please make them feel welcome."

One by one the girls said their name, school, age, parents' names, and something they enjoyed. One girl liked horseback riding, another cooking, and yet another playing golf. I would have expected Summer to say she enjoyed cosmetic surgery, but she only admitted to "beach vacations." Taylor said simply that she enjoyed spending time with friends. They stayed on their spots as they spoke, microphones picking up their voices from some-where else, until all were introduced.

"Thank you, girls," the emcee said. As if this were a cue—which it probably was—the girls filed off the stage and behind into a small room at the back.

The emcee smiled. "While the girls change into their formal wear, I would like to take this opportunity to thank our sponsors. She named several big name companies who donated money, none of which were Sunburst Studios. So that wasn't the connection.

"And here they are again, after that quick change. Our Lovely Miss Pennsylvania contestants!"

The audience clapped as the girls came back onstage, this time to different spots and poses. I was about blinded by the colors and sparkles. Summer again defied tradition—and safety—with her skin-tight, silver tube of a dress. Taylor had chosen a much more tasteful dark green number, which fit her well, without being obnoxious.

The emcee called one of the girls forward, and the contestant stepped forward to answer an interview question. The process went down the line, each girl asked something different, and we heard all sorts of answers—most of which were fairly intelligent—until we got to Summer. She joined the emcee and batted those horrid tarantulas pasted on her eyes, and simpered and posed and generally scared the room. At least I was terrified. It was like she'd been taken over by some unknown entity and would soon explode into lots of little pieces, or else just eat us all.

"What is of daily importance to me, making my life worth living?" she said, repeating the emcee's question. "Oh, so many things, it's hard to choose. Helping the homeless, feeding the poor, working for world peace, finding homes for abandoned pets, how can I pick one?"

The emcee's smile was like the barnyard in winter. "Try."

Summer paused, as if thinking, then smiled,

searing us with artificial brightness. "The most important thing in my daily life is my dog, Sally. She is so full of fluffiness and is about the happiest person I know. She likes other people, too, and is so nice to the kids who live next door. I just love her so much, and so I have to say she's the best. So, so important to me."

The room was so deadly silent, it was like we'd been hit with a stun bomb. The question came back to me—*Who got this girl/creature into this pageant, anyway?* Wasn't there any kind of "normal" quota she had to pass first?

Eventually, the emcee regained consciousness and said, "Well, that's interesting, Summer. Thank you for sharing."

Summer blinked some more, causing shudders to reverberate around the fair, and shared another one of those hideous smiles. Somehow, no one fainted.

"You may take your place again, Summer," the emcee said. "*Summer.*"

"Oh, sure! Bye!" She flounced back to her spot.

Next in line was a sweet girl from Lansdale, who spoke about the best book she ever read (*Pride and Prejudice.* Yawn. Everyone knew she had to read it for school) and finally it was Taylor's turn. She was like a breath of country air, and not the kind after someone spread manure. She was fresh and smart and real.

"Hello, Taylor," the emcee said. "Would you please describe for us an accomplishment of which you're very proud?"

"Thank you, I would be pleased to talk about that." She took a moment, and looked into the audience, ending at her mother and keeping her gaze there. "When I was nine years old, my father died. It was a very hard time for me, but also for my mom. She was suddenly a single mother, and besides the trauma of losing her husband, she was faced with how to survive financially. With the help of family—" she smiled at her Aunt Amy "—my mom went back to school, received her cosmetology degree, and got a job at Serenity Salon. She worked hard and now she is the manager. She has begun all kinds of programs and special events there, and she works hard to make health and beauty a possibility for all people, not just those with a lot of money. I'm very proud to call her my mom, and very proud of all she has accomplished."

There was an awkward pause before a smattering of applause. Mothers of the other contestants glanced around at each other, like "What the heck was that?" and the other girls on stage seemed confused. It seemed nobody was used to someone talking about someone other than themselves. Nick and Miranda clapped hard, and Zach looked like… good grief, like a proud boyfriend. He'd known her two days. Daniella and Amy both had tears running down their cheeks, and Claire, well, she just looked sad. Perfect cousin strikes again.

I checked out the judges' table. The tall lady and the guy were busy scribbling on their sheets. Valerie sat back in her seat, mouth partly open, eyes wide. After a few seconds her mouth snapped shut, and she smiled. After a glance at her judging partners, she began writing, too.

So, she was glad with Taylor's performance. Interesting. I guess that meant her "job" might not be so hard, after all, if what she had to do was make sure Taylor won. Unless that selfless answer meant she wouldn't win. I was so confused. But assuming Taylor had just scored well, that still left the question of "Why?" Why did Gregg want Taylor to win? Did he think it would give him an "in" with Daniella? And how would Mrs. Gregg feel about that? And what, if anything, did that have to do with Rikki's death? Too many things to think about.

Another girl answered the emcee's question, and then the interviews were over. Time for individual talent. The girls left the stage again, and after a short break, during which last year's Lovely Miss PA winner talked about her "amazing" time as the winner, they came back one by one. We were subjected to bad karaoke, a decent flute performance, tap dancing, a recited Joan of Arc monologue, and—most disturbingly—Summer's baton routine. Batons in themselves aren't disturbing, of course, but when they're in constant danger of being snagged on elephant boobs, it's a bit distracting. Finally, we got to Taylor's talent, which, as her mother had described before, was a lovely sign language performance, set to a song describing how we need to look outside ourselves and see the greater good. Again, the other mothers seemed a bit confused by the whole "talent with meaning" thing, and Valerie Springfield looked smug, while the guy judge clapped and the tall lady nodded.

Hmm. Maybe good girls do win once in a while.

After all of the contestants had demonstrated their talent, the emcee took her spot up front. "The judges need just a few minutes to confer, ladies and gentlemen, and then we will be thrilled to announce our finalists, and this county's Lovely Miss Pennsylvania representative!"

The room relaxed into excited buzzy chatter while the three judges put their heads together, sharing scorecards and, I assume, their favorite candidates. Valerie seemed to be making a case for someone, with lots of gesturing and serious pointing at scorecards. It was hard to tell what the other judges were thinking, but they were at least listening. I wished I was a fly on that table, and believe me, being at the fair, no one would think twice about a fly hanging around.

Nick bumped me with his shoulder. "Why are you glaring at the judge's table?"

"I'm not glaring."

"Are so," Miranda said.

"Are you a part of this conversation?"

"Well, excuse me. I was part of the deception, or whatever that was with Ms. Springfield before the pageant. I deserve to know what's going on."

I hated it when she was right. "I'm studying them, okay? I'm trying to read their minds. Or Valerie's mind, anyway. From the text I saw, Gregg is expecting her to 'Do her job.'" I explained what I was thinking, and how I wasn't sure why he would care about a teenage girls' pageant so much he would resort to cheating. But then, cheating was sort of his thing, wasn't it?

Before Nick and Miranda could respond, the girls were back, re-dressed in their formal gowns, to stand on their pedestals. I watched the judges, and it seemed like they were giving Taylor special glances, but I could have been reading into it. I supposed they could have been giving other girls looks, too. None of the three judges seemed especially happy about the decision they'd had to make.

The tall woman looked hard at Valerie, shared a meaningful glance with the other guy—although I didn't know what it meant—and marked up a piece of paper, folding it and holding it up toward the emcee.

"The judges are prepared to reveal their decision!" the emcee chirped, as if nothing in the world could be any more exciting. She flounced over to grab the paper, but I wasn't really watching her. I was watching as the blood drained from Valerie's face. She was obviously doing her best to keep it together, but her eyes were darting all around, mostly toward the back of the building, where— gee, what a surprise—Gregg had slipped back in, along with his thugs. Why on earth did he care so much about this stupid contest?

"We want to thank all of the contestants who participated today. Our county is blessed with an abundance of beautiful and talented young women, and today proved that once again. Let's give a hand to everyone up here on the stage."

The audience applauded, and the girls up front tried to smile and act like the next five minutes weren't going to change their lives—which is a sad statement, isn't it? Taylor was the only one who seemed relaxed and natural, but then, that would be natural, wouldn't it, if she expected to win because the judging was rigged? Wouldn't she be surprised when it was revealed that she wouldn't come out the winner? At least, that's what I suspected from Valerie's behavior, smiling at Taylor's performance and now so worried. But why was she arguing with the other judges? Could they really not see how much better Taylor was than all of the others?

I swear, I would never understand this world.

Summer, the medical miracle—or should I say, experiment—smiled her hideous smile and thrust her chest out to the Atlantic. I wondered just how many brain cells made their home in that head of hers. Looking at her next to those other girls, how could she possibly think she had even a ghost of a chance?

The emcee opened the paper and glanced at it, getting her bearings. "Our third runner-up today hails from the town of Westbrook, where she is a junior at the local high-school."

It was easy to see who that was, because the girl's shoulders slumped about a mile before manners kicked back in, and she smiled and straightened. The emcee announced her name, and the girl went forward to receive her banner and wave at the audience. Her disappointment at not winning seemed almost more than she could bear, since her lips trembled, and her eyes shone with tears. Good grief. She should be happy she placed. A bunch of the other girls, in a few moments, would do anything to trade places with her rather than be relegated to the losers.

The emcee announced the second runner-up, who was much more gracious, and actually seemed excited, like she hadn't expected to place at all. She smiled big-time, and waved and blew kisses.

Nick patted my leg, and I realized how tense I'd become. I relaxed, and let my neck droop. What was I so anxious about, anyway?

"And now, for our first runner-up and alternate. She will step into the role of the county's winner, should the crowned Lovely Miss winner be unable to perform her duties for any reason. What a privilege and honor. To fill this role for her county and the Lovely Miss organization, please congratulate our first runner-up, Summer Moss!"

There was a pregnant pause, which I felt in my own gut, and then the applause began gradually, until most people were clapping. Summer's mom sat in the front row, mouth gaping, face red. She really had expected Summer to win. She really had thought all that surgery and cosmetic warfare was going to gain her daughter the title. She was apparently so stunned by the turn of events she couldn't clap.

But then, Summer was apparently so deaf, she couldn't hear. She still stood on her pedestal, smiling and looking around like her name hadn't been called.

"Summer?" The emcee waited until Summer turned her way. "Are you coming down?"

Summer blinked, and then her brow furrowed. Or, it would have, if she still had any flexibility in her face. "Are you talking to me?"

The emcee laughed. "Yes, dear, you are our first runner-up! Congratulations!"

"But…" Her mouth puckered into an O, and she looked out at her mother. "What is she saying?"

"Come on, Summer," the emcee said, a little stronger. "Come receive your banner."

When she still didn't move, the emcee glanced offstage, and one of the helpers came up, took Summer's elbow, and led her to the front of the stage.

"Congratulations, Summer. You represented both your town and your county very well." Better than expected, was what she should have said, seeing how she was a work of science, not unlike the bionic man. Except she wasn't, well, a hero.

Summer blinked rapidly, frightening small children in the front row, and stood like a statue as she accepted her banner, which announced she was the First Runner-Up. She looked down at it, where it bulged grotesquely over those pounds of fake flesh, and followed the helper robotically back to her place with the others.

"And now," the emcee said, "it is time to crown our county's Lovely Miss Pennsylvania winner. This contestant has proven herself to be everything the judges—and we all—look for in our young women. Strength of character, a desire to make the world a better place, and, of course, a lovely countenance to look upon. Please welcome this year's winner, Taylor Troth!"

The girls up front simultaneously slumped and cheered, all now plenty aware that they were lacking in some fashion. Taylor herself looked about as stunned as Summer had, although on Taylor it was a lot more attractive. She accepted congratulations from the girls around her, and by the time she arrived at the front of the stage, she was smiling. The emcee placed a banner around her shoulders declaring her the winner, then set a sparkling silver tiara on her head.

Zach, Randy, and Bobby, along with Daniella and Amy and a good bunch of people sitting around them, stood up and hooted and hollered. Claire was the sole family member still in her seat. Her mom looked down and nudged her, and Claire finally got to her feet. Eventually, she clapped. And even smiled.

Taylor waved as music swelled, and television cameras rolled forward down the aisle to capture the moment. I glanced over at Valerie, and caught her giving a triumphant look toward the back of the building. But Gregg was gone, along with his entourage. I guessed there was no point in staying.

Mission accomplished.

For whatever reason.

Chapter Thirty-five

"Results are in," Carla said. "It was exactly what , we expected."

She found me on the home phone. Nick, Miranda, and I had come back immediately after the pageant to avoid the dramatics, and I got to spend a spectacular evening doing nothing but farm stuff. Heaven. My tired brain struggled now to remember what Carla was talking about.

"The Greggs' dairy cows," she said.

Right. "Rotten food?"

"Practically toxic. We're lucky the cows didn't get hurt worse. And it was no wonder they acted like drunk old men."

"They'll be fine, though?"

"Sure. But they're out of competition for the week, of course. Seeing how they missed their event today."

"Well, there goes Gregg's money down the toilet."

She laughed. "He'll probably just sell them. Or try again at next year's fair."

"If his girls still care. No, if he still cares. His girls are obviously already way over the whole thing."

"Whatever, that's not my concern. I'm just glad the cows are okay. And I'm praying nothing more happens."

"If it's about the Greggs, you should be out of it. They have no one else to threaten, if their events are over."

"True."

"No idea who did it, though?"

"None. It's not like the cops could get fingerprints off a wooden stall. And who knows where the feed came from. The feed bin the Greggs were using had only their prints on it, and that feed was perfectly fine, so…" She yawned so loudly I could practically feel it. "A few more hours and I can go to bed, just to do it all again tomorrow. Tell me again why I agreed to this?"

"Because you had to go through it at least once. Now you'll know to refuse if you ever get asked again."

"You got it. Thanks again, Stella. I sure appreciate your having my back."

"Anytime, Sister. And thank that man of

yours, too. He's the one who let me know what was happening."

She paused. "Is there something wrong with your phone?"

"No, sounds fine on this end."

"All right. It's just, I could have sworn you said something nice about Bryan. Must be the phone line."

"Hardy-har. Goodnight, Carla."

She laughed, and hung up.

Talking to Carla about those results made me wonder what was happening with Rikki's toxicology report, so I called Willard.

"Sorry," I said, when he answered. "Did I wake you up?"

"Just from a sound sleep."

"Did you hear anything yet?"

"I'm assuming you mean about Rikki Raines?"

"What else would I mean?"

"Stella." He breathed into the phone. "Didn't I tell you I'd call as soon as I heard anything?"

"Well, yeah."

"Don't you trust me?"

"Of course I do."

"Then good night." He hung up.

Whoops.

Chapter Thirty-six

Thursday dawned hot and muggy. As if there were any other kind of weather. The only plan I had, other than working around home, was to attend Zach's showmanship judging in the afternoon. Until then, I puttered around the house, fixing things, mowing, and taking a late morning nap.

After lunch I headed to the fair. Since Nick was keen to stay home and get some work done, and Miranda had done all the bonding with me should could take—thank God—I suited up and took the Harley. When I got to the fair I found a safe spot in a corner where I stripped out of my leather and locked it in my saddlebags. I debated carrying my helmet with me, since it wouldn't fit in the bags, but really didn't want to drag it around, so I tucked it under the bike and hoped no one would be dumb enough to touch it. I considered leaving a note threatening bodily harm, but decided that could be taken the wrong way.

I grabbed a drink at the food tent, then settled in at the arena. Taylor, wearing her tiara and banner over a pink, cotton dress, sat in the front row, next to her mom and another woman I recognized as one of the pageant organizers. A very pouty Summer sat down the row next to her mother, who looked not so much pouty as disillusioned. Perhaps the whole thing would serve as a lesson to her, but I didn't hold out much hope. It seemed a little late for that, since her brain had probably been affected by all of the chemicals shoved into her body.

Zach's parents had made it to the arena this time, and I waved across at them, and the whole Granger clan, who had shown up. Corn must have been all done. Mallory and Brady were even there, sitting behind Jethro and Belle. Brady wore a t-shirt declaring SMASHMASTER RULES, but it was a little outdated, seeing how his friend had gotten knocked out in the first round of the combine demo. Oh, well. It was nice to know he wasn't a fairweather friend.

The youngest classes of showmen went first, with the bucket calves, and the kids looked absolutely adorable in their whites. The whites weren't exactly, well, white on all of them, but then what do you expect from eight-year-olds? I'm sure they kept as clean as they could. By the time Zach's group came in, everything looked a lot more professional.

Zach and Barnabas did terrific, as did Bobby and Laura. Austin was a no-show, which surprised me, but then, I supposed he was so freaked out from everything, it would have been impossible to focus. Plus, he'd as much as said he didn't really care about winning that ribbon. The Gregg girl was also a no-show, which was only natural. All she could have done would have been to let her calf do its thing, since she didn't have a clue. Gregg probably didn't want to take a chance on losing, since she'd already won the ribbon that to him really mattered.

Loser.

One of the kids' calves acted up during the judging, so the calf was switched out for another, better behaved one, since what was getting judged in this round was the showman, rather than the calf. The kid involved showed real poise as it all happened, so that had to go in her favor.

When the final lineup was announced, Randy and Laura both made the top ten, and Zach stood in the Reserve Champion spot. I was so proud of him, but he didn't even look for me. Instead, he smiled at Taylor, who clapped and grinned like it was her victory, too. Wow. My little boy really was growing up.

I stayed in my seat for the dairy cow showmanship class, because both Claire and Bobby would be in that one. In this class, it didn't matter the breed of your cow, but your age, so it was all mixed up with the Holsteins and Ayrshires and Guernseys. A bunch of gorgeous animals. Both Claire's and Bobby's cows behaved perfectly, and Claire again won Champion, with Bobby following at third place. This time, Claire gave a gracious smile, and even congratulated the Reserve Champion before breaking formation. I was glad to see her enjoying her win. Taylor stood and clapped as Claire walked out, and Claire smiled at her. Finally.

When judging was over, I made my way to the calf barn. Zach and Taylor were with Barnabas, placing his ribbon prominently on the stall. I held out my fist, and he bumped it.

"Awesome job, Zach. All of your hard work paid off, for sure."

"Yeah, I guess so." He grinned. "Maybe next year you won't get on me so much to get my other work done instead of spending time with Barnabas."

"Oh, you think?"

He laughed, and gave Barnabas a pat. "We've gotta go. Taylor needs to make a bunch of appearances today."

"Heavy weighs the crown."

They both frowned. "Um, what?" Zach said.

"Nevermind. Have fun."

They took off, Zach reaching to grab Taylor's hand. Interesting.

"Where'd he go?" Jethro and Belle made it to the stall.

"Already gone," I said. "Off with the new girlfriend."

Belle's eyebrows rose. "New what?"

"Oh, uh, he hasn't mentioned her?"

She looked at Jethro, who smiled hugely. "That's my boy."

I laughed. "I gotta go talk to some more winners. See ya."

I found Randy and Laura, who took a few seconds to accept my congratulations, then slipped over to the dairy barn. Bobby had already put up his ribbon, and Claire was in the middle of hanging hers—right next to the other ribbon she won.

"Decided to show them both, huh?" I said.

She looked down at me. "You were right. I should be proud of them. And of Breezy. She deserves for people to know how awesome she is."

"Good girl."

She smiled, and I continued across the barn, ending up at the Greggs' empty stalls. It was a shame, the way the cows had been cut out from the judging. As Claire had just said, it certainly wasn't the animals' fault they were seen as cheaters, and they really were impressive to look at. But I couldn't feel too sorry about the Gregg girls not receiving false rewards.

"They're going to be okay."

I started, and realized Mrs. Gregg stood next to me. She was clean again today, and her face had lost its redness, along with the puffy eyes. In fact, she looked much more relaxed than she had all week. I glanced around, ready for battle, but it seemed she was alone. Perhaps her reason for not being anxious and worried.

"The cows?" I said. "I'm glad."

"Yes. It would have been such a shame if they'd been hurt. As it is…" She shrugged. "Things could have been a lot worse."

"Yes. I guess they never did figure out who poisoned your cows, did they?"

She stared at the stalls for a few seconds, then closed her eyes, shaking her head, as if she just didn't want to think about it anymore. "They never did. But it's done now. The cows are gone, the fair's almost over. I hope they let it rest."

"It was a crime."

"I know. But I'd like to just…move on."

I guess I couldn't blame her.

She gave me a pinched smile. "I came back to collect a few things. We're done with these stalls now. Then we'll just have Melody's, over in the calf barn."

"You think you'll be back next year?"

She gazed at me, unblinking. "David says we could use these same cows again, but after everything that happened this year, I'll try to convince him, somehow, that it's over. Makes me a little sad, but everything needs to end sometime. I wish…" She shook her head.

"What?"

"I'll make sure that this is our last year. It's just not worth it anymore."

I tried not to show my relief. Having the Greggs gone from the fair would be good in more ways than one.

"Goodbye," Mrs. Gregg said. "I'm sorry about…well, I'm just sorry."

"Yeah. I'm sorry, too."

I didn't tell her I was sorry she was married to such a creep, and that she'd gone along with the cheating stuff for so long. I'd just let her interpret it however she wanted. Because when it came down to it, she *was* sorry—a sorry excuse for a 4-H mom.

Before I left the fair, I found Carla, where she was taking a much-deserved break in the corner of the goat barn. Not the least smelly place she could think of, but she didn't seem to mind. It was nice to see her smiling again, and she told me she'd had no more texts, and no more strange animal behavior to figure out. Just "run of the mill" stuff, she said, in her technical lingo.

I got a message asking me to come by the cops' building, and since I just so happened to still be at the fair, I stopped by.

"Still no actual toxicology results," I said to Watts. "What a surprise."

She had the grace to look embarrassed.

"So what do you want?"

"Finally got your statement typed up. Wanted you to sign it."

"Really? You called me for that?"

"And to ask if you remembered anything else. Or had any more ideas about who might have killed Rikki Raines."

I skimmed the statement and signed it. I then held it up in Watts' face. "Did you read this?"

"Yes."

"Then you can see that my sole role in this whole sad affair was that I happened to be in the wrong place at the wrong time. I heard a girl scream, I went to help, I pulled Rikki's body from the shit pile. I didn't know her. I never talked to her. She was a complete stranger to me. What about that statement says to you, 'Hey, if I keep on asking her the same stupid questions over and over, maybe she'll remember something that she had no possibility of ever knowing'?" I thrust the paper at her, and she clutched it, looking around as if making sure nobody was watching. "Goodbye, Watts. Don't call me again unless you have something to tell me that I'd actually care about."

That concluded any obligation I had at the fair that day, thank the good Lord, so I got back on my bike and went home.

Chapter Thirty-seven

Friday morning was already hot, and I'd taken my first shower of the day, feeling too disgusting after the morning milking to do anything else until I was at least in dry clothes. I was feeling better than I had all week, after a good night's sleep and the slower fair schedule the day before, along with the nice ride on the hog. I'd come right home after talking with Watts, taking a long way around, enjoying the trip, and got home in time for a nice cookout with Nick, Miranda, and Lucy's family. We sat in the shade, and the heat wasn't too awful. At least the high, dry temps kept the worst of the bugs away.

Now this morning, Nick and I had just finished breakfast, and we were discussing how the only fair event that sounded even remotely tempting today was the fireworks in the evening. They always put on a good show for the Fourth, with special ground designs and lots of those sparkly fireworks that twinkled. I liked those.

Nick was running his fingers down my back, imitating those very fireworks, when I noticed Miranda standing in the kitchen doorway, fresh and clean and…up really early for her. I eased away from Nick, rinsed our dishes, and stuck them in the dishwasher. And then I remembered Miranda's plans for the day.

"Right. Have fun," I said.

She frowned. "What do you mean?"

"What do you mean, what do I mean? I said, 'Have fun.' How hard is that? This is the day you're going to Daniella's salon, right?"

She looked at Nick. "Are you going to tell her, or am I?"

He held up his hands. "I am so not getting in the middle of this."

A cold, clammy chill ran up my body. "What are you not telling me, Nick?"

He kept his hands up, and backed out of the room.

Without moving any other part of my body, I swiveled my eyes toward Miranda.

She smiled, way too brightly. "What he's not telling you is…you're coming with me."

◇◇◇

"We planned it all out," Miranda explained later. "We wanted it to be a surprise."

A surprise? More like an ambush.

Miranda and I had made a run for the R5 train out of Pennbrook Station, and had found forward-facing seats in the second car, where I tried to avoid the greasy hair goo on the window, left so thoughtfully by the last passenger. The train itself was fairly clean, other than that, but I would need to concentrate on not getting queasy with all the starts and stops on the regional commuter.

I had done my best back home to argue that I couldn't waste an entire day in Philadelphia—after the past several days I had work to do on the farm ("Lucy's got it covered, right, Luce?"), the fair was still going on ("Zach's judging is over, as is the dairy class, the showmanship, and Taylor's Lovely Miss PA pageant, so what is there left to see?"), and Rikki Raines' so-far unsolved murder ("Not your problem, and anyway, if you're so hung up on it, we'll check things out at the salon. She used to go there, right?").

I was so not going to enjoy this. Just on principle.

Nick, the weasel, had slipped away to who knew where—dashing out the drive in his Ranger before I could throttle him. For once he wasn't answering his phone, and Lucy and Miranda weren't afraid of me as I argued. Tess watched with either shock or disbelief, her eyes darting back and forth between Miranda and Lucy and me, and Queenie made it quite clear she didn't care what I did, as long as she could stay home and sleep in the shade. Loyal friend, my foot.

Miranda ignored my blatant crabbiness and went on and on—and on—about our schedule for the day. Massages, facials, mani-pedis—which she assured me was something to do with our finger-nails and toenails, and not something I would regret later, although I couldn't imagine not regretting having my nails done—and, finally, makeup and hair. She didn't need to know I would be refusing the great lot of these adventures.

We were almost to Glenside, eight stations down the line, before she finally took a long enough breath I could say, "This is going to cost a fortune."

"Oh, no, remember? Daniella is giving us a discount."

"However much the discount is, it will still be one hundred percent more than I can afford. Or would ever spend on something like this."

"Oh, Stella." She slapped my arm. "It's my treat."

Holy crap. This Miranda was not the woman I'd gotten to know. And there was nothing I could do about it. It wasn't like I could kill my future sister-in-law in the middle of public transporta-tion. Then Nick and I would never get married.

I couldn't see his surviving sister or his mother attending a prison ceremony.

I was feeling righteous. "You'll spend money for a day of personal luxury, but can't stand it that Nick is spending a few dollars on our home?" Dangerous territory, I knew, but then, if I couldn't kill her on the train, she couldn't throw a hissy fit there, either. I knew where to fight my battles.

Her eyes flashed. "This is for your wedding, Stella. How do we know how to dress you that day unless we have a trial run?"

"I know how to dress myself."

She snorted. "Sure, if you want to wear boots and a T-shirt to get married in."

So, she was getting to know me, after all.

I stared out the window as we got closer to town, amazed, as always, that the train takes its passengers by the parts of the city that would be best avoided for the sake of tourism. Abandoned townhomes, trashy, overgrown lots, and factories with broken windows and missing bricks. Not exactly signs of a thriving city. But then, we were on the outskirts, where people live and work who can't afford to live in the pretty spots. That's why, if you look closely enough in the classifieds, you can find that specific real estate for bottom-of-the-bucket cash. You just wouldn't want to actually live at those spots, unless you're used to living in fear, crouched behind the barred windows of your not-up-to-code house.

That took me back to thinking about my own house, and the maintenance it needed, and how it was finally going to get paid for, now that Nick was in. And then I thought of that slimy David Gregg, and the monstrosity he'd built out on the Main Line. That was paid for by the hard work—and debasement—of some of the area's finest musicians.

"Oh, look!" Miranda exhaled slowly. "There's the city!"

We scraped around a curve, and the cityscape rose up before us. Even for a country girl like me it was a little awe-inspiring.

Miranda leaned over me to see out the window, and I pushed myself back into my seat, not wanting to plant a facial on the window hair grease, or have my nose stuck in Miranda's ear.

"It's been so long since I've been here!" Miranda said. "I wish we could stay overnight and go shopping tomorrow."

Oh, Lord, deliver me from evil.

The city disappeared as we were sucked into the underground tunnels, and Miranda settled back into her own seat. She took a deep breath and squeezed my arm. "Oh, Stella, this is going to be so much fun!"

The train lurched to a stop, giving me an

excuse for not responding, and for freeing my arm from her death grip. We started and stopped several more times until Miranda finally jumped from her seat at Suburban Station. "This is it! Come on!" She blocked the aisle, right in front of an elderly man who was also waiting to get off the train.

"Sorry," I said.

"No problems, young lady. Your friend seems excited."

"That doesn't begin to explain it."

He chuckled, and gestured for me to go in front of him.

Miranda dodged and weaved through the station, like we were in *The Amazing Race*. I tried to keep up with her, but she ended up waiting for me at the bottom of the stairs. She dragged me up to street level, where I just about collided with a woman in a black suit, sneakers, and earphones. The glare she gave me would have destroyed anyone not ready to return it in kind.

Miranda pulled out her phone, where she'd programmed in a walking path to the salon. We sweated our way just a few blocks—wouldn't that be lovely for the folks at the salon—until we arrived in Rittenhouse Square. Miranda practically ran the last half of a block until we arrived at Serenity Salon and Spa.

Miranda looked up at the building and said,

"Here we go, Stella! I can't wait to see what you look like by the end of the day!"

Give me strength.

Chapter Thirty-eight

A cloud of odors enveloped me as we walked in the door. I gagged, then acted like I was holding back a sneeze when Miranda glared at me. I took my hand away from my nose and tried to breathe normally. *What was that smell?*

"It's heavenly," Miranda low-toned into my ear, "and if you don't wipe that look off your face, I'm going to poke you with a nail file. Believe me, I won't have to go far to find one."

"What look?"

"The look like you're about to throw up."

"But—"

"Hello!" A waxed and shined receptionist popped up from behind a high counter, her smile on high beam. For a second I was transported back to the food tent at the fair, when we'd been assaulted by Summer and her gigantuous boobs. This woman had been plucked and shaped and colored and pulled just about as much as the pseudo-teenager, although this one couldn't hide the fact that she was at least, well, some years older than the LM Pennsylvania contestant.

She clasped her bejeweled and painted hands and said, "You must be our nine o'clock!"

"We are!" Miranda galloped around to meet her halfway, and shook the woman's hand.

The woman batted her eyes at Miranda. "My name is Misty, and I'll be getting you started. You must be the bride. I'm so thrilled for you!" The woman's smile escalated to an even higher wattage.

"Oh, uh, no," Miranda said. "That would be her."

The two women swiveled slowly toward me. I held up a hand. "Hi."

Misty's smile dimmed just a smidgen, but she quickly bucked up and hustled my way to shake my hand so hard she would have torn the arm off a weaker specimen. "So glad to have you here... Stella, right? I understand you're a personal friend of Daniella's?"

"Well, I just met her—"

"She is!" Miranda gushed. "Daniella thought it would be wonderful for Stella to have a practice day here at the salon, and worked her magic to get us in. We can't wait to see what this salon has to offer."

"We are a full-service spa," Misty said, "which

of course you know, since you're starting out the day with a massage." She gasped, in an excited, you-won't-believe-this and look-what-time-it-is way. "And speaking of that, we need to get you started! Come this way, ladies."

Ladies. Uh-huh.

Miranda pushed me to follow Misty through gauzy yellow curtains into a waiting room filled with gold and cream couches, glass-topped coffee tables, ankle-deep white carpet, and gooey music. The windows were swagged with thick gold curtains, and antiquey-looking lights drooped from the ceiling and perched on shiny gold stands. Again, the fragrance was almost more than I could take, and I concentrated on taking shallow breaths.

"If either of you needs to wait for the other at any point today, this room is for your use," Misty said. "There are snacks and hot drinks or cold water over here, and you are welcome to them. Of course, you will be having your catered lunch at noon, so you don't want to fill up too much!"

Catered lunch? What the—

Miranda beamed at me.

"So now," Misty said, "if you two would like to come this way, I'll show you to your room. Our massage therapists are wonderful, and I'm sure you'll—Stella?"

I'd stopped listening, because I'd noticed a wall of signed photos. Famous people who had taken advantage of the salon's services, I supposed. I didn't recognize all of them, but there were famous television personalities, movie stars, singers, athletes. And Rikki Raines. There she was in her cowboy boots, fringed vest, and bright white hair.

"She was a regular here, right?" I pointed at the picture.

"Oh, yes, it's so sad about her, isn't it?" Misty came over to stand by me, and her eyes grew… well…misty. "She was such a sweetheart, always with a smile, always kind words to say. She was a beautiful girl, but also very real. Everyone loved working on her."

"When was the last time you saw her?"

"A week ago Wednesday."

"You remember that clearly?"

"Certainly. She's been coming in every Wednesday and Friday this summer, because those are the days of the Lovely Miss Pennsylvania pageants, for the most part. Every once in a while there's a change, but they try to keep it fairly regular. Rikki came in each time to have her hair and makeup done. She wanted to look good for the girls, you know, and since Daniella is so involved, we were glad to help out however we could."

Yup, I was sure the publicity and star-power had nothing to do with it.

"You take care of a lot of the girls, too, don't you?"

"The ones who live in the area, yes. Those who live out of the region go to their own salons, but since we are the official salon of this area's pageants, we get the majority of them."

"You take care of a girl named Summer?"

Her forehead wrinkled. "Summer…"

"Fake everything, boobs out to here."

"Oh." Her face went blank. "Yes, she is one of our clients. I believe she and her mother were just here last week. Now, if you'll come this way, you really need to get started."

I followed her to the nearest door. "You take care of people from the recording studio, too, right?"

"You mean Sunburst? Yes, we're their official stylists for album covers, videos, press conferences. Whatever they need us for. It's quite exciting. We even get the men. They're helpless when it comes to makeup, of course, but they need it for their camera work. Sometimes we even get to go on-site where they're shooting."

"I suppose that means you're in touch with David Gregg."

She hesitated. "Of course we deal with Mr.

Gregg. He is in charge of Sunburst's production, after all."

"So he's in here a lot?"

"Stella…Ms. Crown, I really shouldn't be talking to you about other customers."

"Was he ever here when Rikki Raines was getting done? Did you see how they interacted?"

"Stella." Miranda grabbed my arm. "Misty has a job to do."

Misty swallowed, and wouldn't meet my eyes. The gauzy curtains over the door parted, and two women came in. They looked surprised to see us.

The first one, a short, pleasantly plump, middle-aged, used-to-be-redhead smiled. "Not ready yet?"

"Sorry," Misty said. "We were checking out our Wall of Fame."

"Of course. We can take it from here, Misty. Thanks."

Misty threw me a quick glance, then scurried back out to the front lobby.

"You are such a bully," Miranda muttered.

"I was only trying to find out what she knew about Gregg and Rikki."

"Exactly."

The short woman gestured to the door that said "Massage Therapy." "If you'll please come this way."

We followed her and the other woman, a younger, African-American woman with stick arms, into a dimly lit, smelly room. Smelly in that overripe garden way again. There were two tables set up head-to-head that looked sort of like the ones at a doctor's office, except these were covered with sheets and blankets, rather than paper. One of those tiny water fountains gurgled in the center of the room, and some kind of New Age-y music played so quietly I almost couldn't hear it. Besides the tables, there were two soft chairs, one at each end of the room, a table with bottles and towels, and what looked like a bathroom through an open door.

"My name is Sondra," the shorter woman said.

The other woman smiled. "And I'm Petra."

"We'll be doing your massages. So, if you want to leave your clothes on those chairs, we'll be back in a few minutes. Feel free to use that restroom, and go ahead and lie on a table, covered with a blanket. We'll begin with you lying on your backs. Any questions?"

"Our clothes?" I said. "What do you mean leave them there?"

Sondra blinked. "Is this your first massage?"

"By someone other than my fiancé, yes."

"Sorry," Miranda said. "I didn't know. I would have told her."

"It's not a problem." Sondra waved Miranda and Petra away, and led me toward the chair in one corner of the room. "From the appointment book, I see that you are a bride, and you are having a spa day with your maid of honor."

Maid of Honor? That Miranda. After our day of pampering, I was going to kill her.

"The first thing on the schedule is this side-by-side massage. For that, you need to undress, placing everything but your underwear on this chair. You can leave your panties on."

I coughed a laugh. "Seriously?"

Sondra smiled. "Don't worry, whatever body part I'm not working on will be covered, to keep you warm."

"I'm not worried about staying warm."

She leaned toward me. "Believe me, I won't be looking where I'm not supposed to. And remember, I've done hundreds of these massages. I won't be seeing anything I haven't seen before. Please, try to trust me." She watched me. "You okay?"

"I'm fine."

"All right, then. I'll be back in a few minutes."

She left. Miranda's girl, Petra, was already gone. Miranda was almost done stripping, and was down to her bra and underwear.

"We're going to be naked in here together?" I said. "Really?"

"Oh, Stella, stop being such a prude."

"Prude? I'm not a—"

"Then shut up and take your clothes off." She tossed her bra onto a chair and lay on the table, pulling the blanket up over her. "They're going to be back in a minute. I promise I won't look." She made a show of squeezing her eyes shut.

I huffed, and kicked off my shoes. This was ridiculous. I could have had Nick give me a massage, and it would have been much more fun. And less embarrassing. I pulled off my jeans and shirt, and dropped them onto the chair.

Someone knocked on the door.

"Not ready yet!" I yelled.

"Trying to relax, here," Miranda murmured.

I threw my bra on the chair and dove under the blanket. "You're going to owe me after this."

"Right," Miranda said. "We'll see who owes whom when this is all over."

I didn't have to see. I already knew. This was going to be the single most bizarre thing I'd ever done.

This time when they knocked, Miranda called out a welcome. The door opened, and the women came in and began their work.

You know, there are some times when I'm happy to be wrong.

Chapter Thirty-nine

I noodle-legged my way to the next room, where again I lay on my back. This time the technician concentrated on my face, slathering layer after layer of lotions over it, then bagged up my feet and hands with some other kind of moisturizers. When that was over, I sat in our private dining room, big enough only for two people around a little round table, and stared at the mound of lettuce, grilled chicken, and bright red cherry tomatoes.

"Do I look as shiny as you do?" I asked Miranda.

She laughed. "Shinier than I've ever seen you."

"I thought I was going to melt into the floor."

"See? Told you."

After the delicious lunch of grilled chicken on organic greens, we sat side by side as different women went to work on our fingernails and toenails. That mani-pedi Miranda had talked about. Whatever.

"So, what kind of color would you like?" The lady held out a palette with about a hundred shades, from bright red to a deep, dark, almost-black maroon.

"Clear," I said.

"Are you positive?"

"Clear."

Miranda didn't hesitate to express her disgust.

"You do Rikki Raines' nails?" I asked my girl.

She kept her eyes on her work. "Sure. Sometimes."

"When was the last time?"

She didn't answer for so long, I thought she wasn't going to. But when she'd finished massaging goop onto my fingernails, she set my hand down. "Last week. Wednesday."

"How was she?"

"She was fine." She glanced at Miranda's girl, who said, "Oh, go on and tell her. It's not like everybody in the whole salon didn't hear."

Miranda's eyes widened. "Hear what?"

The girls stared into each other's eyes for a moment, then glanced around to make sure no one else was listening. Miranda's manicurist leaned forward. "It was huge. I'd never heard a fight like that."

Now that was news. "Rikki was fighting with someone?"

"No. I didn't mean her. It was him."

"Him? Him who?" It dawned on me. "Gregg? Gregg was here?"

"Shh." My girl shrank down. "Mr. Gregg comes here sometimes, when we're working on one of his bands, or singers, or whatever. He wants to make sure we're doing everything right, and making them all happy. And making sure they're doing what they're supposed to, because sometimes, you know, they want their own look."

"Who was he fighting with? You said it wasn't Rikki?"

"No, it was his wife."

"Mrs. Gregg? What was she doing here?"

Again with the shared look between them.

"She's been hanging around more and more," my girl said. "Whenever Mr. Gregg is here, she's here, too. It's almost like…" She shook her head, and put her head down again, working on my nails.

But she didn't have to finish the statement. I could finish it myself. *It's almost like she doesn't trust him.* And I didn't blame her. From the little I'd seen of him—and heard about him—just that week, I wouldn't trust him either.

"What were they fighting about?"

"What do you think?" Miranda's girl this time, her eyes wide, like the answer should have been obvious. "Or, should I say, who do you think? I mean, she was right there."

"Who, Rikki?"

"Uh-huh. Mrs. Gregg pulled him in the other

room, and we could hear everything they said, because, like, there's no door."

Right. Just beads and curtains and wispy things that couldn't keep out smells, sights, or sounds.

"She was saying she'd had enough of the cheating. That she was done pretending, that the girls would just have to make it on their own from now on, that she wasn't going to go along with it anymore, and if it didn't stop, she was going to do something about it. The girls would have to pay."

The beads hanging from the door clicked, and Misty appeared, looking as chipper as ever. Or even chippier. Had she frosted her hair over lunch? Or whitened her teeth? "So, how are we doing in here?"

Miranda smiled. "Doing great! Your manicurists are wonderful!"

How could Misty not notice the tension of gossip in the air?

"I know they are." Misty patted my girl on the shoulder. "Glad you're having fun."

She swept back through the beaded curtain, but the girls never spoke again of what we'd been discussing, even when I asked straight out what more had been said, and if the Greggs had been talking about any girl or girls in particular. I guess they'd realized they'd crossed the line earlier. Too bad.

I didn't recognize my own hands and feet when we were finished, even though they were attached to my body. When had my nails last been buffed and shined? Well, I suppose the answer to that would be never.

From there, we followed a guide into yet another room of smells and swivels chairs. The hair salon.

"Not much you can do with mine," I told the stylist, as she tipped my head back into a sink.

She smiled. "Just you wait."

Twenty minutes later, I would have sworn I'd started with long hair. Somehow she had made it look like I wore my hair up in some kind of a knot.

Miranda just smiled. "And now, for the final touches."

"Which would be what?"

"You'll see."

I was placed in a leaning back chair, and yet another person went after me. I relaxed, almost falling asleep, while she placed something warm on my eyebrows. It felt sort of good, but sort of weird, too, like drying mud. After a few minutes, she said, "Ready?"

"For what?"

Pain exploded on my face.

I screamed and grabbed her shirt. "What the hell was that?"

She stumbled back, my grip on her shirt pulling me upright. She held up what looked like a slice of my face. With hair. "I'm shaping your eyebrows."

"What?" I looked in the mirror. I now had eyebrows like…like Miranda's. Perfect arches. My right eyebrow looked like I'd just been really surprised by something. Which I had been. "What is that? I'm look like I'm terrified."

"No, no, you don't," the girl said. "It looks great."

I spun to glare at Miranda, who had just had both of her eyebrows done. Without her screaming, mind you. She grinned. "Now for the other side."

"I'm not doing that again."

"Then you'll look like an idiot."

The girl wrinkled up her face. "I'm sorry. I thought you wanted…it was on your schedule. Your maid of honor said—"

I held up my hand and gathered myself. I'd been through worse, right? Broken foot, broken ribs, skin grafts, tattoos…

"Fine." I threw myself back into the chair. "Finish."

She yanked the other half of my hair out, and I didn't scream. But I was done. "Let's go, Miranda."

"Oh, no. One more thing."

"No way."

"This won't hurt."

"Forget it."

"It's just makeup."

"Makeup."

"Oh, come on. It'll be fun. Besides, I'm paying, remember?"

Eyebrow Girl shuffled her feet. "Really. It won't hurt. It'll feel good. Everyone says so."

"Plus, I promised Nick," Miranda said.

"You promised him what?"

"That he'd get to see you fully done up. You don't want to disappoint him, do you?"

"I would never want to disappoint him. And I won't."

"Good, so let's get you into your last chair."

"No."

"But you said—"

"I won't disappoint him by giving in to anything else. He won't recognize me if I come home wearing makeup. He might not even recognize me now." I pointed at my eyebrows. "Especially if these look as red as they feel."

"Stella—"

"You go ahead. I'm done."

I ripped the cape from my neck and stomped out to the waiting room, where I paid a long visit to the wash room. When I came out, I felt a lot better, and sucked down half of the salon's snack and bottled water supply. When Miranda came to find me, I was stuffed, lying on one of the fancy couches with my feet up and my eyes closed. Although I kept my ears open. I wasn't going to be surprised again, because who knew what they could tear off of me this time?

I heard footsteps approach, so I cracked open my eyelids.

"Stella, what did you do?" Miranda stood by the couch, her fists on her hips.

"Ate too much."

"No, I mean to your hair."

"Made it normal."

"But it looked so—"

"Stupid?"

Miranda growled and spun on her heel. "Come on."

I met her in the front lobby, where she was handing over her credit card to Misty. Misty glanced up at me, then got really busy punching numbers. Another woman behind the counter, whose hair was three different colors, set down the phone, and touched Misty's wrist with her blindingly red nails. "She's coming."

Misty nodded, still focused on the cash register.

"Who's coming?" I didn't want to see anyone else. "I'm going outside."

"Stella, don't be such a—"

I let the door slam on my way out.

Chapter Forty

Rittenhouse Square is a pretty area of Philadelphia, if you like the city sort of nature thing. Grass and flowers and trees growing out of sidewalks. Squirrels running around, and birds singing. Just like home. Except for the trees in sidewalks. I wandered over to a bench across the street from the salon and sat, gazing up into a tree. It was the only way I could avoid looking at all the people swarming around me. That, also, was unlike home.

A shadow fell across my face. "Stella?" Daniella stood on the sidewalk in front of me. She wore a gorgeous gray suit, and in no way could I tell she'd had a stressful week. How could the woman look so perfect after all she'd been through, with Rikki, and the pageant, and everything? And there was no question in my mind. Gregg and his wife could have just as easily been arguing about her as about Rikki.

Daniella took her time giving me the once

over, and eventually returned her focus to my eyebrows. Or what used to be my eyebrows. "I'm so sorry."

"They'll grow back."

She sat next to me, crossing her ankles and clasping her tastefully painted mauve nails in her lap. "I mean I'm sorry about the whole day. I wanted it to be nice for you, after the ways you've supported me this week. It's meant so much." She held up her hands, and let them fall back to her lap. "I wanted to do something to give back just a portion."

"You don't need to—"

"Yes, I do."

I thought back over the day, trying to forget the whole eyebrow experience. "Not all of it was a disaster."

A smile tugged at Daniella's lips. "How reassuring. Which part passed muster? The snacks?"

I grunted. "They were all right. And the lunch."

"That's it?"

"No. The massage was heavenly. And the facial was okay. Except I'm feeling pretty oily right now. And every time I move I smell flowers."

She picked up my hand and examined my nails. "These look nice."

"You mean the technician somehow hid the terrible state my nails were in before."

"They weren't terrible. Just short."

"They're still short."

She gave a short laugh. "Yeah."

We sat in silence. She still held my hand. I was just beginning to feel uncomfortable when she shifted to face me. "Stella, why are you here?"

I pulled my hand away. "Because Miranda made me come. It was a conspiracy at home. I'd been made redundant for the day."

"No. I already know you well enough to realize that if you hadn't wanted to come, you wouldn't have. Just like you wouldn't stay for your makeup consultation."

"That was because I didn't want to get hurt again."

"Makeup doesn't hurt."

"Sure, that's what they all say."

We sat in silence again.

"You were asking questions," she said.

"Not enough, apparently. Otherwise I would have known Miranda's plans for torture."

"You know that's not what I'm talking about." She took a deep breath and let it out. "You were asking about Rikki."

Crap, had the nail girls been talking?

"Misty said you noticed Rikki's photo on the wall."

"Sure. I asked when she'd last been in."

Daniella looked at me knowingly. "Was that all?"

I shrugged, and watched a very fat man waddle past with a very fat dog. He nodded at me, but his gaze was drawn immediately to Daniella, and he watched her until his dog strained at the leash. The man swiveled forward, and rolled off.

"I want to know what happened to her," I said. "Rikki didn't deserve that kind of end, Zach and his friends are freaked out, and I'm having nightmares. Plus, the cops won't leave me alone. I don't know why they think I have any answers."

"They think I have them, too."

"Are you sure you don't?"

She looked across at the salon, but I don't think she was really seeing anything, except maybe images in her mind.

"So what was the fight about?"

"What fight?"

"The one last Wednesday, when Rikki was here."

"How did you hear about that?"

I kept quiet.

She shook her head. "Those girls. I tell them not to talk about clients…"

"Well, they did. So was the fight about Rikki?"

She pinched her lips together, and she tipped her head back to look at the top of the tall brick building across the way. "From what I heard, it was partially about Rikki. And partially about Rikki's friends, and all of the other female artists at Sunburst. And partially about their family life. And partially about…me."

"You?" I didn't know why I was surprised, since I'd just been thinking of this possibility. I'd seen the way Gregg had come on to Daniella—or should I say assaulted Daniella?—at the fair. It was obvious he had things on his mind other than business, or how his daughters' cows were faring. "Why would they be arguing about you? You and Gregg aren't…" I tried not to look too disgusted.

"Oh, no! Please!" Daniella looked as grossed out as I felt. "I would never…he's married, you know. Mrs. Gregg and I are sort of, well, maybe not friends, but we understand each other. We've both had to put up with a lot from her husband. She more than I, of course." She sighed. "Even if he weren't married, I would stay far away because, well, he's not a nice man. I've told you that."

Uh-huh. I'd heard that before. How many women said a guy wasn't nice, or that he was married, and went after him for exactly those reasons? How did I know Daniella wasn't exactly that kind of woman? She might think she knew me after five days, but in my experience, it took a lot longer than that to get to know a person.

The door to the salon opened and Miranda stepped out. She looked back into the salon, waving and smiling, but as soon as the door shut her expression darkened like a tornado. She stood as still as a fencepost, fists straight down by her hips, swiveling her head side to side, reminding me of that movie where the alien comes bursting out of that man's stomach.

"Looks like you're in trouble," Daniella said. The twitch was back on her lips.

"Nothing I can't handle." I let Miranda stew for a while, dodging other pedestrians, scanning the sidewalks, her face growing redder and redder, which seemed to be negating all the pampering she'd had that day. And the red really didn't go with all that makeup. Finally, I stood and stretched. "Thanks for the day, Daniella."

"We're forgiven?"

"You are. Miranda's not."

She smiled. "I can live with that."

Miranda caught sight of us as we crossed the street, and let us come to her, where she stood tapping her foot. I could see the desire in her eyes to strangle me right there on the street. "Where have you been?"

"Sitting right there. Not trying to hide."

"Miranda." Daniella stepped between us. "Thank you so much for spending a day here at Serenity. It means so much to have customers who appreciate what we do here."

Miranda's nostrils flared as she visibly changed her attitude from being pissed at me to being awed by Daniella. Her mouth worked, and she finally smiled. "It was our pleasure. Thank you for fitting us in so quickly. I'm sure we'll be back before—" she choked "—Stella's big day."

"Wonderful. Now, before you go, I was wondering if you had a few more minutes for a surprise."

"I am not going back in there," I said.

"I wouldn't ask you to. I'm taking you some-where else."

Miranda's eyes lit up. "Bridal shop?"

Oh, Lord, help me. I'd gone to one with Lucy the summer before, for her wedding, and it about did me in.

"No." Daniella smothered a laugh. "Some-place better."

"What could be better than a bridal shop?"

The morgue? Hell? *The Price is Right?*

Daniella smiled. "You're getting a tour of Sunburst Studios."

Chapter Forty-one

"I can't go there," I said. "Gregg will sic the guards on me. I'll be lucky to get out of there alive."

"See?" Miranda said. "If you'd let them give you a makeover, he'd never recognize you. Now you just look like...you."

"I'll flash my nails. They're all buffed out. They'll never know it's me."

Daniella laughed. "No reason to worry. I know all about how David feels about you."

"You do?"

"Sure. He told me. As did his wife. And one of the daughters. I think maybe Annie. Anyway, he won't be there today. He's busy getting photos taken at the fair."

"Of his sick dairy cows?"

"No, of his prize calf. And his family. And him, doing down-home events. Now that the showing part is over, he's concentrating on the marketing aspect."

"At a county fair?" Miranda sounded disgusted. "Who cares about that?"

"Half of his customers," Daniella said. "His country music line is growing day by day." Her face darkened. "At least, it was. Losing Rikki will set him back."

I guess that took him out of the running for who would be glad to see her dead. Except it seemed he had Valerie Springfield ready to step in where Rikki left off. At least, she was young and pretty. Even if she was more mainstream than country.

"Come on," Daniella said. "It'll be fun. Maybe you'll see somebody famous."

Miranda clapped. I was beginning to think that was her involuntary response to everything giddy.

Daniella walked us around the square to another shiny building, where we had to show our IDs and walk through a metal detector just to get past the front desk. Nice. We took the elevator up to the ninth floor, and the door opened into a plush lobby. A young, gorgeous woman in a revealing black "dress" sat behind a huge wrap-around desk. As soon as she saw Daniella, she gave a huge smile. "Ms. Troth!"

"Hello, Chrissy. Okay if I give my friends a little tour?"

"Sure! If they could just sign here…"

After Miranda and I signed our lives away saying we wouldn't disclose anything we saw or heard there that day, I guess so no one could copy it, she gave us VISITOR badges. I pointed out a small shrine in the corner, dedicated to Rikki Raines. A poster-sized photo of Rikki in concert was perched on the top of a pyramid kind of thing. The stair-steps down from the top held more photos—Rikki with other singers, on-stage, on the covers of magazines—and her first and only CD, surrounded by a garden's-worth of flowers, taking up a good portion of the lobby. Cards stuck in the arrangements were signed by all sorts of people and companies. Other singers and record labels, actors, television and radio personalities, towns in other areas of Pennsylvania. According to all of them, Rikki had been loved, and would be missed.

A lump formed in my throat. "Can we go now?"

"Sure. This way." Daniella led us down the hallway, where we passed several closed office doors, then entered a large area with couches, a small kitchenette, and bathrooms.

"The green room," Daniella said, "where artists get ready to perform. All sorts of people come through here. There are several studios, some big enough for an orchestra, some smaller, for bands and soloists."

We passed through the green room and came to a large space full of equipment so complex it might as well have been a spaceship. Buttons and tables and slides and microphones, all on the other side of glass, which looked into what I figured was where the artists would go to perform. No one was in there at the moment, so we weren't interrupting anything.

"This one is used for larger groups, which you can tell," Daniella said. "Let's go upstairs and you can see a smaller one."

We walked up stairs, decorated with framed photos of musicians who I assumed must have recorded there, but soon realized that wasn't possible, since Sunburst hadn't been around when some of them had been alive, or still recording. I soon figured out it was just a showcase of artists with a Philadelphia connection: Boyz II Men, Frankie Avalon, Will Smith, Hall & Oates, The Beastie Boys, Patti LaBelle, DJ Jazzy Jeff, Jim Croce, Marian Anderson. I wasn't familiar with all of them, but their names had been conveniently signed on the photos.

"Here we are." Daniella opened the door, and we filed into a smaller, loft-type space. Again, a comfortable room with a refrigerator, but this time the doors on the other end were closed, and a light above them indicated that they were recording.

"Ooh, can we see?" Miranda said, heading over.

I choked. "Miranda!"

"It's okay," Daniella said. "As long as she doesn't start banging on the door, we're okay. This place is soundproofed."

Miranda didn't do any pounding, but she shielded her eyes and peered in the window. She gestured me over, eyes wide. "You'll never guess who's in there."

I joined her, putting my hands around my eyes. I had to look past people in the first room, the one with all the machines, and focus on the room beyond, where Valerie Springfield sang into a microphone.

I stepped back. "Doesn't she record with another label? What's she doing here?" Although I was getting a creepy feeling that I knew, after that weird performance at the pageant.

Daniella also took a look. "I haven't seen her here before. Maybe that's new. Or maybe she just never came to the salon. She is fresh on the scene." She looked troubled. "But we usually get them first thing, for studio shots and appearances. Although I don't think she came to us before the Lovely Miss pageant on Tuesday, not like Rikki did." From what I could see on Daniella's face, she wasn't all too pleased to find Valerie in the building.

"I wish we could hear it," Miranda said, still watching, her face pressed up against the glass.

Daniella strode over to what I thought were light switches, and pushed a button. Music came over some speakers, and we heard Valerie's voice.

Miranda clapped. Again. "It's happening right now!"

Daniella rejoined me in the non-fan section, looking thoughtful.

"Any way to find out when this recording session got scheduled?" I asked.

"Sure." She picked up a house phone, tucked away in the corner, and pushed a couple buttons. "Chrissy, you know Valerie Springfield, who's recording up here in the Penthouse Studio?" She held the phone away from her ear, while Chrissy's voice came over loud and clear and…loud. When it went quiet, Daniella replaced the phone. "When did she get scheduled for this session? I see. How did that happen? Okay. Thank you."

She hung up. "Took a cancellation today. She hadn't been on the books before that."

A gift for helping Taylor win? If so, I don't think Daniella knew anything about it. But how could I be certain?

"Daniella…what were you arguing with Gregg about that day Nick and I saw you?"

"What?"

"Out by the campers. You guys were fighting, and he grabbed you. You, um, kneed him in the boys."

Her face went red. "You saw that?"

"Sorry. Nick and I were just walking through. We didn't even know who you were then. But we were impressed."

Her mouth pinched, and she dropped onto one of the couches. I followed, sitting catty-cornered on an easy chair. She leaned forward, clasping her hands between her knees, and spoke without looking up. "He's a cheater. In every way you can imagine. The cows, of course. With women. Money, I'm sure. Even…"

"The Lovely Miss pageant."

She looked up. "You know?"

"I figured it out."

"And you still talk to me?"

"Yes, because I also figured out that you wanted nothing to do with cheating. Isn't that what you and Gregg were arguing about the other day? You telling him that he was insane if he thought you'd go along with it? If the two of you aren't involved in any other kind of relationship—" I raised my eyebrows, and again she waved off the idea "—you wouldn't have anything to fight about over that, and unless you're bringing your salon business to the fair, it had to be something else. But

I saw him at the pageant, after someone got Valerie in there to take Rikki's place, and I read a text he sent Valerie, telling her to 'do her job.' So for some reason he wanted Taylor to win. What I can't figure out is why. And what would make it so important to him that he would have Rikki taken out so he could replace her with someone else who would help your daughter get the crown. But that just seemed ridiculous to me. So then I started thinking about that marketing thing you'd mentioned that Rikki wouldn't do, and how she'd rebuffed all his advances, so I thought maybe Gregg was tired of her saying no to stuff, so he got rid of her. But then I hear that Valerie's not a true country singer like Rikki was, but more mainstream, so she can't really replace Rikki in the recording industry. She's a different brand."

I leaned my head back on the chair's high back. "If it wasn't Gregg who killed Rikki, I'm at a loss. What if it really was about the Lovely Miss thing? And who would possibly kill someone over a beauty pageant?"

Daniella laughed, but it wasn't a happy, that-was-funny laugh. "You'd be surprised."

Unfortunately, I probably wouldn't. "But you have to know why."

She blinked. "Why Rikki was killed? You think I know? She had only just told me that day what he wanted her to do at the pageant, and I couldn't believe he'd stoop so low. Well, actually, I could, but I couldn't let it go when it involved my daughter. But I knew Rikki wanted no part of cheating, so I trusted her to do the right thing. I had no reason to make sure she wasn't a judge. David called me after her concert to try to convince me again, saying if I would do it, he knew I could convince Rikki, too."

I remembered her getting that call, and the look of annoyance on her face. Nick and I had guessed right about who was calling.

"No, I didn't mean you knew about Rikki and the pageant," I said, "although I'm starting to think it had something to do with her death." A door clicked behind us, but I wanted to know the answer to this question, so I kept on. "What I meant was, you have to know why Gregg wanted Taylor to win the pageant."

"He didn't." Valerie Springfield stood at my shoulder. "He paid me to make sure Summer Moss took home the crown."

Chapter Forty-two

"Summer?" My jaw about hit the floor, for two reasons—one, because who would want that chemical repository to win? and two, because Valerie Springfield was entering our conversation like she'd been a part of it from the start. And like she knew us. When I recovered, I asked, "But why would he want her to win?"

"Don't know." Valerie shrugged, and dropped into one of the other seats. She took a slug from a water bottle and slung her leg over the arm of her chair. "All he told me is to make sure that monstrosity won, and I could do a record with Sunburst. I tried telling him there wasn't a chance in hell that she could come out on top, but he seemed to think I could work magic. I told him, no matter how well she did at the interview and talent, which she was crappy at both, there was no overlooking her distorted body. Now listen, I like to look good, and I'm not afraid to have a little work done to get there, but everything she did, huh-uh. Can you imagine her representing an organization that's supposed to be about health and beauty and 'youthful freshness?' Ugh." She took another drink.

Miranda sat down next to Daniella, and Valerie frowned, looking back and forth between us. "Don't I know you two from somewhere?"

Miranda's eyes widened, but I didn't think the singer would be mad, not after how she'd just spoken to us so frankly. "At the pageant," I said. "My fiancé had you go talk to Miranda, saying she was a big fan, but too shy to talk to you."

Valerie was still frowning. "You're not?"

"Well, sure I am," Miranda gushed. "Not shy, I mean. A fan. But only after hearing you sing right now. You're amazing. But I'd never heard of you before the pageant. Sorry."

"But you'd heard of Rikki."

"Well, yeah. It's kind of hard not to, since she's from around here."

"I guess. But why did you say you wanted to meet me?"

I jumped right in. "My fault. I needed to see your phone, to check out what Gregg had texted to you, so I needed to get you away from the judges' table."

"You looked at my phone?"

"I suspected he was blackmailing you or

something, and I thought the text would be about the pageant, since he'd gotten you placed there."

There was a war on her face of whether to be mad at me or not. Finally, good won out, and she took another sip. "Whatever. There's nothing on there I'm ashamed of. Not like I would've been ashamed—no, more like totally embarrassed—if that hideous girl had won."

Hideous. My word for Summer. I was liking this Valerie, after all.

Valerie smiled at Daniella. "Taylor did so well. With her being the top fave and Summer being, well, herself, I knew there was no chance, even if I put all perfect scores, that the Disgusting Girl would win. So I tried not to sweat it."

"That's why you were happy when Taylor did well," I said.

"How do you know?"

"You were smiling."

"Oh." And then she smiled again. "Guess I couldn't hide it."

"So you're not in trouble with Gregg?" Miranda asked. "I mean, you didn't get his candidate to win."

"I did my best. Sent him a screen shot of my scorecard, which wasn't perfect, because that would've completely raised flags, but was better than she deserved. And I tried to talk her up to the other judges. They thought I was a crazy person. So even though Gregg's a creep, he had to stick with our agreement, which my agent knew all about."

"Your agent went along with all that?"

Valerie was young, but it was obvious in her eyes that she was already jaded. "You keep within the lines all the time, you never get anywhere in this business. Ask Rikki."

"But she was going somewhere, even with her principles. At least it seemed like it."

"Yeah, but look where she is now."

Awkward, sad pause.

"I didn't mean that like, snarky," Valerie said. "Rikki was my friend. She was helping me, introducing me to people."

"But what about that war over the zombie guy? It was in all the magazines."

"Nicholas?" Valerie snorted. "What a joke."

"You weren't both after him?"

"Hardly. I mean the guy's eye candy, for sure, but oh, my God. No brain at all. It was no wonder he was in a zombie show. Completely typecast."

"Then why the publicity about you and Rikki fighting over him?"

"We were all at the same party. He got his picture taken with me and then with Rikki. Turns out, Gregg thought it would be good publicity to get it in the papers. So he leaked the photo of

Rikki and Nic first, then mine a while later. Made it look like it was a love triangle. No way. The guy's an epic dork."

Interesting. No wonder Rikki wanted to keep her relationship with Austin out of the public eye. Who knew what Gregg would do with that. Probably crucify Austin for being a down-home country boy. Or else use him to foster country fans. Either way, I couldn't imagine Rikki wanting the poor guy thrust into the spotlight.

"But Rikki's boyfriend—"

"She had a boyfriend?"

"—said you were worried that she was keeping you from becoming a star."

"Please. The only thing that could keep me from that is my own stuff. Or industry stuff, which I guess could mean her, but didn't. She was cool. I've been doing okay on my own. I had nothing against her. If she thought I did, it was because Gregg or somebody told her so. And seriously? She had a boyfriend? Who was it?"

"What I want to know," Miranda said, going back to the original subject and saving me from having to give up Austin, "was why Gregg wanted Summer to win in the first place."

"I know why he wanted Taylor to win," Daniella said, "but I can't imagine it was the same for Summer."

"Which was?"

"He was going to make sure she went all the way to the top, became the spokesperson for Lovely Miss Pennsylvania, then on to win Nationals. He wanted to use her for marketing Sunburst Studios."

"Kind of lame, isn't it?" Miranda said. "Using a teenage girl's pageant for marketing?"

"Not when you think about who listens to most of the music he's putting out," Daniella said. "Teenage and tween girls are a huge audience, the biggest. Know who votes the most on *American Idol*? All those singing reality shows? Those girls. They basically pick the winner each year. Getting someone like Taylor in a position where she would have influence would be a perfect in-road for someone like Gregg."

"But what about Summer?" Valerie said. "Like, ugh. No girls are going to listen to someone who looks like she got stung by ten thousand radioactive bees."

I laughed. Yeah, this girl was all right. But I still had questions. "So how do we find out why he wanted Summer to win? And more importantly, if this all somehow led to Rikki's death?"

"Would he keep information on it?" Valerie asked. "Like on his computer or in his desk or anything?"

"I doubt it. That would be kind of dumb."

"Besides," Daniella said, "there's no way to check. His office would be locked and loaded, wouldn't it?"

Valerie stared at Daniella, but she wasn't really seeing her, I didn't think. Her face had gone all serious, and she popped the sides of her water bottle in and out, in and out.

"Valerie," I said, "what is it?"

She fidgeted with the bottle. "You know how I said he's a creep?"

We waited.

"It's not just about public events like the pageant. He also wants…other stuff."

"Like degrading marketing campaigns?" I looked at Daniella. She had never told me exactly what Rikki had said no to.

Daniella's nose wrinkled, like she smelled something rotten. "It was a calendar."

"A calendar."

"With practically naked female singers."

"Oh."

"He wants more than pictures," Valerie blurted.

I tried not to show my disgust by puking. "Sex, you mean?"

Valerie looked at the ground, then sat back in her chair, her face hard. "He tried to push it on me. Said if I wanted to get started here, that was one of the *perks*." She spat the word. "I don't know how his wife puts up with him. He goes after anything that moves. I'm not dumb. I know I'm not the first. Rumors were flying during the past few weeks about him and Rikki. I don't know what happened for real, but I do know his wife hated her."

Miranda looked appalled. "What did you say when he propositioned you?"

"What could I say? The man held my career in his hands, I couldn't exactly give him a flat-out no."

According to Daniella, Rikki had told him no, despite the rumors, but then, not everybody could be that strong.

"So I gave him a maybe. This week he said to sweeten the offer, he would let me have this 'job' with the pageant. That if I got good results he would get me in the studio this week, and find a featured artist for my album, like maybe Kelly Clarkson, or even Maroon 5, or somebody." She waved a hand at the studio door. "My agent made sure he followed through." She smiled, looking more like a shark than a young woman. "Gregg hadn't expected me to tell my agent. I guess he thought I wouldn't want to look shady. But my agent's been around a long time. She knows how these things work. And she knows how Gregg works."

"Anyway," I said, "were you going somewhere with this?"

"Actually, I was." She sat up straighter. "Do

you really think this whole pageant thing is the reason Rikki's dead?"

"It's looking more likely all the time. You were a prime candidate up till now, but I'm kind of off that kick now." I smiled, to show I was only half serious.

Valerie's chin trembled, and she rubbed her mouth. "And if we find out why Gregg wanted Summer to win, you think you'll know if he did kill Rikki?"

"I don't know, Valerie. We're sort of grasping at straws here."

She nodded slowly, like she was making a decision. She was here at Sunburst, recording her first album, hoping to make it big, only because of her deal with Gregg. If she screwed that up, who knew what would happen to her. She could just as easily disappear into the wanna-be void as end up on the charts.

Finally, she made her choice. "Would it help to get into his office?"

"It might. There's no way to know."

"But it could?"

"It could."

"Then leave it up to me."

Chapter Forty-three

Gregg's ancient secretary, according to Valerie, was used to his conquests, and while she didn't condone them, she didn't do anything to stop them, either. So when Valerie told her she was supposed to meet him in his office that afternoon, the secretary took it in stride and let Valerie into the inner sanctum. And then Valerie let the rest of us in through a door in the hallway that wasn't marked, but was locked with multiple deadbolts.

"He likes having an escape route," Valerie whispered. "At least, that's what I've been told. Plus, when he's here, he can bring people into the office without anyone knowing."

"Security cameras?" I said.

"Not that I know of. He doesn't want people seeing what all he does in here."

I tried not to think about what exactly she meant, but it was hard not to, with the comfortable couch, the thick carpet, and the heavy curtains, which served as much for showing off money as for privacy and comfort and the whole brothel feeling. I wasn't going to get anywhere close to the couch, because it looked like the main place for Gregg to get up to those things he didn't want anyone to see. That wouldn't be a problem, staying far away from it, because the room was the size of my barn.

"So what are we searching for?" Miranda said, and we all shushed her. She rolled her eyes. "Sorry," she hissed. "If the secretary's that's ancient, she won't be able to hear us."

"Anything that has to do with the Lovely Miss pageant," Daniella said. "Or Summer."

Valerie stayed by the door, probably thinking about how her career was going to blow up if we were discovered, and wondering if it was worth it. Daniella had sat right down at the desk, and turned on the computer. While it booted up, she looked through desk drawers.

Miranda opened a closet door and was struck silent when she saw the contents. Clothes. Shoes. A full-length mirror. Not all for Gregg, unless he made a habit of trying on women's lingerie. Miranda dove in with enthusiasm.

I kept my hands in my pockets and wandered around—avoiding the sofa—thinking that maybe something would pop out at me. Platinum records? Nah. The artists weren't my type, and couldn't possibly be threatened by a white, country girl. White baby grand? For heaven's sake. Did Gregg even play piano? Or was Liberace going to stop by? A stocked bar, a conference table so shiny I could see my reflection, photos of Gregg with every famous Philadelphian he'd ever come into contact with. Bill Cosby, Pink, Dr. J., Supreme Court Justice Alito, Kevin Bacon, Chase Utley, and Cliff Lee. In addition, there were plenty of other celebrities from other places, including politicians, actors, musicians, and models.

Moving around the room toward his desk, I studied another set of photos. These were more focused on local charities, where Gregg had lent his studio name and celebrities to further a cause. Or, more like, to further his own cause. The photos centered around him and people I supposed were the organizers of various benefits, rich folks who wanted to either make the world a better place, or avoid paying taxes by pretending to care about the needy.

Yes, I know how I sound.

Rikki was in several of the photos with him, sometimes in formal wear, sometimes in her concert dress. In all of them she smiled brightly, standing in groups with Gregg and the philanthropists, also dressed to the nines. Men, women, children… Summer's mom.

"Hey," I said, too loudly. "Look here."

The others trotted over and followed my finger to the photo.

"That's her," Miranda said.

"But who's with them?"

"Gregg," Miranda said.

"Gee, thanks."

"Just trying to help."

Daniella leaned close to the photo. "I don't know any of those other people. They would be part of the charity, I guess. Does anyone know the organization?"

Physicians United. Who'd ever heard of them?

"Let's look it up," Miranda said.

I took a step back. "But not in here."

"Right," Valerie said. "Let's go." She turned to leave.

"Valerie," I said. "You'd better lock up after us and go out the way you came in."

"But Gregg didn't get here."

"Tell the secretary he called to say he was running late, or was in the hospital. Or found a girl at the fair he liked better."

She made a face. "I'm sure that wouldn't surprise the old lady. Okay, you guys go on. But make sure there's nobody in the hallway."

"Where should we meet?"

"Back up in the green room. I have another

recording session starting—" she looked at her phone "—in twenty minutes."

We peered into the corridor, and when the coast was clear, we hustled out and up the stairs. Miranda had her phone out and searching before we'd even sat down.

"Physicians United. 'To make the world a more beautiful place.' It says here they're a group of plastic surgeons who go on mission trips to help kids in developing countries, you know, who have been born with cleft palates or whatever."

"A worthy cause," Daniella said. "Where do they get their money?"

Miranda poked around a little longer. "Private donations. Federal grants. Some software pioneer guy. And—" she looked up at me, wide-eyed "—the Wilbur and Sherry Moss Foundation."

It took me a second. But then it hit me. "They're named specifically. By name."

"We got that," Miranda said. "It says their names."

"But you know what that means."

"They like to give away money?"

"It means they *have* a lot of money. And Gregg would know that."

Miranda kept messing with her phone. "Wilbur's dead. Died of a heart attack six months ago."

"Ms. Moss doesn't seem to have taken her

husband's death very hard," I said. "You saw the way she drooled over Nick."

"Everybody drools over Nick."

"Not Daniella."

Daniella gave a small smile. "Not that he's not very good-looking, of course."

"What did I miss?" Valerie burst into the room. Miranda filled her in.

Valerie made a face. "What do you want to bet one of those physicians rewards the Mosses' contributions with free plastic surgery?"

"Not a bet I want to take," Miranda said, "because it's plain to see."

"So." I sat in the easy chair again. "What does this all mean?"

"Duh," Miranda said. "That's obvious, too. Gregg wants to tap into that money. This studio takes tons of money to operate, plus look at his office. How expensive was that to furnish? And his mansion up north? When Daniella and Taylor wouldn't go along with the whole cheating thing, he moved right on to the next thing. If he couldn't get her as his Front Page spokesperson to make money that way, he'd go on to the next best thing, which might actually be a better thing—cold, hard cash. Which means he needed Summer."

"Like a runner-up?" I said.

Valerie laughed. "Yes. Just like that."

But it wasn't funny. "Runner-up. Summer is the runner-up."

They all looked at me. "So?" Miranda said, speaking what they all were thinking.

"Remember that emcee's description of the runner-up? That she would take over if something kept the winner from being able to perform the role?" They still didn't get it. "Just how important is it to Gregg that Summer actually be Lovely Miss Pennsylvania?"

The blood drained from Daniella's face. "You mean—"

"—if Gregg wants the Mosses' money, he's going to get it. Even if it means forcing Summer into Taylor's role."

Chapter Forty-four

We were flying back to the fair in Daniella's car, although I was driving. Daniella was in the back seat and on the phone, texting Taylor, texting Zach, calling whoever she could think of. I had Watts' phone number, as well as several other cops', seeing how they'd been hounding me for more information, so she was sending them information, too. Watts said she'd be on the lookout for Taylor, who wasn't answering her phone, and would also be watching for Gregg and his thugs.

"Take the wheel for a second," I told Miranda.

"What? Why?"

"I'm going to call Willard."

"But, traffic!"

"Miranda. We're not moving."

The Schuyllkill was not only packed, like on any regular day, but at a complete standstill. This meant it was Friday, which caused traffic to behave even worse. We were moving at a lame snail's pace, if at all.

I got Willard's voice mail and told him what was going on. I was sure he would at least be in touch with other law enforcement, even if he couldn't get there himself.

Zach texted Daniella back, saying Taylor was fine. He was watching her at that very moment, awarding a junior 4-H prize to a kid who'd made a photo collage of her dog.

"So she's okay," Miranda said. "That's good, right?"

"Of course it's good," I said. Had the woman turned into an idiot? "But it doesn't mean she's safe."

"Do I call Gregg?" Daniella said. "Should I let him know we're onto him, or would that just make him act sooner?"

"Call him," Miranda and I said together. We glanced at each other, not quite sure what had just happened. Had we actually agreed on something?

Daniella punched some numbers, but was soon groaning. "He's not answering. I'll try again." But the same thing happened. The third time, she left a message asking him to please call her, and to not do anything rash, that it would just be bad for everybody, and that the cops were keeping an eye on Taylor. She hung up and sank back into the seat. "I knew I never should have let her be in that pageant. I knew it couldn't be good for her."

I glanced into the rearview mirror. "Daniella, she's going to be okay. And listen, it's not the pageant's fault." Again, like when I'd complimented Bryan, I thought maybe the week's heat had fried my brain. "The pageant has nothing to do with this."

"Of course it does. If she hadn't won—"

"She won because she deserved it. She's in danger because Gregg is a crazy man. It's his fault. Nobody else's."

"His wife," she said, like I hadn't been talking. "I'll call her." She dialed, and held the phone up to her ear. I expected a repeat of what had happened with Gregg, but suddenly Daniella was talking. "Edie? Hey, is your husband with you? No? Do you know where he is? I need to talk to him. No, no, it's about…business. Okay. I understand. If you see him, could you please—Great. Thank you." She hung up, but didn't look appeased. "I don't know who else to call."

"Miranda," I said, "call Nick. Tell him what's happening."

"We don't want him going over there."

"He'll want to know."

"I don't think—"

"Call him."

"Fine." She did, and explained the situation.

When she was done, she thrust her phone toward me. "He wants to talk to you."

"Stella?"

His voice made me tear up. "Hey."

"What do you want me to do?"

"I don't know. I just…wanted you to know what was going on."

"Thanks, Babe. Maybe I'll go over there. See if I can help."

I figured that's what he'd do, and it was the last thing I wanted, to put him even close to danger. But he was an adult, and he cared about people. I couldn't hold out information from him just to keep him safe.

"Be careful, okay?"

"You know I will."

"I love you."

"You, too."

For once, Miranda didn't make a gagging sound. Or even look like she wanted to. "How about Carla?" she said, instead.

"Sure."

She called her, and let her know what was happening. Carla said she and Bryan would keep an eye out. Taylor was going to be watched over well, whichever way you looked at it.

Traffic finally began moving once we reached Route 476, and before we knew it, we were only a couple miles from the fair. Daniella was sitting forward on the seat, looking out the front window, as if she could see her daughter from there. As soon as I pulled into the grassy lot, she shrieked at me to stop the car, and went bounding across toward the entrance.

"Go with her," I said.

Miranda, for once, didn't question me, and took off without a backward glance. I found the closest spot and pulled the car in. As I trotted toward the entrance, I called Nick. "Where are you?"

"With Zach and Taylor, and about twenty cops. We're in the home arts building."

"So she's safe?"

"She's fine. And there's been no sign of Gregg."

I stood inside the gate and looked around, like I might see him right there. "Okay. I'll be there in a minute. I want to check a couple places first." I began walking toward the calf barn, where I knew Gregg's daughter Melody still had a stall.

"I'll join you."

"No, stay with Taylor."

"Stella, she's got a couple dozen bodyguards. Plus Zach. He's not going to let anything happen to her."

"Which worries me. He's not equipped to be facing a killer."

"Neither are you."

"I've done it before."

"That doesn't mean—"

"I'm going to the calf barn. Meet me there."

He hung up, and I moved faster. The calf barn was empty when I got inside. A few kids just leaving, but that wasn't surprising, since all of the animal judging events were over. There was really nothing left to do with the calves except make sure they were fed and watered before taking them home the next day, so the 4-H'ers were ready for a last night on the fairway, leading up to the fireworks display at dusk. I knew Zach and Taylor weren't at Barnabas' stall, and there was no sign of Randy or Laura, either, or even Austin. The place was deserted. Except…there was some movement over on the other side of the barn.

I tried to see who it was, but whoever it was was kind of skulking around. It was weird. Like a shadow, or a really slow-moving slug person. Quietly and slowly, I made my way around the outside of the stalls to come up behind the slug person, in the row.

It was Mrs. Gregg. She was standing all the way up now, and petting her daughter's calf with her left hand. And she held something else in her right, that was shiny and long and…it was a syringe.

I crept closer. What was she doing? Whatever it was, it couldn't be good. Not with a shot in her hand. She was murmuring quietly to the calf, rubbing its ears, telling it that everything would be okay. That it would go quickly. And then she put the needle against the calf's neck.

I shot my hand out, knocking the syringe onto the wood chips. The calf balked, stepping back, right on the syringe, breaking the tube and spilling the solution into the ground. I grasped Mrs. Gregg's wrist as she tried to squirm away. "What are you doing?"

Her eyes were wild. "Nothing. I didn't do anything."

"You were going to."

"Stella?" Nick hustled up the row.

"Call Carla. Tell her we need her here right now."

He didn't question me, but pulled out his phone and made the call.

"I thought it was over," I said to Mrs. Gregg.

She sobbed once. "I did, too. I thought it was over, but he said no. He said we could use them all again. That it was important to the girls. To our family. I tried to tell him that he was the only one who wanted it, but he wouldn't listen." She looked up at me with wide doe eyes. "After that happened the other day with the lemon, it all became so clear.

If the cows couldn't compete, we could end all this."
She sobbed again, sinking toward me, rather than
pulling away. "Everyone hates us here. They always
have, but David doesn't care. He says it's good for
the girls. Good for business. And I just…" She
deflated, her wrist hanging loosely in my hand.

"What were you giving to the calf?"

"Just something calming. Something to make
him sleep."

"Forever?"

She gazed at the sweet little calf. "It wouldn't
have hurt. He would have just—" She dropped
toward the ground, like she was demonstrating. I
caught her and laid her over some straw bales. Her
skin sagged, and gray touched the roots of her hair.
Her clothes draped on her bony arms and legs, and
her mouth hung slack. She looked…pathetic.

Nick and I stared down at her.

The 4-H fair criminal mastermind.

Chapter Forty-five

"Mrs. Gregg sent me the texts," Carla said. "She said so, and they checked out the number. It was hers. She hadn't even tried to disguise it. She had nothing against me, not really, but she wanted to make it seem like it was someone else making the animals sick. Someone who was out to get me, rather than someone who was out to get her. And all because that first night I told her she was imagining things when she'd called me about her animals. Well, I didn't say it exactly in those words. I was more polite. But she figured, why not blame me, or someone connected to me?" She shook her head. "It's not hard to get Acepromazine, that's the sad part. She was going to shoot that calf so full of it, he'd never wake up. Sick."

I thought about Ace, and how it acted. I still hadn't heard what had paralyzed and killed Rikki Raines, but I really didn't think it was the same medicine. Ace would have put the calf to sleep, but it wouldn't have choked it to death. It would have just…made everything stop working. Rikki had been smothered by whatever it had been. Paralyzed so her throat no longer allowed air through. Maybe not a huge distinction, but the only one I'd heard about so far.

We sat on blankets in the grassy area of the grandstand track. We, along with all the other fair families, had free reign of the space. The public had to watch the fireworks from the grandstand, or the parking lot. I leaned back against Nick, nursing my tired foot, and Carla curled up with Bryan. Miranda occupied a corner of the blanket, pretending to ignore us all. We had a clear line of sight to Zach and Taylor, and their group. Taylor apparently hadn't taken her mother's warnings too well. "Mom, Mr. Gregg is not going to do anything to me. Nobody cares that much about this pageant. Geez. Will you chill?"

So the adults had to make believe they were "chilling," which we all actually were, since Gregg would have been called to deal with his wife, the wanna-be-calf-killer, and I couldn't imagine he'd get away anytime soon, especially since he couldn't exactly say, "I need to go to get rid of this girl who's keeping me from a lot of money." But then, there wasn't that huge a rush. He could get rid of her in a much more private venue after the fair was over.

Not exactly a comforting thought.

Even with the very slim chance of Gregg trying anything at that particular time, people didn't take a teenage girl's safety lightly. Willard sat with Taylor and her friends, under the pretense of hanging out with Brady, and Daniella and Amy hung around, too. Several cops, including Watts, hung around just in general, since, as Brady had mentioned all the way back on that first day, stupid stuff happens at the fair. The cops all knew Gregg by sight, of course, since he was a personal friend of the sheriff, so tension was rather low. They had no evidence that Gregg had harmed Rikki, and nothing tangible to show that he was out to get Taylor. Just the brains of us women who had put it all together, which the cops weren't exactly keen on. Watts listened politely, then said she'd look into it. Great. That kind of enthusiasm inspires so much confidence.

Speaking of brains, mine was tired. I looked forward to watching bright lights explode in the sky.

Several girls I recognized from the pageant had come over to talk to Taylor, including the second runner-up, who had been so excited to place. She wore her banner proudly, and gave Taylor a big hug before skipping off with a guy her age who looked like a gentle, love-crazed linebacker. Cute. Summer hadn't dropped by, thank goodness, and

I hadn't even gotten a glimpse of her, which made the evening much more pleasant.

I would be glad when the show was over, and Taylor and her mom were home safe. Although I think the plan was for them to spend the night at Claire and Bobby's, so they wouldn't be alone.

"How long till the fireworks start?" Nick asked.

I snuggled up against him. "With any luck, before I fall asleep."

He squeezed me. "I don't mind if you do. But seriously, how long?"

"Well, it's not dark yet. A half hour, maybe? Why?"

"Can we move around a little bit? I'm feeling a bit tingly."

I sat up fast. "Are you having an episode?"

"No. I'm okay. I think it's just sitting on this hard ground. It's pinching my nerves." He smiled, and I almost believed him that he was okay.

I stood up and gave him my hands to pull him up. "We'll be back," I told Carla and Bryan. "Save our spots."

We picked our way through the other people scattered throughout the grass, until we made it to the outer edge, and the racetrack, which was fairly clear, because who would want to sit on cinders?

"Want to walk?" I asked him.

In response, he took my hand and we headed

counter-clockwise, taking our time, not moving fast. I kept my eyes open for Gregg, but he was nowhere to be seen, which was lucky for him. I was ready to take him down.

Several times people called to us and we waved, but we kept going, not wanting to make small talk with folks we hadn't seen for ages, or talk about the week's adventures with those we had. It was nice just to walk and not have to think.

Almost fifteen minutes later we made it back to our starting spot. I shook Nick's hand. "Want to go again? It's still light enough."

He slid his hand out of mine and stretched his arms above his head, causing several women in our vicinity to hyperventilate. I watched him, too, enjoying the view, and saw the exact moment something caught his eye.

"What is it?" I turned, but didn't see anything that stood out.

"Isn't that Summer's mom?" He pointed, and I had to do that thing where I got eye level with his finger in order to pick her out of the crowd. She was standing far behind our group, her phone at her ear. I didn't see Monster Daughter with her, but that didn't mean she wasn't around somewhere, waiting to take over for Taylor, should something happen. Looking past Sherry Moss, I saw another familiar face, headed our way. Laura. I guess she hadn't made it in time to come with the crowd. I saw the moment she noticed Taylor's group, and angled her approach that way, although it was slow going through the crowded grass. My phone buzzed, and I checked it. A text from Willard.

just heard med called botulinum toxin A. like botulism. more soon.

I shared the text with Nick. "Weird, right? Food poisoning doesn't paralyze you, does it?"

"Actually, I think I've heard it can in severe cases. But food poisoning doesn't paralyze you, and then shove you in a manure pile."

I hoped more answers were coming, because this wasn't really helping.

There was movement up at Zach and Taylor's group, and Taylor stood, talking on her phone, then looking somewhere off to the side. I followed her gaze, but saw nothing that stuck out. Taylor was frowning, and searching the area, so I guessed she didn't see what she was looking for, either. She took a step away from her group, and about five pairs of arms reached for her. She waved them off, saying something, probably, "Will you guys cut it out?" She waved at Zach, and he stood up. I watched for Claire's reaction, but for once, she didn't seem to notice. She was too busy talking to Randy. Hmm.

Zach and Taylor picked their way through the

crowd toward a stand selling peanuts and cotton candy. I looked back at Daniella, who seemed torn. Yes, her daughter was possibly in danger, but also yes, she was in a very public place, with all kinds of people watching out for her. And there was still no sign of Gregg, and a very low possibility he'd come anywhere close.

I waved, catching Daniella's eye, and indicated by pointing two fingers at my eyes that I would keep watch over Taylor. Daniella nodded her thanks.

"Where are they going?" Nick said, watching as Zach and Taylor passed the stand. "I thought they were just hungry."

Hustling to catch up, we went to the food vendor, then looked past it. Taylor and Zach had disappeared into the crowd.

"Where'd they go?" Nick said.

Blood rushed from my head until I saw Taylor's reddish hair, bobbing as she and Zach walked away from the grassy area. "There they are. Come on."

Nick followed me, but his attention was on his phone, where I spied that he was checking out the medicine Willard had just named. I grabbed his elbow and pulled him along with me, making sure he didn't run into anything, or anybody. Taylor and Zach were moving ahead.

"Nick, we need to keep moving if we're going to stay with them."

"Sorry." He walked faster, but kept his eyes on his phone.

"Where are they going?" I muttered under my breath. I hoped they weren't sneaking away to make out. That was not something I wanted to walk in on.

We kept going, until it became clear they were headed for the calf barn. Great. Just where I wanted to go, after finding Mrs. Gregg almost murdering the calf. We stopped just outside the door, and I peered in, not wanting them to know I was watching.

"See anything?" Nick asked.

"Just calves." I checked out the row where the Greggs' calf was, since that was where I'd last seen someone skulking around, but all was quiet.

"Laura?" Taylor's voice sounded loud in the barn. "Where are you?"

Laura? I wondered. *Why would she be looking for her here? I'd just seen Laura over at the grandstands, headed for Taylor and her crowd.*

"She used her mom's phone and said we should meet her here," Taylor said to Zach. "She was afraid she couldn't find us with all the people over there."

"Maybe she meant the dairy barn. I'll go look."

"I'll stay here in case she comes."

Zach came our way, and we jumped around the corner while he went between barns. I went right back to my spot once he was out of sight. Taylor stood in the middle of the empty barn, hands on her hips. "Laura?"

"Oh, God," Nick breathed. "Botulinum Toxin A."

My heart stopped at the look on his face. "What about it?"

He held out his phone. "Commercially called Botox."

The name hung in the air between us. Botox. That cosmetic drug I'd thought about so many times that week, always in conjunction with two people. Summer. And her mother.

"It's used to paralyze parts of your body," Nick said. "If your body is paralyzed, it can't wrinkle. So if enough of it got injected into the right place, it could paralyze other parts of you, like…"

Like Rikki Raines' throat.

I thought back to a few minutes ago. "Summer's mom was just back at the fireworks. I saw her. She was talking on her phone. She couldn't possibly be—"

Sherry Moss crept out of the shadows at the side of the barn, right behind the stall where Taylor was standing. She stood still for a moment, then made a sudden move toward the girl, raising her arm.

I burst into the barn. "Taylor! Run!"

Taylor jumped and turned, causing Sherry to miss with whatever weapon she held in her hand. She stumbled against a stall, then spun to swing at Taylor again. I sprinted down the aisle and cannoned into the woman, knocking her to the dirt floor. Something sharp jabbed into my arm and I jerked away, then clutched Sherry's wrist, banging her hand against the ground until the syringe in her fingers skittered away.

Nick ran up behind me and grabbed Sherry's arms. I scooted back on her legs so she couldn't kick.

"Nick?" Sherry said. "Nick, what are you doing? You need to listen to me."

"Rope, Taylor. There!" I jerked my chin toward a lead hanging on a post, and Taylor grabbed it and tossed it to Nick, who used it to tie Sherry's wrists together. He didn't respond to her repeated protests. I flipped her onto her stomach, partly to keep her from talking, and partly to get Nick out of her sightlines, and since I just had one rope, I looped one of her legs into the knot already tying her wrists. When I'd finished, I flopped onto my back, my heart going like a stampede.

Footsteps pounded up behind me, and I

swung up onto my knees to defend myself. I froze. "Zach?"

"What's going on?" He looked incredulously at Summer's mother, squirming and shrieking that, "She doesn't deserve the crown!" and "I paid good money for that title!"

Nick took a few steps away from Sherry's flailing limbs, talking on his phone, a finger stuck in his other ear. I heard him say "Watts" and "calf barn," but other than that I just had to guess the rest of the conversation.

"Ms. Moss?" Taylor squeaked. "What are you doing?"

Sherry spat dirt from her mouth. "Trash. That's all you are. Not an image of perfection, like Summer. She was supposed to win, not you."

Taylor's forehead furrowed. "I'm sorry you're disappointed."

"Disappointed?" Sherry let out a high, maniacal laugh. "I'm not disappointed. I got cheated. I paid a fortune for that crown. I was supposed to win!"

"I don't understand. *You* were?"

"Watts is coming," Nick said.

"The detective?" Taylor said. "Why?"

"Are you really that stupid?" Sherry hissed. "You think I'm going to work this hard, then let you walk away with the title?"

And suddenly Taylor seemed to get it. Her eyes widened. "You mean you—"

"—killed that cheater Rikki Raines, with her famous white hair. And I would do it again. You were going to go along with it, too, with all the conspiracy. In fact, you did, didn't you, with that new judge? Took the crown away from me and my beautiful girl. We deserve that title. I'm going to make sure we get it."

"Mom?" Summer was suddenly there, staring down at her hog-tied mother. I'm sure her brow would have been furrowed, like Taylor's, if it had had any flexibility. But her face was a smooth, blank mask. Perhaps it was from Botox. Perhaps it was just because the girl had no brain cells that knew how to function.

"Summer!" Sherry cranked her neck to look up at her daughter. "Summer, go get Mr. Gregg. Get him now! He'll vouch for me. He'll tell them how I deserved to win that pageant!"

Summer still looked like she'd been frozen in a very dumb place, her grotesque lips sticking out in a pucker. "What do you mean, you deserve it?" she finally said. "Wasn't I the one in the pageant?"

Surprisingly good question, coming from that surprisingly outrageous mouth.

"Has anyone seen Laura?" Taylor said. "I got a phone call saying she needed me to meet her here."

Summer frowned. "No. But Mom texted me, saying you wanted to talk, so that's why I'm here."

The girls looked at each other, then down at Sherry, who lay face down on the dirt, pounding her forehead.

Loud voices and the sound of many footsteps came from the doorway, and we were soon overrun by Watts and her gaggle of cops.

"Syringe," I said, pointing.

Watts bagged it immediately, then came back to me. "Tell me."

So I gave her my theory, that Gregg had approached Sherry about trading the win for money, but that they had to find a way to get Rikki to cooperate. Sherry found a way. To get rid of her and bribe someone new. But then Taylor spoiled it all by actually winning.

Rotten kids.

Watts patted my knee. "We'll need to talk more."

"I know."

"But, hey. Thanks."

I nodded, and watched as Watts looked over my shoulder, her face brightening. She jumped up. "Dad! I mean, Sheriff." She smiled. "I believe we've solved the case."

He smiled indulgently and squeezed her

shoulders. Not exactly a boss/underling response, but a great dad/daughter one.

"Hey." Nick came over and squatted beside me. "You okay?"

I rolled my shoulder. "I think she got me with that syringe."

"Are you going numb?"

"Just tingly. I don't think she got a chance to push the plunger."

Nick shook his head. "We'll get it checked out."

"Maybe." I held out my hands and he stood to help me up. "Shall we go outside?"

"Don't leave!" Watts called after us.

I gave her a backward wave, but kept going. She had her hands full with Sherry and Summer, Taylor and Zach, and Daniella, who had already arrived, having sprinted from the grandstand after Nick had been so thoughtful as to call her. The woman didn't even look out of breath, or the slightest bit disheveled. Disgusting.

I limped outside, glad to breathe the fresh air, and took a minute to watch the fireworks, which had begun bursting over the grandstand.

"Don't really need those, do we?" Nick said.

I leaned into him. "How is it that we have so many of our own?"

He kissed the top of my head. "Most of the time that's a good thing."

A movement across the way caught my eye. A shadow. A person. "Hang on." I speed-walked over, just in time to catch Gregg when he peeked back around the corner. His eyes widened, but he couldn't move fast enough to get away. I clutched his shirt, wanting to beat the crap out of him, but knowing it would only make things worse.

"Let go!" he demanded.

I didn't. "Do you realize how much trouble you've caused?"

"Where?"

"Everywhere."

He jerked, trying to get away, scrabbling at my hands.

I leaned into his face. "You are a cheater in everything you do. Work. Family. Life. Even cows. How does that not bother you?"

He finally ripped himself away from my hands. His shirt hung open, the buttons popped, but he stood tall. "I don't cheat. I take advantage of opportunities. It's how you survive in this world."

"No matter who it kills?"

He blinked several times. "What do you mean? I didn't kill anybody."

"Really? You have no idea what you did? You

can't see that what you began ended up with Rikki's death?"

"Rikki? I didn't touch that girl. She made her own choices. She knew how things worked. She knew what she had to do in order to get ahead in this worl—"

And then I couldn't help it.

I punched him in the face.

Chapter Forty-six

"Where are we going?"

Nick smiled. "Just get in the truck."

"We're not going somewhere embarrassing, are we? No surprise party or anything?"

"Stella, your birthday is over."

"Engagement party?"

"We got engaged a long time ago."

"So why won't you tell me?"

"Will you just get in?"

He slid in his side, so I really had no choice except to follow suit. It was Monday, three days after the fiasco at the fair, and I was back in the truck, not exactly willing to go somewhere that hadn't been explained. My shoulder was back to its usual self, the tingling I'd experienced just from the prick of Sherry's needle, rather than any Botox actually making its way into my arm. And my brain was fried from too many police interviews.

At least that was all over. Taylor was safe.

Sherry Moss was locked away. Carla's job was intact. Life was back to pre-fair parameters. Mostly.

It had been a long and exhausting weekend. All those loose ends to tie up, and interviews to attend, and statements to sign. It was also educational—not that I wanted to ever learn how Sherry stole Botox from one of her Physicians United contacts, swiped Austin and Taylor's numbers from her daughter's phone—remember how Daniella had said the pageant girls shared everything?—and basically decided life wasn't worth living without a stupid tiara. Talk about twisted. Summer was now without a parent or a tiara, Rikki was dead, and the Gregg girls had lost both their father and their livelihood because of his collusion in the whole pageant-fixing thing. Not to mention that Mrs. Gregg was having her own troubles with the law for mistreatment of animals.

It was a sick, sick world, and I was ready to distance myself from all of it.

Miranda came running out of the house. Nick sighed, and rolled down his window.

"Where are you going?" she demanded. "When are you coming back?"

He rested his head on the steering wheel. "What is this, the Inquisition?"

"I just want to know."

"Why?"

She blinked. "Because."

"Uh-huh. Okay. Miranda, my fiancée and I are going on a date. We'll see you later."

"A date in the middle of the day?"

"People have been known to do that. It's called…doing stuff. See ya, sis."

He closed his window and drove out the lane, reaching over to grab my hand once he hit the road. He pulled my hand up and kissed it.

"Nick."

"Hmm?" He grinned.

"Why are you acting so weird?"

"Kissing your hand is weird? Smiling is weird?"

I narrowed my eyes. "No. You're just…I don't know."

"Trust me. You'll be happy you came. You do trust me, right?"

"Of course I do."

"And you love me? You don't regret saying you'd marry me?"

"Nick—"

"Sorry. Sorry, I won't ask again." But his smile was gone, and little worry lines appeared around his eyes.

"Nick, pull over."

"What? Here?"

"Wherever."

He pulled into the parking lot of the Care and

Share Thrift Store, and put the truck in park. His smile had vanished, and he wouldn't meet my eyes.

I took off my seat belt and scooted to the middle of the seat. "Nick." I turned his face toward me, and he finally looked at me with those gorgeous, blue eyes. "Nick, I have never regretted for one moment that you came into my life. Well, no, that's not true, during those first couple months I regretted it a lot." I smiled. "But never since then. Never since we realized how we felt about each other. Especially after…after this week, I realize just how much you mean to me. I can't imagine life without you anymore. You are…my life. I just… after all that's happened, I'm feeling, well, vulnerable. It's not that my feelings for you have changed. No, actually, maybe they have. I feel even more in love with you than I did a week ago."

Tears glistened in his eyes, and my heart skipped a beat. "Nick, what's wrong? Are you sick? Do you feel bad?" I choked. "Do you wish we weren't engaged?"

"No! No." He closed his eyes briefly, then turned to me and took my hands in his. He searched my face for a long time. "Stella, I feel fine. It's nothing to do with being sick. And listen, I haven't ever, not for one day, regretted that I fell into your life. There were times I've been angry about it. And I've wished I didn't love you, back when you hated me."

"I never—"

He put a finger on my mouth. "But I've loved you since the moment I walked into your office that very first day. There's just something about you I can't resist." He finally smiled again.

"Okay. Good." I let myself breathe. "So why are you acting so weird?"

He ran his finger along my forehead, my cheekbone, my neck. Along the collar of my shirt.

"Nick, if you don't stop, I'm going to jump you right here in the parking lot, and I don't think the Mennonite ladies bringing old clothes to the thrift store would appreciate that."

He smiled, and took his hand away. "Fine. But listen. You said you trust me, right?"

"Of course."

"And you still love me?"

"Nick—"

"Then trust me just a little longer. Please."

I waited, and when I realized he wasn't going to say anything else, I scooted back over to the passenger seat and put on my seatbelt. "Fine. Let's go. Wherever we're going. Even if this is all weird."

He started the truck and pulled out of the drive. "You won't regret it. I promise."

We drove northeast, not saying anything else,

not even listening to the radio. Nick held my hand, and I did my best to relax, and remember that Nick would never do anything to hurt me.

Twenty minutes later we reached the outskirts of Doylestown. Lunch at the Italian Place? Or the gourmet deli? He had made me wear decent clothes, after all. I glanced over at him, but he wasn't giving anything away.

We drove up the main drag, the turned onto Court Street. Nick found a space along the road and parked.

"Nick?"

He smiled. "Come on."

My stomach was doing the whole butterfly thing now. He took my hand, that warm, familiar gesture, and led me up the walk.

"Nick, are we…"

We walked up the wide cement stairs and through the glass doors.

"Nick, are we getting our marriage license?"

He pulled me over to a wooden bench and sat me down. "We don't need to get a marriage license."

"Why not? Are we…Nick, I'm confused. Just a few minutes ago you said you still wanted to marry me."

"Oh, yes. I do." I heard the doors swish open, and Nick glanced over my shoulder and smiled. "Here they are."

"Here who is?" I scooted around on the bench and saw Carla and Bryan. "Wait. Are they getting a marriage license?"

"No. At least, not that I know of."

I stood up. "Carla, what are you doing here?"

She raised her eyebrows at Nick. "Haven't told her yet?"

"No, I…" He reached back and pulled something out from under his shirt, where he'd had it tucked into his jeans. An envelope. "We don't have to get a marriage license, because we already have one."

My mouth drifted open.

"You've been so annoyed with Miranda and all her planning—I can't blame you, of course—and the idea of having an actual church wedding freaks you out so much, I thought, why go through all that? Especially after you came home Friday after being at that salon. No way was I going to let Miranda put you through that again. So…" He waggled the envelope.

"You can get a marriage license without me?"

"Well, um, I know somebody."

"Who pretended to be me?"

"No, who notarized the application."

I stared at him. "Isn't that illegal?"

"Stella!" Carla laughed. "Do you really care? Seriously?"

"No, I guess not, it's just…what exactly are we doing here?"

Nick smiled and handed the envelope to Carla before taking my hands. "You said you still wanted to get married, right?"

"Yes."

"Well, then, how about we do it today?"

Today. He wanted to get married. Today. "But your mom. Miranda."

"They'll survive. They can throw us a reception if they want, some other time. But today…" He pulled me close and put his arms around me. "I want our wedding day to be something you enjoy, too. Something you're not nervous and tense and angry about. It should be just us."

"And us," Carla said, giggling.

"Yeah, why them?"

"Witnesses," Nick said. "We needed two, and I figured Carla was the person you'd choose out of anybody."

"Well, sure." I gave a little laugh. "You want to marry me right now?"

"More than anything."

"Wearing jeans?"

"What else should we be wearing?"

I didn't know what to say.

"So, Stella. Please, will you marry me right now?"

I looked at Carla, who was smiling and nodding so hard she looked like one of those stupid bobbleheads people put on their dashboards. Bryan even looked pleased by the idea, but his reaction was a lot more subtle.

Nick seemed hopeful, and happy, and a little bit nervous. I slid my arms around his neck and pulled him close. "Of course I'll marry you right now, you wonderful man."

"That's good," he said into my hair. "Because the justice of the peace is waiting for us."

"You made a reservation?"

"That's how I roll, Babe."

We filed into the little courtroom, where a gray-haired woman waited for us with a smile and a rose, which she handed to me. "You must be the Crown and Hathaway party."

Nick squeezed my hand. "We are."

"Congratulations on this momentous day. Shall we begin?"

"Yes," I said. "Let's begin right away."

And so I promised to love, cherish, and honor Nick, forsaking all others, in sickness and in health, for better or for worse, becoming his and his alone. We were bound by the court, and our love, and by all that is holy and good in this world and beyond.

Until death did us part.

"That better be a long, long time from now," I said.

"Oh, it will be," Nick said. "If I have anything to say about it."

"You may kiss the bride," the justice said.

Carla made a noise, and I looked at her. "Are you crying?"

"No." She sniffled, and Bryan handed her a NASCAR handkerchief. "And why do you care, anyway? Stop looking at me and kiss that gorgeous husband of yours."

So I did.

Eventually, I pulled back. "Nick, I'm afraid death may part us this afternoon."

"Stella, I feel fine. Why are you worried?"

"Because Miranda's going to kill us."

His eyes widened. "You're right. So I guess we'd better go on our honeymoon right from here."

"Honeymoon? Nick, I haven't packed. I haven't planned a trip. There's the farm. I can't possibly—"

Carla yanked my arm and dragged me toward the door. "You are the worst bride I've ever seen. Don't you think Nick's already thought of those things? I've got two suitcases in my truck, just for you."

"You packed my stuff?"

"Well, some of it. Most of it is brand new."

I turned to Nick. "You've really thought of everything?"

"What I've missed, others will take care of."

"Lucy's in on it?"

"Leaving for the honeymoon immediately was her idea."

I stood in the foyer of the courthouse and realized that not only was I a new wife, but I was a very, very, extremely happy woman.

"Come on, husband," I said. "Let's get going. I've got big plans for tonight."

He stepped back. "Should I be afraid?"

"Yes, you should be very afraid."

Carla laughed. "Okay, that's it. We're getting out of here. We'll transfer your luggage to your truck."

"Carla."

She stopped.

"Thank you."

She hugged me so hard I could hardly breathe. "You're the best friend I've ever had. Don't you forget it."

With a few more sniffles, she and Bryan took off out the door.

Nick pulled me close. "I love you, Stella."

I put my hands on the sides of his face and thought how well I knew every inch of it, and how much better I would know it as the years went by.

"And I love you so very, very much." I smiled. "Let's go start the rest of our lives."

We were halfway to the truck when he said, "So. Are you thinking Stella Crown, still? Or would you feel okay about becoming Stella Hathaway?"

"Maybe you should be Nick Crown."

"I could do that."

I laughed. "You really are the best, aren't you?"

"I try. So what do you think?"

"I think I'll see how this honeymoon goes. I have a feeling more than one person is going to call me Mrs. Hathaway. We'll see how it feels."

He waggled his eyebrows. "I'll see how you feel."

"You already know."

"But I don't know how you feel now that you're my wife."

"Hmm. That's right. I guess that's what honeymoons are for, huh?"

"Okay, lovebirds," Carla said, slamming the door of the truck. "I'd say get a hotel room, but you already have one reserved. So you're all set. Have a great trip. Don't get sunburned. Eat a lot of amazing food. Have fun, and—"

"Carla."

"What?"

"We will come back."

She sniffed again, gave me a final hug, gave

one to Nick for good measure, and climbed into Bryan's truck.

"So, wife," Nick said when they were gone. "You ready?"

"Yes. I'm ready for it all."

We climbed into his truck, and left everything familiar behind.

To receive a free catalog of Poisoned Pen Press titles, please contact us in one of the following ways:

Phone: 1-800-421-3976
Facsimile: 1-480-949-1707
Email: info@poisonedpenpress.com
Website: www.poisonedpenpress.com

Poisoned Pen Press
6962 E. First Ave. Ste. 103
Scottsdale, AZ 85251

LP M CLEM
Clemens, Judy.
Leave tomorrow behind

CPSIA information can be obtained at www.ICGtesting.com
Printed in the USA
BVOW03s0953121113

336094BV00003B/75/P

9 781464 202032